DON'T LET THE FOREST IN

CG DREWS

SQUARE FISH

FEIWEL AND FRIENDS

NEW YORK

Content warning: Blood/gore, body horror, panic attacks, grief, eating disorder, bullying, and self-harm.

SQUARE FISH

An imprint of Macmillan Publishing Group, LLC
120 Broadway, New York, NY 10271 • fiercereads.com

The Library of Congress has cataloged the hardcover edition as follows:

Names: Drews, C. G., author.
Title: Don't let the forest in / CG Drews.
Other titles: Do not let the forest in
Description: First edition. | New York : Feiwel and Friends, 2024. | Audience: Ages 13 and up. | Audience: Grades 10–12. | Summary: "Two teen boys attempt to stop terrifying creatures that seem to be coming to life from macabre drawings"—Provided by publisher.
Identifiers: LCCN 2023042937 | ISBN 9781250895660 (hardcover)
Subjects: CYAC: Friendship—Fiction. | Monsters—Fiction. | Forests and forestry—Fiction. | Boarding schools—Fiction. | Schools—Fiction. | Horror stories. | LCGFT: Horror fiction. | Psychological fiction. | Novels.
Classification: LCC PZ7.1.D773 Do 2024 | DDC [Fic]—dc23
LC record available at https://lccn.loc.gov/2023042937

Originally published in the United States by Feiwel and Friends
First Square Fish edition, 2026
Book designed by Meg Sayre
Square Fish logo designed by Filomena Tuosto
Printed in the United States of America

ISBN 978-1-250-89564-6
10 9 8 7 6

Once upon a time, Andrew had cut out his heart and given it to this boy, and he was very sure Thomas had no idea that Andrew would do anything for him. Protect him. Lie for him.

Kill for him.

High school senior Andrew Perrault finds refuge in the twisted fairy tales that he writes for the only person who can ground him to reality—Thomas Rye, the boy with perpetually ink-stained hands and hair like autumn leaves. And with his twin sister, Dove, inexplicably keeping him at a cold distance upon their return to Wickwood Academy, Andrew finds himself leaning on his friend even more.

But something strange is going on with Thomas. His abusive parents have mysteriously vanished, and he arrives at school with blood on his sleeve. Thomas won't say a word about it and shuts down whenever Andrew tries to ask him questions. Stranger still, Thomas is haunted by something, and he seems to have lost interest in his artwork—whimsically macabre sketches of the monsters from Andrew's wicked stories.

Desperate to figure out what's wrong with his friend, Andrew follows Thomas into the off-limits forest one night and catches him fighting a nightmarish monster—Thomas's drawings have come to life and are killing anyone close to him. To make sure no one else dies, the boys battle the monsters every night. But as their obsession with each other grows stronger, so do the monsters, and Andrew begins to fear that the only way to stop the creatures might be to destroy their creator.

Also by CG Drews

HAZELTHORN

Praise for

DON'T LET THE FOREST IN

A *NEW YORK TIMES* BESTSELLER
AN INDIE NEXT SELECTION
A B&N BEST BOOK OF THE YEAR
A JUNIOR LIBRARY GUILD SELECTION
A GOODREADS CHOICE AWARD FINALIST

★ "Drews paints a gruesome narrative with visceral descriptions of monsters and the violence they enact while, with equal vigor, encapsulating the trauma of loss, disordered eating, bullying, and anxiety, all of which is counterbalanced by a gentle touch addressing asexual identity."
—*Booklist*, starred review

"More Brothers Grimm than Disney, Drews's modern-day fairy tale artfully tackles heavy topics, including homophobia, bullying and eating disorders, while skillfully weaving in the dark fantasy elements that anchor the story. Drews's words feel like poetry, almost lyrical in their grotesque execution, and you can't help but keep reading. The story opens with a boy cutting out his heart for love; by the time you reach the final, gripping page, you may feel like doing the same."
—*The Seattle Times*

"Compulsively readable. *Don't Let the Forest In* lures you into a lush world full of terrifying monsters and codependent boys trying to survive their obsessive art—and each other."
—Trang Thanh Tran, *New York Times*–bestselling author of *She Is a Haunting*

"With a lingering terror that will lurk well after you finish, this psychological horror is packed with monsters of fairytale, folklore and so much more. Good luck not getting hooked (and haunted)."
—*B&N Reads*

For the monsters in your head

ONE

It hadn't hurt, the day he had cut out his own heart.

Andrew had written about it later in spidery lines from a sharp pen—a story about a boy who took a knife to his chest and carved himself open, showing ribs like mossy tree roots, his heart a bruised and wretched thing beneath. No one would want a heart like his. But he'd still cut it out and given it away.

Being left aching and hollow was a familiar feeling. A comfortable pain.

Andrew had always been an empty boy.

It was easier to tell a story than say how he felt, so he'd ripped the page from his notebook and slipped it into Thomas's back pocket the day school let out for the summer. Then Andrew had dissolved into his father's car and Thomas had been swallowed by the bus, and that had been it. They would be severed until Wickwood Academy opened again.

It didn't matter if Thomas read the truth in the story or not, how he alone owned Andrew's heart. The thrill of the confession had been terrible and beautiful—and retractable. Just in case.

There were words for people like Andrew Perrault. *Desperate*, maybe. *Awkward* fit, too. *Coward* stung, but it wasn't a lie.

Andrew was probably the only person who didn't crave summer or holidays, but he felt better at school, solid and more real. He'd boarded at Wickwood since he was twelve, and the ivy-smothered walls, the old stone manors, even the rose gardens and forests cloaking the campus, all felt like home. He left everything here—his books, his memories, his school things. He left Thomas Rye here, too.

Andrew was hungry for it. Take him away and he starved.

But summer had ended, and that feeling of wholeness hadn't yet filled his chest as his father drove him back to Wickwood. All he could think about was how this was their final year. Dread already threatened to suffocate him.

Andrew pressed his cheek to the cool window glass as the BMW snaked along winding roads. The forest grew so thick on each side it felt like gliding through a tunnel of dark and wolfish green. It should take an hour to get there from the city, but his father had been driving at a glacial pace. Usually he moved with confident speed, taking calls and dictating emails to his phone, his grip easy on the wheel as his gold watch clinked against matching cuff links.

Today Andrew's father sat rigid, a muscle in his jaw flexing. He kept glancing at Andrew through the rearview mirror, and Andrew kept pretending not to notice. He stuffed in one earbud against the silence. His notebook lay open on his lap, two lines of a new story begun.

This was what Andrew did—told stories. Ones with dark, bitter corners and magic curled into thorns. Ones about monsters with elegant, razor-like teeth. He wrote fairy tales, but cruel.

Thomas loved them.

Once upon a time there lived a prince who wore a crown of rowan to protect him from woe, but a sweet willow maiden asked

him to take it off in return for a kiss. After the kiss, she cut out his eyes.

They're the best, Thomas said. *They make me want to draw. Do they mean anything?*

Andrew had given a small shrug, but a fever lit beneath his skin at the praise. *They're just meant to hurt.*

Like a paper cut—a tiny sting that meant nothing more than *I'm alive I'm alive I'm alive.*

Thomas was the only one who understood the stories. Andrew's father didn't. Even Dove didn't, which felt like a betrayal since they were twins.

She sat in the front passenger seat of the BMW, her arms folded and her posture stiff. She was locked in a frosty war of silence with their father. Over what, Andrew had no idea, but they wouldn't even acknowledge each other.

They looked like twins, Andrew and Dove. Pale skin, honey-gold hair, brown eyes, and not much height difference between them. But Dove was a statue of glittering ice, beautiful and dangerous and impossible to reshape, while Andrew was more like a collection of skeleton leaves, fragile and crumbling. Dove was the one everyone saw, and Andrew was the one they forgot.

She wore the Wickwood uniform of white collared shirt and tie, deep green blazer and plaid skirt, not a single button or wisp of hair out of place. Dove had the graceful poise of someone expecting to stand before an auditorium and give a valedictorian speech while cameras flashed, immortalizing her as an example of perfection. She'd be fine this senior year; she'd own it. Andrew suspected this year would beat him up in a back alley and leave him for dead.

Already his stomach felt knotted, but he told himself he'd calm down when they arrived. Thomas would be waiting with his freckled cheekbones and troublesome scowl, forever angry at everyone except the Perrault twins.

He was theirs, and they his. The three of them had been this way since they met.

The car's tires rolled from smooth road to crunching gravel, and Andrew pressed even closer to the window. His heartbeat sped up. Here was Wickwood, grown from the forests and thorns of middle-of-nowhere Virginia. Cars and buses filled the circular driveway, and students flooded the marble front stairs alongside baggage and fretting parents.

As their car crawled forward, looking for a place to park, Andrew searched for Thomas. Nothing.

He glanced at his phone. His heart still gave a small jolt at the sight of the scars crisscrossing his skin, thin as cobwebs, from fingers to wrist. It didn't hurt anymore. He barely remembered how they had happened.

He checked for texts, knowing there'd be none since Thomas had broken his phone a week into summer vacation.

Andrew pulled up their last exchange and chewed his lip.

phones pretty muvh smaashes exicse typos ill see you when schools back

Andrew had taken an excruciatingly long time to think up a reply that didn't sound panicked. An entire summer. No talking. Thomas could email, except he never did.

Andrew had texted: *How did you break it this time??*

well dad did. hit my heead wth it then thrw it at wall. Its abot to die cabt charge. don't freak out.

How the hell was Andrew meant to *not freak out*? It wasn't the first time Thomas had offhandedly mentioned something like this happening—though it seemed the violence was shocking to Andrew alone—but he couldn't stop thinking of how much it would have hurt. Or if Thomas's father had concussed him with a blow like that. Or about the long weeks where worse things could happen to a boy with a sour mouth who never knew when to stop.

Thomas had that in common with Dove—you'd have better luck softening stone.

Andrew's father pulled up behind an unloading bus and left the engine running. The chaos of hundreds of voices thrummed against the window. Andrew hesitated, fingers on the door handle. As intense as it was out there, it would be better than the strangling tension in here.

"Andrew." His father studied his hands as if they'd been welded to the steering wheel. "There are other schools."

Andrew shoved open his door.

"Andrew."

The sigh was frustrated, but also tired, and it made Andrew slump back into his seat and let the car door thump shut. They'd had fractured variations of this conversation before and he hated it. Last year had been . . . It didn't matter. It was over.

Andrew wasn't changing schools. His life was *here*.

He looked out the window again for Thomas.

"Fine, then listen." The muscle in his father's jaw flexed again. "If it's too much, call me and I'll come. We can transfer you somewhere else, anywhere you want. And talk to the school counselor if you . . . Just talk to her."

Andrew checked to see if Dove was steaming that their father was leaving her out of the conversation, but she must have slipped out while he'd been distracted. Great. No reconciliations were happening today.

"Are you coming in?" Andrew said.

His father's voice was tight. "I have a flight to catch."

Andrew didn't ask where to, and his father didn't say. He was an international land investor and developer, owner of hotel chains and restaurants, with enough charm to convince anyone to do anything. Sell, buy, invest. It was the Australian accent, Dove had said, and added, *Look, Andrew, we're still novelties in America. Lean into your accent and you'll have any girl by the end of high school.*

Andrew decided to speak as little as possible for the rest of forever.

Invisible was best. It was easier to speak less and hide his softest parts so he could fit between the shadows of the rich private school kids with their bored expressions and catlike claws. They took down prey for fun and only left it alone once it knew to stay on its belly. He understood the rules.

"Just don't go into the forest," his father said. "Andrew? Promise me that at least."

"Okay," Andrew said, but he couldn't mean it since the forest was Thomas's favorite place.

This time when Andrew got out of the car, his father didn't stop him.

Andrew set his suitcase on the footpath and propped his satchel against it. Dove hadn't waited. That hurt. He jammed his notebook into his suitcase and fought the zipper as his father's car pulled away.

Then it was just Andrew alone, with sweaty hands and a firm pulse of anxiety in his stomach. By this point, Thomas should have seen him and descended. The three of them would usually crowd together on the steps, an instant hurricane as they caught up. Thomas would sling his arm around Andrew's neck while he teased Dove for already starting to outline their plans for extracurriculars this year.

Friends, best together. They were everything they needed from each other, and it was enough. It had been that way since they enrolled at Wickwood.

Andrew repeated that a few times so it felt solid.

But what if Thomas wasn't here? What if his grades hadn't secured his place or if his parents had pulled him from Wickwood or *murdered him*—

A scuffle from the stairs made Andrew turn. Everything was stone out here, boxed in by manicured lawns and late summer roses, and it carried the air of comfortable tradition. Except instead of gentleman scholars, Wickwood had its fair share of spiteful vultures ready to pick the bones of the weak. A pack of seniors messed around on the stairs, their backslaps and howls of greeting drowning everyone else out. But it was the smack of a hand against a book, the ensuing explosion of pages, and a vicious yell that caught Andrew's attention.

Thomas stood with fists bunched, one hand gripping the railing like he meant to pound up the stairs. His sketchbook looked like a bird shot from the sky, pages flittering around his feet.

The vultures would claim it had been an accident. They'd be believed because they were Wickwood's finest. Well-bred and

rich, white teeth and perfect hair, their family names moneyed and sleek and attached to politicians and lawyers and CEOs.

Whereas Thomas fit none of those criteria, and he didn't have the sense not to hit someone and be expelled before first period.

Andrew cupped his hands around his mouth. "THOMAS."

Dozens of heads turned.

Only one mattered.

Thomas's whole body tilted toward the sound, as if even amid the crush, his name from Andrew's lips would always be heard. He shot one last furious look at the vultures and then burrowed through the masses to arrive breathless at Andrew's side.

A second stretched between them, long enough for Andrew's anxiety to beat like moths behind his ribs. Everything had gone wrong already with Dove vanished and Thomas late. After all, friendship lasted forever until it didn't. Months apart could change someone. Stretch bonds. Break them—

"Are you okay?" Thomas said.

Andrew hesitated before nodding, because this wasn't their normal greeting. But then Thomas launched into him, and the way he crushed his arms around Andrew's shoulders said everything.

It only lasted a second. Then Thomas pushed away and thumped Andrew's shoulder, his smile a blazing star. "There's nothing of you. Didn't you eat this summer?"

"Isn't that what grandmas say?" Andrew let a wry smile play on his lips, and it didn't fade when Thomas shoved him.

"It's what people who are hungry and projecting say. I'm *starving*." He snatched for Andrew's satchel and hooked it over

his shoulder. "Can't believe they don't feed us breakfast first day back. Come on, we'll dump your stuff before assembly starts. How was summer? Hell?"

"Always. How was . . ." Andrew hesitated, doing a precautionary sweep over Thomas. To be sure he was whole.

To be sure he was real.

Everything looked the same—auburn hair and sharp jaw and face like someone had upturned a whole jar of freckles on him. He was at least a head shorter than most boys his age, and he wore his uniform like he'd been in a fight—white shirt scrubby and untucked, tie a mangled noose at his throat. No blazer. No vest. Ink-stained fingers and paint smudged under his jawline—

No, not paint, a scab. Andrew resisted the urge to reach out and rest his thumb over the shape of it.

"I, for one," Thomas said, "want to punch Bryce Kane and his crew, but that's not new."

"Was that sketchbook—"

"Not much in it. Forget about it." Thomas scooped a page off the ground and stuffed it into his pocket. "Do you need anything? Do you need me to . . . I don't know. I just—" He scrubbed at his hair and tilted his head toward Andrew.

He shouldn't be fussing like this. He hadn't even asked why Dove was in a mood or why they'd arrived late. He hadn't even launched into a proper rant about Bryce Kane and his vultures, Thomas's personal nemeses, who he antagonized as much as he got picked on. Instead he seemed jittery, as if he'd had too many coffees and couldn't quite keep eye contact.

"I'm okay," Andrew said, but he didn't add *Why wouldn't I be?*

"After everything last year . . ." Thomas winced, then shook himself a little.

"What about you?" Andrew said. "You survived? But your phone . . . Did your parents, um . . ."

Thomas stiffened, his whole body tucking into itself. He messed with one of his sleeves before jamming his hands into his pockets. "I don't want to talk about them," he muttered, and forcibly took off into the crowd.

He was always cagey about his parents, but this was something else.

Andrew hefted his suitcase and followed. He had to trust they'd settle back into their normal rhythms, but it worried him in a real and deep way how Thomas wore armor when talking about his family. No one looked at the students of Wickwood, with its extravagant tuition fees and high test score demands, and questioned what kind of people their parents were.

He caught up to Thomas and they took the stairs in sync. Two steps at a time. Knuckles brushing as they reached the top.

Andrew looked down on reflex, not sure if the touch had been an accident. That was when he saw Thomas's sleeve—the one he'd tried to hide before.

It could be paint. Thomas was nothing if not a chronic mess of untucked corners and spills and mussed hair and artwork staining his cuffs.

But this stain was the red of spilled wine. Splotchy, as if it had been scrubbed with a paper towel.

Thomas turned, and the stain was hidden. He started talking about the dorm renovations, but his tone felt too light, too forced, and Andrew didn't miss the way his fingers trembled as he fiddled with his sleeve again.

The first question on Andrew's mind was *Whose blood was that?*

The second was, how was Andrew meant to pack down the heat pulsing behind his eyes, spreading through his jaw, burning him all the way down? If someone had hurt Thomas—

Breathe. Let nothing show on your face.

He fell into step behind Thomas, but in his head roared a white static.

Because here was the truth about his friendship with Thomas Rye:

Once upon a time, Andrew had cut out his heart and given it to this boy, and he was very sure Thomas had no idea that Andrew would do anything for him. Protect him. Lie for him.

Kill for him.

TWO

Andrew should be forgotten. That was what happened to the quiet ones, the wallflowers. When people like him made a friend like Thomas, there should be nowhere to stand in the wake of glory and chaos that Thomas left behind.

But Thomas always looked over his shoulder before turning a corner, always reached back to tug Andrew after him. It seemed as natural to him as breathing, that need to check that Andrew hadn't been left behind. He dreaded the day Thomas would drop the habit, but he still hadn't. Even after they detoured past the dorms to dump luggage and joined the stream of students pouring into the halls of Wickwood Academy, Thomas still reached back to stop them from being separated in the crush.

Andrew was drunk with relief. *Let this be one thing that never changed.*

Dove was already changing everything else. She should be here with them, bickering with Thomas about something inane until he shot back a quip that startled her into a laugh.

Instead, Dove's icy war must be extending to Thomas, too. Andrew knew they'd had some massive blowup before school let out for the summer—he'd decided to stay out of it this time—but they usually smoothed things over by pretending it never happened. Andrew couldn't live like that; if one thing went wrong, it festered in his chest until he couldn't bear it, and then someone would have to fix it for him before he spiraled.

Dove could be just catching up with friends. She had a dramatic academic rivalry with her roommate, Lana Lang. The kind where they battled for top of the class all day, but then as soon as 4:00 p.m. hit, they were sharing Sour Skittles and snorting over inside jokes. Dove-plus-Lana did not drift into Dove-plus-Thomas-plus-Andrew, though. They orbited separate suns. Possibly because Thomas had no time, interest, or tolerance for most people, and he let them know it, too.

Other people existed only in Thomas's periphery, but the Perrault twins eclipsed his entire galaxy.

There was something intoxicating about meaning that much to one person.

Addictive.

But Andrew would never admit it out loud.

"I have to tell you something," Thomas said, his words half-lost in the rising chatter of other students. "Tonight when we sneak out to stargaze—Oh. Should we still do that?" He shot Andrew a worried look. "We shouldn't, right?"

Why, because they were seniors now? Thomas had a chronic need to fight every rule ever, so worrying wasn't like him.

"I still want to," Andrew said.

Lines smoothed on Thomas's forehead. "I'll tell you everything tonight, but you have to swear to believe me."

"Well, that's cryptic—" Andrew started, but Thomas's fingers dug into his sleeve hard enough for him to forget what he was saying.

Thomas stared over Andrew's shoulder, his eyes gone waxy with fear. Nothing ever scared him. Confused, Andrew twisted to look, but all he saw were Wickwood uniforms and bright faces.

Then a knot of students cleared and Andrew understood.

Principal Adelaide Grant stood in the foyer with arms folded and a stony expression. She looked as if she had been pulled from a black-and-white photograph—crisp pantsuit, white skin against whiter hair, piercing eyes that noticed everything. Thomas collected reprimands and suspensions from her like confetti.

It meant they knew each other well, Thomas and the principal. Their eyes locked across the room and a frown darkened her face.

"Isn't it too early for you to be in trouble?" Andrew said, but then he noticed who the principal had been talking to.

Two cops stood at her side, stances casual as they glanced around. Wickwood did take a moment to absorb: the heavy Victorian drapes and dark carpets, the chandeliers and oil paintings and gilded cornices, the smell of mothballs and old books, of ambition and timeless traditions. One of the cops wore a cream trench coat and had just finished flashing a detective badge. She followed the principal's gaze.

Thomas turned and yanked Andrew after him, carving them a path into the auditorium with his jabbing elbows and ferocious scowl.

"What did you *do*?" Andrew hissed.

"Nothing. I just got here, same as you."

They needed to find three seats; Dove would catch up to

them before the announcements started for sure. But Andrew didn't have time to voice this before Thomas crammed him into one of the back rows. All of the performances and award nights happened in here, and it had the air of an old theatre with the red velvet chairs and moody lighting.

"Are we *hiding*?" Andrew whispered.

Thomas glared at the row of shiny ponytails in front of them—juniors, all talking with their phones out.

"I'm telling you, she hates me specifically." Thomas fidgeted, trying to get comfortable. "Those cops are probably here to lecture us about drugs or something."

"You'd know," Andrew muttered.

"That was *one time*. I have got to corrupt you all the way this year so you can stop being so innocent."

"I break rules sometimes."

"Only if I drag you into it." Thomas knocked his knee against Andrew's. "You won't even steal a pencil. You know what we need? You, me, stargazing, and vodka. I'm deeply interested in what you'd say with no filter."

Andrew was deeply interested in that never happening. He couldn't risk allowing his mouth to say the things he only dared scream in his head.

He knew he was blushing because Thomas grinned deviously.

One of the junior girls shot a scathing glance over her shoulder. "Excuse me, are you talking about illicit activities?" Her whisper was loud enough for all her friends to hear.

"Yes, we're going to steal all the pencils in the school," Thomas said.

"I can report you," she hissed. "They're cracking down this year, and whoever has been selling Adderall is so getting caught. Same goes for anyone sneaking off campus into the forest, too. You of all people should respect that."

Several more of the ponytail girls turned with lips pursed. A few looked pityingly at Andrew.

"Oh my God, are they the ones from that thing that happened last year?" one whispered to her friend. "I'm surprised they came back."

Thomas started to raise a finger, but Andrew grabbed his hand and slammed it down.

He maintained a neutral expression until the girls turned away, but his heart raced. He didn't know what that was about. Maybe because of what he'd done to his hand? But it shouldn't be something the whole school would gossip over. He wasn't interesting enough to care about like that.

A few rows ahead, Andrew caught sight of the back of Dove's blazer where she sat with her AP class friends. She laughed at something a friend said before casting a quick glance over her shoulder. She must've locked eyes with Thomas, because she frowned and his scowl deepened in response. They looked away at the same time.

A microphone crackled as a professor approached the podium and began the morning announcements. Time for an enthusiastic lecture about giving Wickwood your all, followed by a reminder of all the golden students who'd graduated on to Ivy League colleges. Everyone here was handpicked for excellence. Time to achieve! To thrive!

Except the reality was most of these kids were here thanks to their parents' bank accounts. Dove had aced the entrance exams on her own genius, but Andrew clung on by luck—and their father paying the steep tuition, with a little extra for donations when pressed.

Thomas stood squarely in the middle. His parents were artists and wore wealth like disposable plastic, selling a piece worth hundreds of thousands one day and impulsively burning through the money the next. It meant Thomas went to an incredibly expensive school and yet wore his uniforms to threadbare rags before getting new ones. His grades slumped worse than Andrew's, but at least he had his art.

Thomas was viciously talented. Andrew wrote cruelly beautiful fairy tales, and Thomas could illustrate them with a few slashes from a pen with such macabre beauty even his teachers overlooked his endless attitude problems.

Andrew tried to listen to the professor drone on, but all he could think about were those cops. It couldn't be about Thomas. It just—no, it couldn't.

Except one look at Thomas and anyone could see his mouth was crammed full of thorns and lies. If Dove had sat with them, she'd have surgically removed all of Thomas's bullshit and figured out the truth by now.

Andrew kept his voice low. "You and Dove fought before summer break, right? You never made up?"

Thomas bit his thumbnail. "No."

That explained it. One of them had to give first, and this time it seemed like their individual stubbornness was winning.

The principal took over the microphone next for a motivational speech about exams and excellence—and subtle threats about zero tolerance for substance abuse or prank wars. No police lurked by. Maybe they'd left.

Andrew realized he was still pinning Thomas's hand to the seat, his fingers with their web of delicate scars resting over Thomas's charcoal-smudged knuckles.

He snatched his hand away.

Thomas didn't look at him, just folded his arms and slouched deeper.

Andrew had to get Thomas and Dove to make up . . . but later. He was too tired right now. Summer at his father's Australian house had left him thinned, and the flight back to America was always brutal, jet lag leaving his eyes bruised. He fantasized about dissolving into his blankets back in the dorm while Thomas went off on a rant about how math was offensive, or how he belonged to the forest like some sort of fae child who planned to run away to the trees and never look back.

By the time assembly let out and the halls flooded with students headed for class, Thomas looked gray from choking back his own secrets. It didn't help that the principal made a beeline for them.

"Pretty sure she'll walk past," Thomas said.

She did not.

"Hello, gentlemen," Principal Grant said. "I hope you're both well. Mr. Perrault, you had a safe flight? And Mr. Rye, I see you've neglected your blazer. Good thing you have time to rectify that before class. But first, I must borrow you for a moment."

The cops hadn't left, Andrew now saw. They stood at the stairwell leading up to the faculty offices. Students flowed around them, whispering behind cupped hands.

"I didn't do anything," Thomas said, too high-pitched.

Concern softened the principal's face, and that was more terrifying than a reprimand. "Unfortunately, this is about your parents. Those officers need to ask a few questions."

Andrew glanced at Thomas, but the other boy's face had gone blank. Did he seem smaller than usual? Messier? His auburn hair stuck out in unkempt tufts.

Then there was that blood on his sleeve.

Principal Grant turned for the stairs, but Thomas stood frozen.

Andrew unbuttoned his blazer. "Take this." *Cover the stain,* he didn't add.

Thomas tugged it on, the sleeves a little long on him. "Come with me?"

The principal had made it to the stairs and cast him a stern look. "You may catch up to your friends in class, Mr. Rye. Come."

Thomas trudged up the stairs, the cops at his heels. A gallows march.

Andrew's chest tightened, and he felt light-headed all of a sudden. Returning to Wickwood and Thomas was meant to make everything better. Nothing should be unraveling this fast.

Andrew couldn't follow, but—

Damn it. He had to.

He waited a few moments, chewing the inside of his cheek, and then ducked up the stairs. The faculty floor was forbidden without a permission slip, but Thomas had whispered *Come with me,* so nothing else mattered.

Andrew slipped soundlessly down halls of antique burgundy carpets and dark mahogany doors set against chestnut wallpaper. Priceless art covered the walls in gilded frames. It was hard not to feel smothered by the decadence of this place.

He put his ear to the principal's closed door and tried not to breathe.

Muffled voices. The thump of feet on carpet. Andrew knew two leather armchairs sat before the principal's intimidating desk, and behind it were ceiling-high bookshelves stacked with classics and antiques. It didn't sound like anyone had bothered to sit.

". . . explain the situation to you, son."

"My name is Detective Stephanie Bell. Why don't you take a seat?"

"I'm fine." That was Thomas, his fury tightly laced.

"First off, can you tell us when you arrived at school?" Bell's voice sounded chill and efficient, a frost that would unapologetically burn anything new and green.

No one asked *Where were you*–type questions for good reasons.

Andrew's skin felt too tight.

"This morning," Thomas said, guarded.

"You live in the city? An hour's drive, isn't it?"

"I took an early bus."

"Do you still have your ticket? Is it time-stamped?"

"Officers." The principal had an odd edge to her voice. "I was informed this would be a meeting to relay sensitive information, not an interrogation. Do I need to place a call to his guardians?"

"Unfortunately, that's why we're here, Mrs.—"

"Doctor Grant."

"My apologies. This is following up on a concerning 911

call. Neighbors reported hearing loud noises coming from your home last night, Mr. Rye. Screams."

Andrew forgot how to breathe. The moment didn't seem real: kneeling bunched up next to a keyhole, listening to his best friend, his *heart*, be dissected.

"Nobody was home this morning," the detective went on. "House was trashed. Looks like an animal tore through. And there's . . . blood. Due to the volume of blood, we surmise it's not yours, so we're just wondering if you knew anything about that."

"Excuse me." Footsteps sounded like the principal had marched out from behind her desk. "Does Thomas need a lawyer present? What exactly are you implying?"

"Not implying anything, ma'am. We are merely trying to get ahold of the boy's parents, but no one is answering calls. Did they say they were going out of town, Thomas?"

Silence. It lasted a beat too long before Thomas mumbled, "I don't know. Maybe."

"It was quite a lot of blood."

"Did you inquire at local hospitals?" the principal said.

"Of course, ma'am. So, Thomas, was there a fight last night? Or a party, maybe? Anything get a bit rough?"

"No." Thomas bit out the word like he wanted it to eviscerate the detective. "I don't know anything. I'd already left."

Bell's voice sharpened. "But you said you only left this morning."

"Yes . . . really early. It was still dark. That's what I meant."

"All right, no need to get agitated. We're sure you're worried about your parents."

Thomas didn't sound worried—that was the first thing Andrew had noticed. But maybe he could read Thomas too well. He imagined Thomas's body language right now, taut and defensive, fingers picking at his bottom lip or a loose thread.

Or at the bloody sleeve hidden under the borrowed blazer.

"I'm sure your folks are fine, but we'll have the blood tested and continue trying to locate them. Dr. Grant, would you reach out to his emergency contact and alert them of the situation?"

The voices continued for a minute as information was exchanged, and then the doorknob turned.

Andrew's brain caught up a beat too late as the office door started opening. Then he remembered to run.

He made it to the top of the stairs before realizing flinging himself down would look even more guilty. He was so bad at subterfuge. He pretended to stare at one of the vaguely impressionistic art pieces on the wall as the cops passed behind him.

"—did you think?"

"Kid is lying." The detective said it with finality. "And I want to know why."

Her eyes met Andrew's and she immediately cut off. Her smile came thin, barely polite, then she continued downstairs after her colleague.

Behind him, the principal cleared her throat.

Andrew turned slowly, his cheeks burning.

"Why, Mr. Perrault," Principal Grant said, unimpressed, "I believe you are missing first period."

"I . . . lost something?" Andrew said. "I, um, a pencil."

Next to her, Thomas had been attempting to control his scowl, but at this, he raised one eyebrow at Andrew. So it was a bad lie, fine. But Andrew wasn't exactly well practiced at sneaking about.

"Despite my better judgment," the principal said, "I will believe you were not lurking at doors where you don't belong. This meeting contained private information, and I won't have gossip in my halls, Mr. Perrault."

Andrew nodded far too fast.

The principal turned back to Thomas. "I'll inform your aunt, but I'm sure there's no cause to worry. Your parents are . . . eccentric, as we are all aware. I'm sure we'll hear from them before the day's out."

Thomas said nothing.

The principal gestured for him to go downstairs before casting Andrew a stern look. "You may leave." The grim set of her mouth said *Get going or get detention,* so Andrew shot after Thomas.

They fell into step as they headed for English, but Andrew felt so shaken he couldn't even remember where the classroom was. Thomas still wouldn't look at him.

Kid is lying—

"What's going on?" Andrew's voice barely passed a whisper. "Is this what you were going to tell me about?"

"Nothing. You heard them. My parents are weird about their art. It's probably not even blood. I-I-I don't know. I don't—" He broke off and tugged at his bottom lip.

Andrew nearly tripped. Thomas never stumbled over his words. He also never lied to his best friend.

The corridor was empty, classroom doors closed. They'd be marked tardy before the school year had taken its first proper breath. Andrew started to say as much, but Thomas snatched his wrist and dragged him into a small alcove.

They pressed close to the thick velvet drapes by a huge window, dust motes dancing against the glass. The world felt too quiet. Too heavy.

Every breath seemed to tremble in Thomas's lungs. "It's not going to be like last year." Something desperate shone in his eyes. "Nothing bad will happen to you. I swear."

Bad things were happening to Thomas, not Andrew. *He* was the one who needed protecting right now. Andrew couldn't help noticing that not one adult had asked Thomas if he was all right.

"I'll sort this out," Thomas said. "I don't want you making yourself sick over it. I'll fix everything. Do you believe me?"

If they stood any closer together, they could fit into each other's skin.

"I want you to say it." Thomas's voice steadied. He could pin Andrew to the wall with the way he shaped those words.

"I believe you," Andrew whispered.

THREE

The day would never end.

The whispers unraveled Andrew the most. Furtive glances. A conversation cut off as he slid into his desk. That crawling feeling at the back of his neck that warned him someone was staring.

Thomas ignored everything with a deliberate stoicism that Andrew couldn't muster, and their packed schedules left no time to talk. Dove's AP classes kept her far away from both of them, so Andrew was left with a mouthful of pins instead of answers about why she was avoiding Thomas.

By the time dinner arrived, he felt too sick to be hungry.

Stepping into the dining hall meant being pounded by a wave of chaos. Every room in Wickwood was nothing if not antiquated and stately, but the dining hall rarely seemed under such control. Hundreds of voices tangled with the clatter of plates and cutlery. Mealtimes had been broken into two halves and the seniors dined second. It meant less supervision—they were supposedly "responsible"—and therefore meant way more noise.

The hall itself looked like something from a medieval king's court: three long oaken tables with benches on either side took up most of the room, and a huge fireplace that smelled of evergreens and hazelnuts covered half a wall. The seating style was meant to "prevent cliques" and "encourage peer conversation," but Andrew suspected it had been specifically designed to torment introverts.

Thomas had detoured to the bathroom, so Andrew decided to catch Dove in the serving line. He slid into place behind her and resisted the urge to slump his forehead on her shoulder and moan.

"I hate everything." He pressed his fingertips to his temples. "Have you talked to Thomas?"

"I haven't seen him." Dove crossed her arms over her stomach. "It's roast chicken and apple turnovers. They're giving us false hope before the weeks of meat loaf start." She inched toward the serving table stacked with plates and passed Andrew one.

"So," he said, "are you and Thomas going to fight the whole year or . . . ?"

Dove huffed. She looked worn after the long day, wisps of hair escaping her tight ponytail. "He can talk to *me*."

Sometimes Andrew thought Dove and Thomas were in the midst of their own three-act play: first friends, then enemies, and then—

Lovers. That would inevitably come next.

Andrew was sure of one bitter truth: He'd rather have his lungs punctured than watch Dove and Thomas fall in love.

Sometimes he'd lie awake at night and unpack all his feelings about this boy-shaped hurricane named Thomas Rye. He didn't know if he wanted to *be* Thomas—reckless and uncontainable—or if he wanted to kiss him. He could imagine Thomas's soft lips on his for approximately five seconds before the entire construction crumpled like wet paper. Because there was always *after*. There was always *more*. People didn't just kiss and continue on with their lives. They undid buttons and touched mouths to hot skin and lost themselves within each other.

And Andrew didn't want to think about any of that. At all. Ever. He didn't have crushes and didn't think celebrities were hot and, honestly, the whole thing was stressful and overwhelming and better left boxed up in the back of his head. He was just this . . . this *mess* who felt things about Thomas but couldn't shape them into coherent sentences. And he was almost definitely certain Thomas liked Dove.

Dove reached the front of the line and tried chatting with the servers, though they ignored her, more interested in the line moving faster. A few students had begun staring at Andrew, but he kept his eyes on the ground as he trailed after his sister and had his plate filled with a heaping serving of roast chicken, peas, and a roll.

At the condiments table, Andrew fussed with the butter while Hyder, who sat behind him in history, helped himself to gravy.

"Hey," he said. "Glad you're back. Sorry about . . . everything. You doing okay?"

Andrew's scarred fingers clenched around his plate. "I'm fine."

Any more of this and he would ask the walls to devour him.

He cast about for somewhere to sit while Dove got cutlery, then followed her to the crowded tables. "It's just I don't know what you and Thomas fought about. And I don't know why everyone keeps looking at us."

Dove sighed. "Sometimes I don't know what reality you live in."

He frowned. "What's that supposed to mean?"

But then Dove nodded to where the boy with a mess of auburn hair was slipping out of the dining hall in an illegal escape.

"Do you need me to stay with you, or should I chase him?" Dove said.

It felt like a trick question. Eating alone would be hell, but of course she had to go after Thomas. Fix this. Andrew had to stop being such a coward about being left by himself.

"Go make up." He hoped she didn't interpret that as *make out*, too.

Dove vanished and Andrew walked slowly down the long rows of benches that had turned into hostile territory. No one would notice if he tossed his food in the trash and escaped. But when he turned, Lana Lang stood there with one hand on her hip.

She was Chinese American, wore deep mauve combat boots despite school regulations, kept her hair pulled back in a jagged ponytail, and had an expression flat as a severed heartbeat. To be scared of Lana was common sense: Fake smiles and false fronts melted before her. You had to be real or she took you apart.

She flicked a glance up and down Andrew, her mouth a thin line. "You're wandering around like a lost puppy. Did Thomas misplace you?"

Andrew never knew whether to be meek or defensive with Lana. Their paths didn't cross often—she was firmly Dove's friend, not his. "He's busy."

"And yet all the seniors are required to be at dinner. I swear he has a compulsion to do the opposite of what he's told. C'mon. Sit with me."

Panic set in. "It's fine. I'll sit—"

Lana stalked toward a mostly empty section at the farthest table. "I won't make you sit with my loud friends, Perrault. It'll be just us."

He was tired and it was easiest to just obey.

They sat down across from each other. Lana had drowned her plate in gravy and now set to executing her chicken as if it weren't dead enough already.

"For future reference," Lana said, "you can sit with me anytime."

Dove must have put her up to this. Apparently Andrew looked so pathetic and lost when left to his own devices that even his twin was embarrassed.

Andrew started to ask Lana what Dove had told her, but she glanced over his head and sucked her teeth.

He followed her gaze and was almost thrown into his plate by an almighty backslap that could be considered a jovial greeting. Or assault.

Bryce Kane leaned between them, a hand squeezing Andrew's shoulder. It looked friendly, but Lana gripped her fork like a weapon and Andrew thought his shoulder was about to break. The school had a zero tolerance policy against bullying, so Bryce had curated his image to be described as *charming* and *energetic*. He was one of Wickwood's best tennis players and a "delight to have in class." He had wealthy parents on the school board, and kids flocked to pay tribute to his court—and he got off on making them grovel. He knew how to be terrible without looking like he was being terrible.

"Hey, it's the goth and the Vegemite boy," he said. "An unlikely couple. How was your summer, Andy? Eating shrimp on the barbie and banging kangaroos?"

"I'm a goth because I wear combat boots?" Lana said. "Wow. Original."

Andrew shrugged off Bryce's arm. No point reminding him that July was winter in Australia. "It was fine."

"Weird seeing you without Dove." Bryce scrubbed Andrew's hair. "Or your girlfriend. Where's Thomas Rye the Psycho these days? Heard he's getting visits from cops already."

Lana half rose from her seat, her face gone white with fury. "*Back off.*" The level of venom in her voice surprised even Andrew.

Bryce raised both hands in mock fear. "No need to get hysterical. Just trying to joke around, be chill and normal, you know?"

"You're lucky Thomas isn't here," Lana snapped. "You'd have a broken face by now."

Bryce had the gall to look annoyed. "And that's why I'm not surprised the cops are already on him. Don't even know why Wickwood let him back after everything that happened last year."

He strode off, already shouting across the hall at a friend, who hollered back a greeting.

It took Lana a while to stop steaming and sit down. Protecting Andrew was Thomas and Dove's job, so Lana stepping in should have felt condescending. Andrew should be mad, but at least she hadn't asked him if he was okay, or said anything cryptic about last year, or commented on his ruined hand.

Andrew ate half his roll before he noticed Lana watching.

He absently rubbed his healed hand against his cheek. "The scars aren't that bad. I don't know why everyone's looking at me."

"The problem isn't the scars," Lana said with clipped precision. "It's that you smashed your hand through a mirror."

He wished she wouldn't say it aloud. It sounded blunt and ugly.

Lana went back to stabbing at her food. "They'll stop staring eventually. Some senior will get into a ridiculous scandal in a few days and, boom, attention gone. They're all a bunch of airheaded gnats." She chewed, deliberate and angry. "But what was with those cops? It's day *one* of school. Thomas is unbelievable."

"What are people saying about it?" Andrew asked quietly.

"You don't want to know, trust me." Her voice turned to steel. "The thing you need to do this year is keep your head down and graduate. Survive. Don't"—she pointed her fork at him—"let Thomas get into fights for you. They *want* a reason to expel him. If the gossip gets bad, come to me. I'll help. Got it?"

Andrew felt a little dizzy. Lana and Thomas should've been friends, what with the way they were all teeth and knives out. Except Lana was a cold scalpel, and Thomas was a wild machete with blazing emotions he'd never learned how to moderate properly.

It still didn't make sense that Lana had taken a sudden interest in Andrew. He was fine.

It had been one mirror.

One minute of lost control.

Andrew, a string drawn taught—

s n a p

Blood all over Thomas's shirt as he dragged Andrew away from the wreckage—

"There's something else you should know." Lana's voice sounded odd. "They've put up a fence between the school and the forest."

Andrew shredded the rest of his roll into tiny pieces. "Okay."

"No more class hikes. No more exploring. Immediate expulsion if anyone's caught climbing the fence."

She had to be warning him for Thomas's sake.

Thomas, who breathed best with his cheek pressed against a tree and never wasted a chance to slip out and be as wild as his soul demanded.

"Everything is shit." Lana propped her chin against her fist and sighed. "No offense, but I have no idea why you wanted to come back."

The reason was obvious; it didn't need to be said.

"I should go find Thomas." Andrew slid from the bench. He flexed his scarred fingers and slipped his hand into his pocket. Paper crunched and he frowned at the unexpected scrap. He hurried away from Lana before he took it out and smoothed the corners.

Thomas's work, unmistakably. A stark winter forest, every tree burned white with frost. A boy with horns and roses grown from his eyes held a knife, and he was midway through carving the heart out of another boy with moth wings who knelt in the leaves, his face tilted upward in supplication. Vines blossomed around them, tangled and unruly.

Thomas always drew like this—murderous and dark, sentient forests with teeth and claws, boys made of thorns, studies of hands with flowers blossoming from cuts. Beautiful and horrible all at once.

He drew like this because Andrew wrote like this. They fed off each other relentlessly, their fever dreams bleeding through their eyes long after they woke.

Andrew burst out of the dining hall. He'd barely eaten, but it didn't seem important. If Thomas had illustrated Andrew's story, it had to mean something. Or maybe it didn't. Thomas drew Andrew's work all the time—how was he to know that last story had been a confession about how Andrew felt about him?

Andrew hated the way his brain did this. Destroyed beautiful things. It was like he couldn't just hold a flower; he had to crush the petals in his fist until his hand was stained with murdered color.

The corridors lay empty. No sign of Thomas and Dove. They'd probably be outside, letting the dusk eat their angry words.

The noise from the dining hall turned muddy the farther he walked, and he kept waiting to bump into other students. Counselors touring new kids around. Clumps of friends catching up. Teachers coming and going from offices. The manor should be busy.

Andrew paused in the darkened foyer. It was a rare thing to be so perfectly alone. He breathed out slowly and tried to shake the anxiety thickening in his stomach, but all he could smell was the forest. Damp leaves and mud and the fresh smell of snapped, green sticks.

He shouldn't be able to smell the forest all the way up here.

Someone moved behind him. He didn't turn because it was obvious the person was trying to sneak up, feet too heavy and breathing muffled as if they were on the cusp of bursting out laughing. He knew it was Thomas about to pounce on his back. Andrew relaxed slightly. His fight with Dove must be resolved. Everything would go back to normal.

"I can hear you," Andrew said, a small smile forming.

Thomas flung his arms around Andrew's back and they stumbled forward a few steps. Andrew grunted, but he secretly enjoyed it. He started to jab an elbow into Thomas's ribs.

But something soft and warm pressed against the nape of his neck. Mouth to skin.

For a minute, Andrew did not move. His stomach swooped so violently he didn't know how he stayed standing.

The foyer was so still, darkening around the edges.

He heard Thomas stop breathing.

The weight hanging off Andrew's back felt heavy now, too much to hold. He had to say something. He was *ruining* everything. What did Thomas want from him?

Hot breath brushed the back of his neck again and then, inexplicably, a tongue slid soft and wet up to Andrew's ear. It was a line of heat, sensual and terrible and confusing. What was Thomas doing? This wasn't—this—

Andrew whirled around, shoving Thomas off. But the force of dislodging another body threw Andrew off-balance and he fell down to one knee. When he scrambled up, breathing too hard, the foyer was empty.

Silence stretched in front of him. He touched the back of his neck.

Wet.

He realized now that the feeling of a body pressed against him had been all arms. There had been no legs.

Stop it. There hadn't been anything there at all. Obviously.

"You're losing your mind," Andrew whispered, not sure if he was embarrassed or horrified at what he'd imagined.

It had felt so real. He could still feel the tongue licking toward his ear.

He stuffed his trembling hands into his pockets and hurried outside.

Get ahold of yourself.

But he didn't know what part of himself was safe to hold on to.

FOUR

Their story had begun in the forest, a collision both violent and beautiful.

It had been Andrew and Dove's first year at Wickwood, both of them twelve years old with awkward limbs and amorphous personalities. If the Perraults' father wasn't traveling, he was chained to offices and meetings in the States while his business grew faster than he could hold on to it. He couldn't leave them in Australia, and his unpredictable hours meant boarding school was the logical choice. It meant the twins arrived in Wickwood midyear, when the other students had already settled into their cliques.

Andrew and Dove stood out painfully with their Australian accents and strange phrases and the way their edges melted together. They weren't used to wealth, to listening to kids talk about their opulent homes and extravagant vacations and famous parents. But Dove could be tossed into anything and she'd bounce. Andrew was a glass figurine. Drop him and he shattered.

While Dove made spreadsheets of who she'd befriend and planned how to hit top of every class, Andrew started getting horrible stomachaches. The worst part was how Dove loved it here. Andrew was ruining everything, like always.

"We just need to make friends," Dove had said firmly.

"Do it, then. Stop hanging around me." Andrew was in tears but firm. She didn't have to drown with him.

Except she chose him every time. She sat with him instead of other girls, and she pulled him into games and did his assignments when he was too stressed to concentrate.

Outside, at least, it was easier to breathe. Wickwood Academy sprouted between thorny rose gardens and wide, manicured lawns, and it prided itself on an enthusiastic sports curriculum that included supervised hikes and nature walks in the surrounding forest.

The class would walk the compacted dirt paths, a teacher up front and another behind to herd the stragglers, and everyone had to finish a nature sketch or trace a leaf while listening to a lesson on ecosystems. The other kids mucked around, but Andrew fell in love with the woods. It was quiet there, and the trees seemed like they could keep secrets.

But there was one boy who obviously loved the forest more than Andrew, a freckled kid with a reckless mouth and hair kissed by the devil. Once Andrew started watching him, he couldn't look away.

Thomas Rye was a wild thing. He was everywhere at once, climbing trees and throwing rocks, racing ahead and exploring off the path. The entire forest rang with his name because a teacher was always shouting for him. Only Andrew saw Thomas kiss the tree. It wasn't a performance. This boy did what he wanted on impulse and regretted nothing.

Andrew wanted that—to be so full of fierce life it spilled over his edges.

Instead, he'd walk next to Dove, who already had seven pages of leaf tracings, perfectly labeled and colored, and kept putting up her hand to ask complicated questions. Her enthusiasm was only dampened by the boys behind them mimicking her accent.

"Teach us some bad Australian words." Bryce Kane had bright eyes and a bright smile, a white all-American golden boy.

"They're the same as yours," Dove said, exasperated. "Can you stop stepping on our heels?"

They didn't stop; they found it hilarious. Then they discovered it was even more hilarious to trip Andrew.

The first time could have been an accident. The second time, Andrew's knees hit the dirt and he got up bruised and muddied. Dove snapped at the boys, but they didn't care. Teachers never got mad at Bryce Kane, and his little posse shared the immunity.

The third time, Bryce hooked his foot around Andrew's ankle, and he went down hard enough to shred his knees. He climbed to his feet, bloodied and shaky, wanting a teacher to step in but also embarrassed that he still needed that. He was too old to be so delicate.

"Oops!" Bryce said. Then the others made fake-crying noises between snickers because it was obvious Andrew was on the edge of tears.

Then Thomas Rye appeared.

He came out of nowhere, dirt on his face and his pockets distended from collecting seedpods and pebbles. He tucked his sketchbook under one arm and wedged himself between Andrew and Dove without invitation. The three of them barely fit shoulder to shoulder on the narrow path. He was half a head shorter than both of them, which surprised Andrew, because from a distance Thomas seemed like he could fill up the whole world.

Thomas didn't seem to care about their arms bumping together. "You're the Australians, right?"

"Who are you?" Dove snapped, in case he was one of Bryce's vultures.

"I'm Thomas. Whenever I'm annoying, my mom says I'm a little shit and she's shipping me to Australia." He sounded unfazed. "I think it sounds fun. What stuff do you like?"

Bryce Kane and the others backed off, as if Thomas was something to be wary of, and Dove relaxed.

"I like running," she said—she'd recently added "conquer track and field" to her spreadsheet. "I read a lot, *adult books*, too."

Thomas picked up a stick and dragged it in the dirt as they walked. "We should race and see who's fastest. I think I am, but"—he sounded factual—"you might be because you're taller." He turned to Andrew. "What about you? What do you like?"

Andrew's eyes went wide. People would clock Dove as the friendly one and assume Andrew was rude, not shy. No one bothered with him.

"I like to write," he said quietly.

"He writes *amazing* books," Dove added, forever his one-person hype team. "I'm researching how we can publish them and become millionaires, but I got stuck designing a cover."

"I could draw you a cover," Thomas said. "But I only draw monsters, so you probably couldn't handle that."

He looked at Andrew as he said it, his mouth a serious line with a challenge tucked into one corner.

"I can handle you," Andrew said.

He'd meant to say *I can handle* it.

A smile broke across Thomas's face, all sharp edges and cleverness. Andrew loved it.

Then a hand shoved Andrew's shoulder and he stumbled. "Excuse me! Trying to get past!" Bryce shouted, and his friends cracked up, because of course he wasn't. He reached out to shove Andrew again.

Dove whipped around in fury, but Thomas was faster. He leveled his stick right at Bryce's chest.

"Touch him again like that," he said mildly, "and you'll wish you hadn't."

Bryce towered over them with a mocking smirk. "Is this even your class, runt? I think the preschoolers went the other way." He began to reach toward Andrew again. "We're just messing around. Didn't mean to make Andy cry like a little—"

Thomas slammed the stick down so hard the forest echoed with the crack of wood against skin. Bryce's howl was of both shock and rage as he doubled over, a vicious red welt on his hand.

A horribly delicious feeling flooded Andrew's chest. He could taste pain in the air and for once it wasn't his, and *he loved that.*

The teacher stormed toward them.

Thomas casually tossed his stick into the trees and didn't look concerned. "He won't touch you again," he said.

Andrew could hardly breathe. "You'll be in trouble."

The light in Thomas's eyes was bold and ferocious. "But he won't touch you again."

FIVE

Instead of waiting up until the witching hour to sneak out and stargaze, Andrew fell asleep. He'd found Thomas in the dorms after dinner and they'd fallen into their usual first-day routine of haphazardly unpacking until Andrew had nodded off on his still unmade bed. He dreamed brambles wrapped around his throat, a briar rose resting on his tongue. Dove kept knocking on his door, begging him to come to the forest with her, but he couldn't squeeze words out past the thorns. She went without him.

His best talent had always been letting people down. Even in sleep, apparently.

When he woke, it was dark and he felt feverish. Pinpricks of pain rippled through his right hand, and he gave a sleep-fogged moan before looking down.

Blood streaked his knuckles, every scar flayed open again. When he made a fist, skin peeled apart to show stark white bone against raw tendons.

Andrew shot upright with a cry. A light burst on and he whipped around, an arm flung up to defend himself from the glare—or an attack. But it was just Thomas clicking on his desk lamp, one boot on and worry furrowing his brows.

"Are you okay?" he said.

Andrew glanced back down at his hand.

No blood. Only a lattice of thin, white scars.

Thomas dropped onto the mattress beside Andrew, and they both stared at his hand for a minute. Then Thomas traced from the tips of Andrew's fingers down to his wrist.

A shiver shot down Andrew's spine. He had to breathe out hard to hide it.

"It healed well," Thomas said. "The scars almost look like lace. Do you still want to sneak out? We don't have to."

Andrew pulled away and reached for his sweater. "You owe me like seven hundred answers."

"It'll feel wrong to go without Dove." Thomas said it so softly, Andrew paused with his sweater half tangled over his head.

When he turned back, Thomas still sat on Andrew's bed, his head bowed, fingers picking at old, dried paint on his jeans. Out of school uniform, he always looked lawless, as if the loss of rigid lines turned him into a passionate painting spilled all over a page.

Well, this meant Thomas and Dove hadn't fixed their argument, but if they were in a fight, they weren't kissing. He hated himself for the selfish relief. "I still want to."

They climbed out the window, feet wedged in the cracks between bricks, hands gripping window frames and trellises to lower themselves down. Thomas first, then Andrew, dropping into a crouch on the dewy grass. The night was cool for September, but then Andrew was always cold. Everything felt more alive out here. An energy thrummed between the rosebushes and up through the ivy-covered walls.

There was a stickiness to the shadows, the night so dark that staring into it made Andrew feel unsteady. A shadow moved with

the softest scrape of scales against gravel before slithering out of sight around the dorms. Hair prickled at the back of Andrew's neck, but he scrubbed his eyes and shook himself. He wasn't properly awake, was all. Nothing breathed out here but them.

They took off, the velvet dark cloaking them. Both had notebooks in hand, and Andrew had shoved a packet down his sweater at the last minute. Plastic crinkled as he walked, and Thomas mimed at him to hush several times before giving up and hiding his laugh. They crept through the deserted gardens to the sheds and used a firewood stack to climb onto a low roof. Thomas's sweater rode up, his bare stomach scraping against tiles. A hiss escaped him before he rolled out of the way.

Andrew vaulted up behind him.

"Stop doing that so easily," Thomas muttered.

"Start growing." Andrew pulled a packet of Tim Tams from under his shirt. "Surprise."

"Oh, *yes*, yes, you freaking godsent *saint*."

Andrew bit back a laugh as Thomas snatched the Tim Tams and then scurried like a goblin over the roof. They'd discovered this spot back in freshman year, when Thomas realized no windows from any of the dorms or the school manor overlooked the neat little garden sheds. It was rebellion, but safe. Even Dove allowed it instead of doling out her usual lectures about Thomas's rule breaking.

The way she clung to rules and Thomas mocked them fueled most of their wars, but Andrew suspected they fought because they liked it. Or because Dove needed the relief of an excuse to be less than perfect for a second. Or because Thomas only knew how to bite people for attention.

Andrew settled on his back next to Thomas. The slope was gentle, the tiles cushioned by decades of moss and papered with old leaves.

"I bought original because you have low standards anyway," he said.

"True." Thomas tore into the packet. Tim Tams were nothing more than malted biscuits with a creamy filling, dipped in chocolate and then blessed by an Australian brand name, but for some reason Thomas worshipped them.

"They're not even that good," Andrew said.

"Be disrespectful somewhere else. If I eat enough, I will *turn* Australian. I will be a *bloke*."

Andrew jabbed Thomas in the ribs. "I'll take them back."

"You can't if I lick them all. Actually wait, I'll give you one and you give me your notebook."

"One, wow." But Andrew passed over his notebook.

This was their tradition, a chance to cram in updates about everything they'd missed over the summer. Without Dove, it did feel strange, but so what if Andrew had Thomas to himself for once? It was an excuse to lie beside each other, skin brushing skin, knee pressed against leg. Only the stars could judge.

Thomas sat up and nestled Andrew's notebook on his lap, handing over his own sketchbook. "Give us some light."

Andrew obliged, propping his phone on his knees so a soft glow bathed their swapped books.

An extraordinary amount of intimacy lay in exchanging art. Not for critique and not for class. Just to look. To feel. To understand each other.

Andrew paged through slowly, chewing his lip as he looked

at Thomas's drawings from the summer. Everything here had been cut from the cruelest fairy tale.

Towers wrapped in thorns, with monsters hung by the throat at the gates.

Thistle fairies with their wings cut off, teeth sunk into their prey's flesh.

A princess with fingers grafting into tree bark.

The final portrait made Andrew linger. A boy with arrow-tipped ears, his face a constellation of freckles, and eyes cut out for roses to claw through the sockets. His mouth had been scribbled out in dark pen.

Andrew loved it. He loved them all. He could tell many had been based on his stories, which meant he had been on Thomas's mind all summer.

Thomas flipped pages in Andrew's notebook, getting crumbs and smears of chocolate everywhere as he made small noises of appreciation. "You should write a whole book someday. Your stories are too short and I always want more."

"They're meant to be paper cuts." Andrew turned to the last sketchbook page. "This one is inspired by my story, right?"

A boy, done in charcoal, leaned over the lip of a wishing well with fingers outstretched to the silver water. Behind him, a monster with elegant human hands and a hacked-off wolf's head for a face devoured the boy's parents.

Thomas snatched the sketchbook from Andrew's hand.

Andrew stifled his yelp and had to grab for his phone before it skittered off the roof. He shot a confused look at Thomas.

Thomas ripped the page out and scrunched it up. "I hate this one. It's . . . the shadows are wrong."

Andrew's phone flashed a low-battery warning. He turned it off. Truth felt safer in the dark. "Tell me what happened with your parents."

Thomas sighed and stuffed the last Tim Tam in his mouth. "Or we could look for shooting stars and I could annoy you?" He handed back Andrew's notebook.

"You already do. No extra effort needed."

Thomas wrinkled his nose.

The lightness slipped from Andrew's voice. "Are you even okay?"

They never did this—never confronted each other or asked what was wrong to be mapped out in words that made sense. Andrew was the worst about it, the one who clammed up or outright lied so people would stop trying to pry apart his bones and see why he was riddled with peculiar agonies. He couldn't explain himself, which meant he couldn't ask Dove why she fell into manic study spirals, or Thomas why he had a wine-colored scar on his shoulder blade. So Andrew tucked his problems away—his panic attacks, his suffocating shyness, the way he disappeared into daydreams.

Thomas flung an arm over his eyes. "I'm fine. What about you? You looked haunted after dinner."

No way was Andrew confessing about the . . . whatever that *thing* had been that licked his neck. It hadn't been anything. A waking dream. Lurid, and not his.

"Nothing," Andrew said. "Why did you lie to the detective?"

Thomas went still.

Even whispering, their voices seemed too loud in the night. When Thomas peeled his arm off his face, something harrowed

lived behind his eyes. Fear didn't suit him. He was meant to be invincible.

"Because it looks bad." Thomas's voice came low. "I-I can't explain it. I don't want you to worry, all right? I knew the house was—things were messed up before I left. I left anyway."

"Did your parents hurt you?" Andrew hated the pitch to his words. He thought of the drawing Thomas had ripped up.

"What? No. I told you before, they get a bit high and drunk sometimes and they get caught up in their art. All families are dysfunctional. Stop telling yourself stories where I'm some damsel in distress."

"Thomas—"

He pushed himself up on his elbow and dug fingers into Andrew's shirt. "Stop asking."

Andrew went quiet.

Thomas pulled him down so they lay side by side again. Billions of glittering stars layered the world above them, blotting out the dark.

"Tell me a secret," Thomas said, "and I'll tell you one."

I'm glad Dove didn't come with us tonight. Andrew swallowed, his skin suddenly hot. "I'm scared of everything except the dark."

Thomas huffed the tiniest laugh. "I knew that. You write the darkest things, and it never keeps you up."

"Tell me yours."

"I think someday you'll hate me." Thomas's voice stretched with a loneliness Andrew had never heard before. "You'll cut me open and find a garden of rot where my heart should be."

Andrew let the silence sharpen between them, waited until

Thomas's breath caught in quiet anguish from being made to wait.

"When I cut you open," Andrew finally said, "all I'll find is that we match."

Below them something scraped softly over the stony path. The world smelled of sweet cloying decay, rotten leaves, and earth.

"Did you hear that?" Andrew scooted himself toward the edge, but Thomas caught his arm.

Shadows stole his face but for the sharp line of his mouth. "It's probably a fox or something. We should leave anyway."

They climbed down in silence together, their fingers cold and lungs aching. It was strange, Andrew thought, how when something moved in the dark, everyone's first instinct was to go inside and hide under the covers.

As if monsters couldn't open doors and crawl into bed with you.

Once upon a time, a cutthroat queen and a wormwood king had seven sons. They loved them all except for the last, who was made of sarsaparilla and foul tempers and had beautifully pointed teeth.

They gifted their first six sons crowns made of willow switches. But they ordered the seventh son to be switched with the leftover rods.

They gifted their first six sons golden apples. But for their seventh son, they put worms on his tongue and made him swallow.

They gifted their first six sons a wishing well. But to their seventh son, they gave the hacked-off head of a wolf cub.

The years passed and the seventh son's skin toughened under the switching, and he developed a taste for flesh, and he befriended the murdered wolf cub and told it all his secrets.

When the wolf decided justice was necessary and ripped out the hearts of the cutthroat queen and the wormwood king and ate their six perfect sons, the seventh son did not even notice. He had found his reflection in the wishing well and liked staring at his pointed teeth.

SIX

On Wednesday, they took Thomas from class.

He packed up his books and left in silence, only pressing his fingertips to the top of Andrew's desk as he passed. No backward glance. Through the open classroom door, Andrew saw the corner of Detective Bell's cream trench coat before she strode out of view.

He sat motionless through the rest of the lesson and tried to make each breath more shallow than the last. He would disappear if he could. Just until Thomas came back.

As soon as class ended and everyone filed out, the whispers began.

"Not surprised . . ."

"He's always so rude."

". . . has that violent streak—"

"Bet he killed his parents."

No one should even know this had something to do with his parents. Either a student had overheard something or Dove had been extra vindictive since their fight and spread the rumor. It left Andrew wading through classes with a feeling of pins being twisted into his skin, one by one, until he could barely speak through the taste of metal in his mouth.

His lower lip bled. He had to stop chewing it.

Thomas didn't return for lunch or when the final period ended. Why did the police even need to keep him this long?

Because it looks bad, he'd said on that first night back at Wickwood.

What could you possibly have done, Thomas?

If Andrew started down a trail of what-ifs and maybes, he'd spiral. He had to stop thinking.

He skipped tutoring and went hunting for Dove. He knew where she'd be.

The Wickwood library had been known to eat students whole. It had its own building beside the school manor, smaller but still built of stone and ivy, and it had been packed with shelves and cozy study nooks. The upper floor had begrudgingly relinquished studios to art students and extracurricular clubs, so the whole building always smelled of books and paint, and sometimes Shakespeare monologues could be heard through the walls.

Since Dove lived to study, and Thomas breathed art, and Andrew craved stories, they all had pledged their hearts to this library.

Andrew wandered between the narrow shelves and ran fingers along the spines of his favorite sections. Leather-bound first editions lined overhead cabinets, and every reference book imaginable could be requested because Wickwood was designed for minds that burned to know *everything*. It was a school for brilliance, for fixating on the stars until you grew tall enough to reach them.

Andrew found Dove and her best friend, Extra Credit

Assignments, holed up in a study nook by the window. It had a clear view to the parking lot—perfect, he'd see when Thomas returned.

Andrew slung his satchel onto her table. "That is way too much homework for our first week back."

"It shouldn't even be called homework, should it?" Dove had a pencil behind one ear and another jammed through her ponytail. "We live here. It should be homeschoolwork. I'm starting my essay analyzing stereotypical gender roles in fairy tales. You could write this better than me."

Andrew thumbed through his notes from today's classes, but he was too agitated to focus. He took out his notebook. "I don't show people my stories, you know that. They wouldn't get it."

They'd had this argument before, but Dove eyeballed him anyway. "Our teachers handle Thomas's art, and he's a drama queen of the macabre. You could get extra credit if you wrote for class. Or—hear me out—you could write something *nice*."

To write something nice, he'd need something nice to say. But his ribs were a cage for monsters and they cut their teeth on his bones.

"Have you heard anything about Thomas yet?" Andrew fiddled with the edge of his notebook and glanced at the window. "Should we worry?"

Dove reorganized her already perfectly stacked homework piles, and then straightened her tin of highlighters. "Not yet. Give it till dinner."

"Then you'll ask about him?" He hated how thin he sounded. Pathetic.

But Dove said, "Yes, I'll do the asking," firm and without judgment.

What were twins, if not one to shout and one to whisper?

She started to ask about his math homework—it was one of his worst classes, and Professor Clemens was a glorified bully—but the library doors burst open and a group of teens clattered in. They were all midconversation and immediately began hushing each other and cracking up because of it. Andrew put his elbow on the table and covertly cupped a hand over one ear to block out some of their noise.

Dove suddenly got to her feet. "I have to go." She crushed handfuls of papers down among her textbooks while Andrew's confusion turned to shock. Dove did *not* mess up her orderly perfection.

"Who are we avoiding?" He swiveled to look at the incoming group.

Lana Lang strode around the shelves. Her purple combat boots came first, her stabby expression followed, and she had a sack of flags over her shoulder, the edges peeking out to show stripes of various color combinations. The motley crew behind her looked liberated from theatre class—different ages, some still in costume or glittering from drama class residue, and a few with haircuts that barely met Wickwood's restrictive dress code. They all whispered or linked arms as they headed upstairs.

Only Lana paused. She put one hand on her hip, an eyebrow raised as she surveyed his shoved-aside homework. "Studying alone?"

"No, I'm with . . ." He looked back, but Dove had cleared out like a puff of smoke.

Was she fighting with Lana, too?

Lana watched the last of her crew disappear upstairs, then readjusted her sack of flags. "Want to come?" Her usual brusque tone had a tentative edge.

"Are you running an art club?" Andrew said.

Lana squinted at him, and he had a flash of panic that he'd said something foolish. He hated talking to people.

"Ms. Poppy runs the GSA club, but we come in early to hang out."

Andrew wanted to turn himself inside out. "It's not my . . . thing." Did Lana look annoyed? She probably thought him a bigot now instead of someone who was an absolute mess about his sexuality and didn't want to talk about it with anyone ever.

"Suit yourself." Lana put her boot on the empty chair beside him and adjusted her laces. "Just know anyone's welcome. Queer, straight, questioning." She let that hang in the air. "I just thought it might be better than being alone."

But people did homework alone all the time . . . unless she thought he was too unstable to be by himself.

Andrew massaged his scarred hand under the table. "Dove ever go with you?"

Lana snorted, but her smile was fond. "A few times. She fixed all the Pride flags we'd hung crooked. Offered to iron them, too."

He stole a quick glance at the window just as a car pulled in. From this far away, he could barely make out faces, but a boy with tousled auburn curls climbed from the back seat and slammed the door hard enough for the shock wave to be felt inside the library. One of the professors walked around the car with keys still in hand, motioning Thomas toward the manor.

But he took off in a flat-out run to the dorms. The professor didn't try to catch him.

"I have to go," Andrew mumbled, aware that avoiding Lana to chase Thomas had become a habit.

Aware that she noticed.

He gathered his homework and flung himself from the library.

Lana was wrong to invite him, anyway. He didn't fit with those kids because he didn't fit with anyone except Thomas and Dove, and he didn't know if he was gay enough when there was only one boy he wanted. A small, reserved part of him knew he must be asexual, and that being *gay enough* wasn't a thing. But he looked at other boys and felt nothing, so maybe the only reason he didn't want Thomas to kiss Dove was so their trio wouldn't change—not because *he* wanted to kiss Thomas.

Or maybe he . . . did?

But it was better this way; Thomas was in love with Dove, and he was not one to think kissing was enough, anyway. Andrew wouldn't survive a gentle, pitying rejection. He just wouldn't.

Andrew went to the dorms, but their room was empty. He dumped his satchel on his bed and checked the bathrooms, then the lounge. Nothing. A quick survey of the garden and athletic fields showed no sign of Thomas.

Afternoon tipped toward dusk. He had one last place to look.

Past the endless green sea of tamed grass, the forest rose up in a sharp, dark line. It had always marked the edge of campus, but it used to be easy for a stray ball to be kicked through or kids to sneak past the tree line. Now there was the fence.

As if that would stop Thomas. The forest was immense and unmappable and monstrous—and it had always belonged to him. He never got caught sneaking in there.

Crossing the stretch of open field without being seen from one of the school's many windows would be a trick, so Andrew sprinted. *Don't see me, please let no one see me.*

The fence looked like a beast up close. Eight feet tall? Maybe ten. Chain links made for easy climbing, but the wires had been left sharp at the top. Andrew hauled himself over and waited for some sort of alarm to go off. It was instant expulsion to those who crossed the fence after all.

It didn't used to be like this, but maybe one too many kids had sneaked out to hook up or drink after dark, and the principal had had enough.

Andrew scraped his arm climbing over. He hissed as he dropped to the soft leaves on the other side.

His shoes hit the muddy forest trail and he tried to talk himself through his swelling panic. Whatever the cops had wanted Thomas for didn't matter. They'd given him back. He couldn't be in real trouble.

Because it looks bad—

Pines sighed as Andrew slipped between them. Already dark places lived in the woods, the promise of night thickening against the trees. He left the worn hiking path and followed a thin track crowded with shrubs and mottled blue flowers. Moss underfoot. Ferns rippling against his ankles.

Then the underbrush thinned and his destination sprawled before him—a white oak big enough to hold up half the sky. It was ancient and lovely, with branches that curled like hands reaching out to welcome him. They called it the Wildwood tree and had been climbing it since they were kids. They used to whisper their fears into the bark so it could swallow their words whole.

Thomas would be here.

Andrew stopped at the base of the oak and tilted his head up. "Thomas?"

At first, nothing moved. An emptiness stretched around Andrew, and his heartbeat felt too loud in his ears as his feet sank into the soft, leafy earth. He was acutely aware of how alone he was, how if he cried out, no one from the school would hear. Why was he thinking that? Nothing would happen. This was their place, where they were best together and comfortable in themselves.

A slow chill slipped down his neck like cold molasses, and he shook himself to dislodge the unease. It shouldn't be so still, the ground this soft. He put fingertips to his temple, to the aching pulse of a headache fluttering to life.

Someone breathed out hard behind him. He made himself turn slowly, but there was nothing there. The wind, it was just the wind.

He refused to freak out over nothing again. But when he shifted closer to the tree to see if Thomas had climbed up, the ground seemed to suck at Andrew's shoes. It shouldn't be so damp out here—it hadn't rained. When he looked down, the earth was as sodden as a bog. Dying afternoon light shimmered over the wet leaves, and for a second they looked almost . . . crimson.

Andrew knelt, careful, and touched the corner of a rotting leaf.

His fingers came away tipped with blood.

Something shifted in the Wildwood tree and Andrew surged to his feet, his heart flinging itself frantically against his ribs.

But only Thomas dropped from its branches, his expression strained and his mouth at an angle that looked almost angry.

"You shouldn't be here," he said.

SEVEN

Andrew didn't know how he was meant to react. He'd never been one to break rules—at least not alone—but obviously he'd come because of Thomas. As he tried to get his heartbeat back under control, he looked at his hand. Only damp soil clung to his fingertips. No blood. Of course there was no blood, what the hell was he thinking?

Andrew swallowed. "I was looking for you?" He hated that it came out as a question.

Thomas left the darkening shade of the oak, his sketchbook dangling from his hand, charcoal smudged near his mouth. It was painful how Andrew noticed Thomas's mouth like that. The dying afternoon light turned the tips of his auburn curls to simmering fire and oh, there was a wildness about him, this boy made of angular frowns and thorny words. He was brilliant and terrible and unmanageable.

Thomas's odd flash of anger faded, and guilt ghosted across his eyes. He picked his way across the mottled roots toward Andrew. His foot slipped once, and he flung out both arms to steady himself, sketchbook pages flapping in his grip. When he leaped off the last root and landed unsteadily, Andrew couldn't help the compulsion to snatch the front of Thomas's shirt and ground them both.

But it was Thomas who took Andrew by the shoulder and

propelled him away from the oak. His grip was careful, as if Andrew was a fragile thing, easily hurt, especially out here, away from school walls and protective fences.

Thomas's breath came too fast. "Don't do this again, all right? Don't come out here."

"You shouldn't be here, either," Andrew said. "Usually you want me to break rules with you."

A strange hollowness stole over Thomas's face. "Let's just go back."

"What were you even doing?"

"Nothing."

They fell into step as they walked toward the fence. Thomas still had fingers hooked in Andrew's shirt as if he was the one dragging Andrew away from bad decisions.

"What happened today?" Andrew said. "Why did the police keep you for so long?"

Thomas didn't answer. Light drained from the sky and the ground turned uneven and treacherous in the shadows. Andrew kept waiting to see puddles of stagnant blood, but there was nothing. He'd truly imagined it. But it felt like something was watching them leave, hungry eyes marking their footfalls and tracing the shapes of their shoulder blades. He almost thought he heard the hiss of flesh scraping against tree bark, and thick, congested breathing. A furtive glance over his shoulder showed only the forest watching their retreat with empty eyes.

By the time they reached the fence, both were sweaty and breathing quicker. The forest had left green smudges on Thomas's white school shirt, and he looked unruly, collar popped and trousers muddied. It would be hard to hide where he'd been.

"Climb." Thomas's voice had a brittle edge to it.

Andrew obeyed. He deserved answers, though. Even if he had no stubbornness of his own, he could pretend he had some of Dove's.

He waited till they'd run back across the athletic fields and into the rose gardens before he spoke again. The windows glowed with soft warm light, and the dinner bell must have sounded. There would be a head count. Marks against names if they didn't show.

But Andrew couldn't let this pass.

He stopped walking.

Thomas ducked under a wicker arch of vines before realizing Andrew wasn't following. He spun back to see Andrew planted with arms folded, his mouth in the tight angle he'd seen on Dove.

The way Thomas looked at him was half despair, half frustration.

"Tell me what's going on," Andrew said.

Thomas checked the garden, but there was no one out here except them. Though Andrew couldn't shake that feeling from the forest—the feeling of being watched by something not yet fed.

Thomas sighed, walked back, and leaned against the low garden wall. "My parents are officially starring in a missing persons case."

"Okay," Andrew said.

"And I," Thomas said as the twilight painted his eyes black, "am a person of interest."

Andrew stared. "Wh-what? Why?"

Thomas shrugged and tossed his sketchbook onto the wall. He hauled himself up and sat there, drumming his heels. "They tested the blood and confirmed it's from two people. They said at least one person could not have walked out after losing that much." His voice sounded flat. "You know how my house is at the end of a cul-de-sac? Well, nosy people can see into the front rooms. Some neighbor heard . . . screaming. Saw us arguing. And saw me . . ." He kicked the wall hard then. "Saw me with, and I quote, 'a knife.' But there's no hard proof. It's my word against his."

Andrew's stomach had cramped so tight it took effort to push words out. "Then what really happened?"

"Nothing. Regular family argument. Then I left for . . . I left for school."

He couldn't look at Andrew.

Lying.

He was *lying.*

Thomas's shoulders hunched forward and he rocked himself before hitting the wall with an open palm. Once, twice. Vicious.

Andrew thought of the scars Thomas hid, the brutal stories he delivered like jokes, the way it took nothing to convince him to drink, how distrust caged his heart, how once he'd said all parents slap their kids around sometimes. Andrew had said no they didn't. Thomas had looked genuinely surprised, and it had gutted Andrew.

Thomas's parents had a lot to answer for.

A strange calm unspooled over Andrew. He let out a breath, long and slow.

"I don't care, you know," he said. "If you did."

Thomas went still.

Time slowed, rusty gears caught and shuddering. Andrew's words suddenly felt wrong in the air.

Thomas's voice came so low it shook. "What the fuck did you just say?"

Andrew's feet had grown into the path, his heart turned to petrified wood in his chest.

Thomas slid slowly off the wall. "You know me the best of anyone. But you think . . . you think the same as they do? You think I'm a *murderer*?" The last word came out in a hissed rage so poisonous it could rot bones.

Andrew had no words inside him.

"Do you think I murdered my parents and buried them in the backyard? Because"—Thomas jabbed a finger toward the school—"that's what *they* think. They've got less than nothing to accuse me with and no evidence, but that's still what they think."

There had been blood on his shirt that first day of school. And no wound.

"I'm sorry," Andrew whispered.

"Take it back if you're sorry." Thomas snatched his sketchbook and stood there with anger radiating from him. Even in the dark, he flushed red to the tips of his ears. He did that when he was embarrassed. Or furious.

But mostly when he lied.

The air had been empty between them for too long. Andrew hadn't rushed to fill it because he'd meant what he'd said, and he didn't think he'd spoken wrong. He'd only meant to reassure.

He reached out a hand, uselessly.

Thomas jerked away. "This is why I can't talk to you about anything real. It either freaks you out so you turn into a goddamn mess, or you respond in the most screwed-up way possible."

It hit like a punch. This wasn't happening. This didn't happen. They didn't fight.

Make it stop.

It had to stop.

"This is when I need Dove." Thomas's eyes were bright, a storm wearing itself out.

Andrew hardly recognized his own voice, raw with a bitterness he never showed. "Go be with Dove, then."

Thomas looked stunned. He was shaking apart—or maybe that was Andrew. Andrew, who was tipping toward a steep cliff overlooking an endless chasm. He had no wings. He'd fall and die and he'd do so in silence.

He'd never made Thomas look at him like this, with rage or hurt or—something worse.

Betrayal.

When Thomas finally spoke, he sounded calm and terrible. "I'm walking away from you now. And I'm not coming back."

The world was melting around Andrew, like a sword had been driven up to the hilt in his stomach. He wanted to whisper, *Wait*. He couldn't survive this, couldn't be left alone out here when the forest felt far too eerily close, as if the hungry foulness of whatever had watched them was attracted by this fight.

Thomas turned, one hand in his pocket, the other holding his sketchbook like it was a dead thing he wished he'd buried in the woods. He walked away.

Inside Andrew, the world was ending. He was breathing too fast and yet not at all. He should never have spoken, even if he had meant it.

But no one who was innocent needed to be so violently defensive.

EIGHT

When Andrew woke, Thomas had already left for breakfast.

Thomas knew how to say *screw you* in very specific ways, courtesy of having roomed with Andrew for most of their time at Wickwood and knowing him too well. He'd started with this:

The soundless escape from their room, so Andrew would wake late.

Eating early, so Andrew would risk breakfast alone if he couldn't find Dove.

The way he'd pulled his mess over to his side of the room in a very clear line. Usually his art supplies and knotted-up jeans and scrunched paper balls wandered all over the floor.

Worst was the return of an old well-thumbed notebook Andrew had written in years ago and Thomas had squirreled away for inspiration. It lay flung on Andrew's bed, pages sagging with rejection.

Andrew felt sick as he dressed, his fingers shaking on the buttons of his white collared shirt. He took too long messing with his tie and couldn't get it straight. He covered the bad attempt with a vest instead of the forest-green Wickwood jacket. It was too warm for wool and layers yet, but he deserved to suffer.

He always ruined everything.

They never fought like this. He'd bicker with Dove all day long, but he took more care with Andrew. If they argued, Thomas would end the day by thumping onto Andrew's bed to demand a discussion on fairy-tale lore and the best way to describe a monster to fix things between them.

Andrew needed it and hated that he did. It never stopped making him feel small, the way Thomas had to nurse his anxiety. It lived between them, this knowledge that Andrew couldn't cope and so Thomas took care of it.

Right up until he didn't want to anymore.

Andrew skipped breakfast and went through morning classes with his skin turned inside out. He slumped at his desk, unable to focus on lessons or take notes. Everyone else seemed uninterested in their work as well. They were too busy staring at Thomas.

Did you hear about Rye?

He totally killed his parents.

The school festered with gleeful horror as juicy gossip swapped hands. The students shouldn't know about it at all, but plenty of them had faculty parents to eavesdrop on and a quick Google search confirmed the Ryes' disappearance. Fame followed Thomas's parents in a glamorous haze, their work eccentric and coveted, and their vanishing meant something.

Thomas did not look okay. His face had gone pale under his freckles, and he zoned out in every class, not even doodling as he usually did. Gone were the paint-stained fingertips, the pencil shavings clinging to his clothes, the sketchbook he always had on hand—as if he'd lost all interest in doing the thing he loved most. He needed his best friend right now, not this icy silence between them, especially when Andrew would accept anything he did and never judge or hate him.

But Thomas had only heard—

I think you're a murderer, too.

Andrew should have said nothing. He needed Thomas, but he'd always known Thomas didn't need him in the same way.

Andrew splashed water over his face at lunch and told himself to pull it together. Wait this out. Accusations about his parents would fade because no one had proof Thomas had done anything wrong.

But just to be safe, Andrew used the thin slip of free time during lunch to duck back to their dorm room and burrow around in the dirty laundry until he found that bloodied shirt Thomas had worn on the first day of school. He crouched there, his fingers tracing the brown stains, and told himself this meant nothing. But what if the cops ordered a search of—

Andrew bundled up the shirt and hurried downstairs with it cradled close to his stomach like something wounded, something alive. He burst outside and hurried around the back of the dorms.

It didn't take long to dig the hole in the damp soil beneath the rosebushes. Muck rimmed his fingernails, stained his palms, but he kept going a little deeper. To be safe. Worms wriggled out of the soft dirt, flexing lurid, pink bodies to tangle with his fingers until he shook them off in disgust. He shoved his hand into the hole for another scoop of dirt—and teeth sank into his palm.

Andrew cried out and tried to jerk his hand free, but it wouldn't come. For a wild, panicked second he couldn't think past the pain jolting into his flesh and that claustrophobic feeling of being trapped, needing to get away, *get away can't move can't move can't—*

The teeth slid out of his skin, smooth as a needle suturing flesh. Andrew snatched his hand from the hole, mud plastered to his palm and beetles crawling over him as if looking for an open wound to burrow into. He wiped them off on his pants, his heartbeat rabbiting in his chest and his breath coming in uneven gasps. He stared at his unblemished skin and then darted a glance into the hole.

Empty. No animal coiled there. Nothing with teeth.

"Calm down," he hissed to himself, fierce and shamed. He massaged his palm, pain a ghost thing lingering at the edge of his nerves, while his mind folded over those hot seconds of trapped terror as if they didn't happen. Nothing could have bitten him. There wasn't even a mark.

He stuffed the shirt into the hole and shoved soft, cloying soil over the top.

Everything would be back to normal soon.

It rained all of the next week.

Thomas left the library when Andrew walked in. He was never in their dorm room. In the afternoons he straight-up vanished. He even managed to leave for the bathroom just as they were being assigned pairs for chemistry lab, and Andrew ended up with someone he didn't know. He spent the whole time trying to squeeze words through his closed-up throat.

Their week continued like this. Thomas would spend lunchtime in detention for mouthing off at a teacher while Andrew holed up in the library with Dove and listened to her rambling analysis of the book she was annotating for English as if nothing were wrong. At gym, the class divided between swimming and running laps. Andrew ran. Thomas disappeared into the pool.

Homework and extracurriculars devoured the weekend as the intensity of senior year gained momentum. Andrew's eyes already felt full of paper dust and broken sentences, his assignments slashed in red ink. The gaping hole Thomas left behind was filled with an inordinate amount of study sessions with Dove, not Andrew's idea of a good time, especially with Dove already sinking into frenzied study fervors and micromanaging his work. He couldn't even tell her about his fight with Thomas because the words bunched like razors in his mouth.

Maybe Thomas had been right and Andrew was deeply messed up. It had just taken five years for Thomas to notice, and now that he had, he didn't even want to sleep in the same room.

Every night, Andrew woke alone to silence, Thomas's empty blankets tangled up and their window open. Dawn would bring wet footprints and leaves tracked across the floor, so it was obvious where he went. He slumped in class with dirt still smudged along his jaw and dark circles under his eyes.

When Andrew noticed Dove looked the same, forest dirt clinging to her shoes as she stifled yawns while they studied—he understood.

Go be with Dove, then.

And Thomas had obeyed.

People only sneaked into the forest at night for one reason.

Andrew kept checking his face in the mirror to make sure nothing showed. To make sure he swallowed his shattered feelings like glass. He rested his palm flat against the mirror and tried to count each of his delicate scars. He didn't break anything.

He decided, oh so quietly, to avoid them both in return.

Except they didn't notice his cold shoulder.

He let it stretch a week, then two. He had never been this alone.

On Thursday, Andrew skipped afternoon tutoring on the grounds of having a stomachache—not a lie, since he did feel like he'd swallowed handfuls of cement. No one had spoken to him all day, no one even seemed to see him, so it was with a hollow sense of desperation that he made the call while trudging up the stairs to his dorm room.

He expected to be sent to voicemail or, worse, hear a perky secretary's voice answer, but for once his father actually picked up.

"Hey, kiddo." Noise thrummed in the background as if he'd taken the call in a busy office. "Holding up?"

Andrew leaned against the banister, adjusting his heavy armload of textbooks, and breathed in the musky silence. Most students were in after-class extracurriculars, leaving the dorm empty and Andrew the sole specter left to haunt the halls.

"Not really." Andrew hated how rusty he sounded.

The background noise over the phone grew louder and then dimmed suddenly, as if his father had stepped out of the meeting. He sounded distracted. "It's not a great time for me right now, kiddo, but how about we pencil in a chat for this evening?"

If Andrew opened his mouth, he might laugh hysterically.

His best friend had abandoned him, he felt so sick he couldn't think straight, creepy things kept crawling fingers up his spine in ways that were definitely not real but also definitely *some*thing—and his father wanted to *pencil in* time to *chat*.

It hadn't always been this way between them. Once, his father and Andrew and Dove had been an infallible trio, the three of them all each other had in the world after their mother had walked out. The twins had been a mistake—though no one said that out loud—an accident between a French boy studying abroad in Australia for his final year of university and a Sydney girl who realized raising babies was not her thing. His father's parents had been rich, the kind of rich that when they died, they left their estranged son a small fortune that took him from living in a dank apartment and feeding his eleven-year-old twins tinned spaghetti to driving a BMW and becoming an internationally respected investor.

Lately, his father didn't seem to have time to remember he had kids.

Andrew didn't know why he'd called his father. What did he even want? His father to suggest he change schools, transfer home to Australia? Dragging Dove away from Wickwood would be a special sort of selfish.

"Yeah, that would be good," Andrew managed to say.

"Great." His father acted like he was on a business call, not talking to his son. "And classes are going okay? You're sleeping? Eating? Did you talk to the school counselor?"

Andrew, who wasn't doing any of those things, said, "Yup."

"Good job, son. Talk soon. Love you." Rote words. His

father had ended the call almost before he finished saying them.

Andrew let himself into his dorm room and dumped his books on the floor, wanting to throw his phone or bite his tongue till it bled or—

"Thomas?"

He lay starfished on his bed in gym shorts, shirt off, his curls stuck to still-glistening cheeks. It didn't look like a lazy afternoon nap. He was so out of it that he didn't even twitch at Andrew's entrance.

He looked softer when he slept, sweet almost. But he'd been crying.

The urge to go to him nearly ended Andrew right there. Thomas was so, so not okay. But *he* was the one cutting *Andrew* out. They'd barely been in the same room for two weeks.

"You could sleep at night instead of sneaking out to the forest, you know," Andrew said since he wouldn't be heard. "Aren't you meant to be at soccer practice right now? Or a study group? Instead of, you know, studying Dove all the time."

Thomas really had the most perfect back, freckles pattering all the way down his spine. But all Andrew could focus on was that deep, wine-colored scar on his shoulder. The missing parents who put it there.

Andrew loosened his tie and opened his wardrobe to look for a soft sweater since uniforms weren't required after classes ended. "For the record, I don't think you killed anyone. You would've been caught by now. You suck at planning." Andrew tossed his shirt into the hamper, proud that he sounded factual and unemotional. He was using his voice, buffing off the rust. "The real question is, why are you hiding what really happened? You're protecting someone. You hate your parents too much to cover for them, so you must be protecting—"

"You."

Andrew spun around, smacking his head on the wardrobe door so hard he yelped.

Thomas stretched out on his bed like a sun-warmed cat. He must've scrubbed his face with the sheets, because his cheeks looked reddened now, not damp. Maybe Andrew had imagined the tear tracks.

He watched Andrew with half-lidded eyes, his voice smoky with sleep. "Thanks for analyzing my success rate of being a murderer."

They were talking again. Andrew's heartbeat skipped. "What do you mean protecting 'me'?"

"By not talking to you." He groaned as he rolled off the bed and snatched up a Wickwood sweatshirt. "You're safer not talking to me."

"That's bullshit," Andrew said, strangely calm. "As if we both don't know what it is to deal with rumors."

Thomas rubbed a palm against his eye and flinched.

That was when Andrew noticed the blisters all over Thomas's hands. Cuts riddled his legs, too. From running in the dark forest?

"I'll say sorry," Andrew said. "I'll say whatever you want."

Thomas made a derisive sound. "I just listened to you say I'm too stupid to get away with murder. Maybe stop talking."

Desperation had Andrew by the throat, and he should have

stayed obediently quiet, but he couldn't. "Anyone could be a monster. In the right circumstances. Motivated by the right thing. To protect someone else or to . . . to protect yourself. Is it that wrong to fight for yourself if no one else will?"

Thomas went for the door. He had no shoes on, and his hair looked electrified, eyes unfocused. "I need some space." He sounded tired, no malice left.

"Self-defense isn't murder." Andrew knew he was babbling, but he didn't want him to leave. "N-not that you did anything. But I don't see why you're so upset when they abused you—"

"They don't abuse me. Accidents happen."

"Oh sure, accidents happen again and again and leave scars."

Thomas cast him a sour look.

"I would do something terrible if I had to protect someone," Andrew said, desperately wishing he could shut up. "I'd do anything for Dove. Or . . . or you."

But Thomas didn't answer, he only slammed the door behind him.

Andrew punched the door. Just once. Every bone in his fingers screamed and he had to shake out his hand and pace their small room to calm down. His heart raced with pure panicked adrenaline. He was losing Thomas, watching him slip between his fingers and sink into the earth. Roots would grow over his face and dirt would fill his mouth and he'd be lost forever.

Andrew snatched his notebook and wrote out the story he'd been stewing over for days. He ripped out the page, and the ragged edges matched his ragged breathing.

He tacked it to the window so that the next time Thomas opened it to sneak out, he'd have to read it.

The story meant nothing, just another vignette, but maybe Thomas would draw it and that would be like talking again. Not that Thomas even had a sketchbook around anymore. Drawing was the reason he breathed, the thing he craved whenever a pencil was snatched from his fingertips.

Something was eating Thomas alive if it distracted him from his art.

Once upon a time there lived a woodcutter who crept into an enchanted forest and took his ax to an enchanted tree. It was said a log from here would burn bright and merry forever. Indeed, the woodcutter spent a comfortable night roasting apples with no care in the world.

But the next morning, he found the enchanted forest had come walking. Acres of trees surrounded his cottage, all crying bloody tears. He ran through the forest, but could not find his way out.

All he found were trees weeping blood and blood and blood.

NINE

The afternoon air felt raw and bloody.

Andrew put all his hate into every swing of his tennis racket and got reprimanded twice about control. The coach liked him, though. He was a very short, very French man, who pronounced Perrault correctly. *Perr-oh* not *Per-alt*. He kept pushing Andrew to practice more, eat more, start lifting weights, all things Andrew had no interest in doing. He only played tennis because Wickwood required a sport—he just had the misfortune to be semi-good at it. Hence why the coach kept pairing him with the other top player.

Bryce Kane.

"Your serve, kitty cat." Bryce's hair glowed in a perfect wave above his sweatband, and he grinned with perfect white teeth. He should have been beautiful, but a foulness sat beneath each smug grin. He'd never been in trouble a day in his life, and he basked in knowing he never would be.

"Why are you so distracted today?" Bryce twirled his racket. "I mean, Rye isn't here for you to perv at, soooo . . . Someone else caught your eye?" He put a hand to his chest. "Me?"

Andrew bounced the tennis ball.

"Too bad I'm taken." Bryce made a pouting face and fluttered his eyelashes. "You'll just have to blow Rye in your free time."

Andrew served with enough violence that the ball shot passed Bryce before he even lifted his racket. Bryce lost the point and his eyes flashed dark.

The coach's whistle sounded as he strode over. "Focus, young men! I want to see practice, not chatter. Perrault!"

Andrew turned stiffly, and the coach clapped him on the shoulder. "Keep this energy up and you will play in the November tournament."

"No offense," Bryce called across the net, "but he doesn't have the stamina. Give it fifteen minutes and then I'll beat him every time."

"Start eating more, oui?" the coach said, voice warm. "Do the weights, footwork. Be faster. We are in agreement?"

"I'm actually going to be an author." Andrew directed it at the ground.

"And I wanted to be Picasso." The coach looked unfazed as he steered Andrew back toward the net. "It is better to study law, play tennis, then kiss many beautiful women."

Bryce barked a laugh.

Andrew served hard. Bryce returned the ball and the real fight began. The coach strutted off to enthusiastically harass someone else.

Something shifted in Andrew's pocket and he nearly missed the next serve. His pocket had been empty when he dressed, but maybe it was a note from Thomas—he often smuggled drawings to Andrew and Dove, and they'd find them during a tedious class and end up smiling. Maybe it was forgiveness in charcoal and ink.

But then Andrew's pocket shifted again, pressing against his thigh in a way that felt less like a folded note and more like an earthy clump of—

A shudder barreled down Andrew's spine and his body twitched. His pocket felt *wrong*. Warm and soft and doughy and—

The ball hit him right in the face.

Andrew felt it in his teeth. Pain exploded across his face, air punched from his lungs as he went blind in a white, hot blaze. His racket slipped from nerveless fingers. He bent double as he cupped his nose and let blood pour between his fingers.

"Holy shit!" Feet running. Bryce's shadow loomed over him. "That was an accident. Why'd you stop swinging, you idiot? Coach!"

Andrew thought about punching Bryce so hard he ate the tennis court. Instead, he dragged one bloody hand from his face and reached into his pocket.

His fingers dug into something spongy. He squinted through his tears at the mess in his hand.

"What the hell . . . ?" Bryce said. "Why are there mushrooms in your pocket?"

The fungi crumbled between Andrew's fingers. His mouth opened in confusion, blood running across his lips. He yanked out another handful, but his pocket still bulged with the fleshy, rotting mess, the smell of foul forest everywhere. This didn't make sense. How could he have dressed without feeling it? He dug out another handful and threw it on the ground.

He wiped his hand on his shorts, but the mess didn't come off.

The coach ran over, rattling off French expletives as he tilted Andrew's face up. "Not broken. But you shall go to the nurse."

“I’m fine.” Andrew swiped the back of his hand across his mouth. Everything throbbed.

“The bathroom, then. Go clean up.” The coach whirled on Bryce. “What was that?”

Andrew escaped while Bryce received his deserved scolding. Andrew found no joy in it, though, because his skin was crawling.

Had Thomas put rotten mushroom in Andrew’s pocket?

The indoor pool building held the locker rooms—of course Wickwood had a private pool—and the bathrooms were always crowded this time of the afternoon. But when Andrew stumbled inside, perfect silence swathed the boys’ bathroom. His tennis shoes squeaked on the white tiles, and blood dripped in a perfect line behind him, each drop as round as a marble.

He stumbled to the sinks, already grabbing at his pocket again. His shorts felt dragged half down his hips from the weight of it. But he’d emptied—

His pocket was full again, bursting at the seams.

The mushrooms were growing.

He dug out more fleshy muck and threw it in the trash. Then more. And *more*. His heart crawled into his throat and he began to shake. He couldn’t find a way this made sense.

He had to calm down. He was breathing too fast.

Stop, *stop*, and breathe. It had to be some weird super fungus. Gross, but explainable. He looked at his hands, stained brown, and tried to wipe it off. It clung to his skin, blooming there as it traced up the blue lines of his veins.

“Please, please, stop doing this.” His voice fractured, and he didn’t even know who he was talking to.

The lights flicked off, then on, and Andrew flinched. He snatched paper towels and scrubbed at his fingertips. Shit, *shit.* It didn't come off. He threw the towels aside and started scratching and then peeling at the mushroom on his fingers. It came off like a sucking mouth that left behind red welts. He flung the shed mess on the floor with a moan and stumbled back.

People should be in here. Where was the swim team? He needed witnesses. He needed Thomas to see this so he knew he wasn't going insane.

The air felt wrong. Alive. *Breathing.*

It felt like the first day back at school, the thing in the foyer with lips and fevered tongue against his neck.

pleasure

Horror.

lovely

Horror.

open your pretty mouth for meeee . . .

NO—

A stall door jerked open somewhere behind him.

Andrew's heart punched against his ribs hard enough to bruise. "Hello?" For the first time in his life, he did not freaking care who walked in and saw his bloodied face, with fungi crawling up his arm as he had the mental breakdown of a lifetime.

Please be Thomas.

But no one turned the corner.

Another stall door slammed so hard it crashed against the wall. Andrew's heart clawed up his throat, sweat slick on the back of his neck, and suddenly he couldn't breathe. He couldn't—

He took a step backward, then another. Then he ran for the last toilet and locked himself inside.

Somewhere down the row of stalls, another door slammed. Then another. Like gunshots against the stillness.

The breathing grew heavier. Something scratched against the stall doors with a high-pitched shriek. Then silence.

Andrew wiped his nose, smearing blood up his cheek. His eyes blurred as he swallowed hard. This wasn't happening. Whatever it was. It couldn't *be happening.*

He squished himself onto the closed toilet lid and pulled his knees to his chin and tried not to hyperventilate. Above him, electricity crackled along the fluorescent lights and they snapped off again. On.

Off.

Darkness fell, absolute. It crawled over his arms and pinned him there, no air to even scream.

Another stall door slammed, *slammed*—SLAM SLAM *SLAM.*

It would get to him next. He'd locked the door, but he had to choose to believe it wasn't happening, couldn't be happening. It was all in his head.

In the green glow from the emergency exit sign, legs appeared under Andrew's stall door. They were hard to distinguish, half eaten by the dark, but he could tell they were slender and furred.

A senior prank, it had to be. They hoped to make him piss his pants and then they'd laugh about it for weeks. He could get through that. He knew what it was to be a target and survive.

His mouth trembled. Too soft, too sensitive.

Pathetic—

Panic bricked up his lungs. He just wanted this to be over.

BANG. Fist against the door. It shuddered.

The legs shuffled and made two sharp, clear taps. Like iron horseshoes on tiles.

Andrew forced himself to peer under the door.

Hooves. Each leg ended in perfectly round hooves.

Fingernails scratched against the stall lock. The lock began twisting, slowly. Slowly—

just a little

a little more

and more and more and

He was whispering out loud now, a numb prayer, crushing his face to his knees. "Please, please, leave me alone—"

"Andrew."

His head snapped up, body jolting backward with nowhere to go.

Dove was there. He had no idea how she'd opened the stall door and slipped in so silently. Her skin glowed green against the emergency lights, her lips in a line of cold fury, the kind she wore when she wanted to absolutely end someone for picking on her brother. She took his hands and squeezed.

He shook so hard.

"Come on, I'll get you out of here."

"B-b-b-but the thing—" He broke off with a sound halfway between a sob and a curse. The hoofed legs had vanished, but the breathing hadn't. Thick and rasping, now coming from across the bathroom.

"Ready," Dove whispered, "set . . . *go.*"

They burst out of the stall together. She held on to him so tightly he felt like a paper kite on a string flying behind her.

Hot breath hit the back of Andrew's neck. He could feel it crawling, *crawling,* down his spine. It smelled of mold, of spoiled meat.

Andrew let out a strangled cry as Dove hauled open the door and they tumbled outside.

He stumbled into afternoon sunlight and fell onto his knees on the grass. Bile rose up his throat and he gagged on the blood slick against his teeth, on the *wrongness* of it all.

"It's just a panic attack." Dove sounded so far away.

Two juniors turned the corner, laughing and jostling, but they broke off when they saw the twins.

"Whoa," said one, while the other asked. "Um, are you okay?"

"Don't go in there." Andrew wiped blood from his mouth. "D-d-don't—"

One of them immediately pushed the door open. Andrew tried to get to his feet, to save them somehow, but he couldn't feel his bones. Couldn't stand. Couldn't think. Couldn't—

"There's legit nothing in here."

Something in Andrew's chest gave a sickening swoop. He didn't realize until that moment how scared he'd been that none of it had been real. But how could it be real, Andrew, *you goddamn fool*?

Dove petted his hair anxiously, no condemnation or embarrassment in her expression. He hated the pity, the lines around her tight mouth that said *My brother's having a meltdown over nothing again.*

It only took moments for a crowd to gather. Someone had gone for a teacher, and the track team had begun filing in from their run. People stared at Andrew with a mixture of pity and embarrassment, not quite sure if they should offer help or put distance between themselves and this mess. Andrew focused on his trembling hands, but they didn't feel attached to him. He would cry soon, he knew it, in front of all these teens who were already staring.

Words volleyed back and forth over his head as Dove fumbled an abridged explanation that would make sense. But they both knew she couldn't salvage this.

"He's not feeling well," Dove said, steel in her tone. "That's all."

"It was just some shitty prank, Perrault," someone said. "You're fine."

"S-sorry, I'm sorry. I'm s-s-s-so—" Andrew couldn't catch his breath. "There was this—this thing in there. It wasn't a prank. It was real—" But he cut off, knowing he needed to stop before he made himself look worse.

He was

l   s i n g

o

his goddamn

mind.

TEN

He curled under blankets in the dark, his spine to the wall, listening to Thomas breathe across the room. The electric clock perching on a haphazard stack of textbooks flicked to 2:00 a.m. He watched the dark melt down the ceiling and wished Thomas would fill the silence between them with a whispered *What happened? I'll take care of it for you.*

Andrew hadn't explained what had happened in the bathroom the day before—not that his supposed best friend had been around to tell. Two seconds before lights out, he had slid into their room and dived into bed, and by then Andrew felt too small to speak. It was all over the school anyway: the boy who'd had a total mental breakdown over an alleged senior prank and landed in the nurse's office for the rest of the day.

He decided that Thomas hadn't heard, instead of accepting the possibility he didn't care.

Everything felt wrong. The way the darkness bled like ink before his eyes, the ghosted memory of things *touching* him as if they wanted him, owned him.

He squeezed his eyes shut. "Thomas?"

The only response was the sound of bedsprings shifting as he rolled over and pulled the comforter over his head.

And suddenly Andrew couldn't stand it any longer. A frostbitten anger surged up his throat and he flung off his blankets and punched the desk lamp on. "*Thomas.* Wake up and listen—"

Thomas wasn't in bed.

Andrew squinted in the lamp's golden blaze and scrubbed his eyes, because he'd *seen* him a second before. Heard him moving. Breathing.

But the bed across from him lay empty, comforter and sheets scrunched up, and when Andrew crossed the room to feel the mattress, no heat remained.

Something had been there—

He had the crawling urge to look under the bed.

No, *no*. Andrew dug fingers through his hair and pulled, hissing through clenched teeth. He wasn't making this up.

A cool breeze slipped under the window. Papers rustled on the floor, and crumpled balls of Thomas's half-done drawings rolled around like tumbleweeds.

Andrew would have to wait till tomorrow to confront him—except, why was he always the one who had to be patient and quiet until someone felt like listening to him? Maybe he should force Thomas to listen.

Andrew's jaw clenched. Surely he deserved that much.

He snatched up a sweatshirt and tennis shoes and shoved the window all the way open. He bit his lip until it felt raw and swollen as he climbed down and landed in the rosebushes. He still wore pajama shorts, the cool evening biting at his bare legs, but this wouldn't take long. None of them would want to linger after Andrew busted them in the woods.

Thomas and Dove. Dove and Thomas.

Mouths against skin and shirts slipping from shoulders and the leafy green knobs of the forest's fingers tangled in their hair.

They could do him the barest courtesy of being honest about it.

He wiped at his eyes with the sleeve of his lumpy sweatshirt. It was time to change the story.

At least, he thought, as he ran across the sports field with the moonlight turning his hair silver, he still wasn't afraid of the dark.

He climbed the fence and dropped down the other side without a sound. The night folded over him as he walked into the woods. As soon as the trees stretched up tall and black on every side, he turned on his phone's flashlight and stomped around until he found the dirt track to their ancient white oak.

He decided to be noisy. No way did he want to surprise anyone.

Everything inside him had turned brittle. He couldn't fit into a love story the way he was meant to, the way the stories were always told. No one would see a point in kissing him and leaving it at that, but he didn't think he wanted anything more.

Sticks cracked underfoot and he plowed through leaves until he sounded like a petulant storm. But the tiniest worm of doubt wriggled through his stomach. Was this even a good idea? If there was *something* in the school, it could be out here, too.

Cloven hooves. Breath like wormwood rot.

"I'm not afraid," he said to the trees. "Nothing bad has ever happened in the forest."

Leaves whipped up around his ankles, and a single word slipped into the darkest places between the roots and thickets.

Liar.

Then the wind died suddenly, a switch shut off. Silence pushed down on his shoulders as if it wanted to drive him deep into the earth.

He stood still, flashing his phone light around. "Thomas? Dove? THOMAS."

The silence *breathed out.*

Goose bumps rippled up his arms.

He turned in a slow circle, his light following in a smooth arc. The beam lit up a dark lump leaning against a pine, but he moved it past before registering something had been there. A person hiding behind the tree? He slashed his light back toward the shape. Nothing. Just a single pine shot up to the sky.

"If you jump out at me," Andrew said, his voice surprisingly steady, "I will hit you so hard you'll bleed, Thomas Rye. I am *sick of this." Of you,* he wanted to add.

No one stepped out.

He clenched his teeth and spun back to continue down the rugged little path.

Something huge stood before him.

Andrew cried out, nearly dropping his phone. The light beam skittered everywhere before settling again on the thing before him.

Not Thomas.

Not Thomas.

It reached out a hand—a claw. Its arm was bone, flesh hanging off in rotting ribbons, skin pulled so tight over a naked chest that ribs punctured through. But its face—Vines poured out of its mouth, eyes, ears, growing and writhing. Blood slipped

between its lips as another vine broke out of its flesh and spooled toward the ground.

Its feet were hooves.

Andrew ran.

He flung himself forward with a cry so terrified it didn't sound like him.

This wasn't real. This *wasn't happening.*

The thing followed. He could feel it coming up behind him, a weight so heavy and intense as it came fast fast *faster— FASTER FASTER—*

His flashlight jittered so hard he couldn't see anything. The path was too small, too rough. He tripped, kept going. Tripped again. Shoved to his feet as roots and rocks cut his hands. Panic blossomed in his gut and rose up his throat in choking waves.

A claw ripped forward.

He felt it, his sweatshirt tearing as bright pain slashed across the back of his shoulder. He plummeted to his knees, scrabbling forward even before he hit the ground. His phone flew out of his hand.

The monster kept coming. The weight of it bore down, growing larger as it blocked out the whole forest above Andrew. It took hold of his leg and slowly, languorously, dragged him backward. Claws cut into his skin.

Andrew screamed and kicked out. The thing was almost all the way on top of him now. He would not get through this. He knew it.

The vines falling from the monster's mouth pulsed forward, tips flickering toward Andrew's face. Searching for somewhere to spear into and *grow.*

His eyes.

His ears.

His mouth.

He shook so hard with fear that he forgot to struggle. *Don't scream.* He had to keep his mouth closed. Don't let it in.

Then something slammed into the monster.

Andrew felt it more than saw it. The weight suddenly shoved to the side as the monster toppled to its knees, vines retracting from Andrew. It let out a roar that shook the trees to their roots.

Andrew scurried backward on all fours. His phone light must have shut off because all he had was the blackness. Pebbles bit his hands, his knees, underbrush clawing at his shirt. He couldn't stand up. He couldn't get his legs underneath him, he couldn't, he—

Hands grabbed his shoulders and hauled him up. Soft hands, warm and freckled and human.

A face shoved into Andrew's, so close he felt someone else's eyelashes on his cheek for one breath of a second.

Then he understood the yelling.

"Get up, GET UP. Andrew! Goddammit. STAND UP."

Behind them, the monster roared.

Andrew allowed himself to be dragged to his feet, but he didn't let go of the hands holding him. He clutched Thomas like he was the only thing real in a world of nightmares.

Thomas grabbed his hand and jerked him forward until they were running together down the narrow track, stumbling but gaining speed. His fingers were sweaty and kept slipping.

Thomas didn't let go.

In his free hand, he held a spike, metal like the ones staking rosebushes near the dorms. But that meant he'd brought it into the forest on purpose.

The monster lunged after them, its vines shooting outward to snatch at their shirts, their elbows, their ankles. Thomas yanked Andrew to take a hard right and they plunged into underbrush of thorny brambles.

Andrew had no air to speak, and his mouth tasted of the forest.

Thomas said, "Jump!" just in time, and Andrew had enough sense to make the leap. Then they were falling.

Terror filled him as they toppled. It was only a few feet, but they slammed hard to the ground and Andrew crashed to his knees, pulling Thomas on top of him. They must've tumbled into a small gully, tree roots making a natural overhang. They barely fit under the ledge. But with legs pulled up to their chins and their backs to the wall of dirt, they had a second to catch their breath.

Thomas wrapped one arm around Andrew's neck and closed a hand over his mouth. His fingers dug into Andrew's jaw so hard there would be thumbprint bruises there tomorrow.

The forest had gone silent.

They were pressed so tight together, hearts pounding and chests heaving in rhythm. Everything smelled of mud and sweat and blood. Dirt crumbled above them and pattered into their hair.

They could hear the monster standing above the overhang, sniffing the air.

Thomas did not loosen his hand over Andrew's mouth, but inexplicably he turned and pressed his lips against Andrew's filth-streaked forehead. It lasted half a second. A kiss, but not. Comfort, but useless. The promise, *I'm here*, without words.

Andrew breathed out, shuddering.

Then the monster jumped.

It landed in front of them in a shower of dirt and snapped roots. Its vines shot forward as it roared, reaching for the boys locked together. They slammed into Andrew first, clawing up his body, and he couldn't scream because of Thomas's hand.

But then Thomas let go.

He lunged forward to run.

He didn't grab for Andrew. Didn't reach back. Didn't try to save—

Andrew flung his arms over his face and folded to the forest floor. The horrible weight of this realization bloomed through his heart—that Thomas would escape alone and Andrew would crumble, and didn't that just fit them perfectly?

Except then Thomas howled.

He came up behind the monster and swung his garden spike, slamming it against the monster's skull. The crack echoed through the forest. Thomas swung again and again, as if it were a baseball bat and he wanted nothing left but splinters.

The monster reeled backward, vines jerking away from Andrew, slashing out toward Thomas instead.

Andrew stayed where he was, curled among the leaves.

Only the thinnest rays of moonlight piercing through the canopy lit the battle. Thomas smashed the spike again and again into the monster's head. Bones cracked. Vines lunged toward his face, tried to catch his arms and pin them, but Thomas moved in a violent kaleidoscope, impossible to catch.

Then the monster slipped and went to its knees. Thomas gave a gravelly cry of feral triumph as he shoved the spike into the monster's eye.

He put all his weight into it, driving it deeper and deeper as the monster went down screaming. Blood splattered across Thomas, murky and black. He didn't stop until the thing lay on its back, the garden spike through its skull and driven into the earth below.

The screaming stopped. Its hooves twitched a few times. Then silence fell in a dense, velvet curtain across the world.

There was nothing but this:

Andrew curled with his knees to his chest, watching in numb horror.

Thomas forcing his fingers to release the spike as he slowly straightened.

He flexed his hands and looked at the blood smeared up to his elbows. He toed the motionless monster and then took a step away from it. Then another.

He wiped his mouth, smearing blood across his cheek.

Finally, he looked at Andrew.

"Please don't hate me," Thomas whispered.

They gently lowered the fairy prince's body into a glass coffin, leaving bloody fingerprints smudged on the case. His chest had been caved in from battles fought and lost, and they'd filled the space between his ribs with flowers. Even now the flowers grew, blossoming as they drank the last of his blood.

The princess's silver tears fell like rain upon the coffin. True love's kiss should wake him, but she had tried seven times and nothing had happened.

Behind the princess stood her brother, a poet with soft lips and soft moss for hair.

He whispered, "Let me try." But no one heard.

They buried the fairy prince alone.

By evening, the flowers had grown over his whole face.

ELEVEN

Thomas pulled Andrew to his feet and led him out of the forest.

They walked slow, adrenaline draining with each step and leaving them with bones of water. Andrew still clung to Thomas's hand, their fingers laced and palms slick with blood and mud. One of them had forgotten to let go.

Climbing the fence felt impossible, but they forced themselves over. Andrew ripped his sweatshirt on the jagged wire at the top, but Thomas slipped and sliced his arm. He looked at it with dull, unfocused eyes, like he didn't even feel it. They were almost back to the dorms before Andrew realized he was in the lead.

He was the one dragging Thomas, forcing him on, holding him together.

Since when did their places *switch*?

When they'd climbed back through their window, their room didn't seem real. Andrew touched his mouth, his eyes, as if phantom vines still dug at his skin. Maybe he was the one who had stopped being real. He was falling outside of himself.

Thomas sank down on Andrew's bed and stared at his shaking hands. His nails were bitten to stubs, blood tracing the creases in his muddy palms.

Andrew dropped down beside him, their bodies jammed tight together, hip to hip. "How bad are you hurt?"

"I should be asking you that." Thomas's voice cracked around the edges as if he'd been screaming too long. Maybe he had, before Andrew got there.

"It got my shoulder, I think." Andrew felt nothing, so it didn't seem important. "This . . . this isn't real."

Thomas let out a laugh that withered into a sob. "They're not always that big. The smaller ones have bones of clay and glass, and they're easier to break. I have to kill them, every time, because if I don't, they climb the fence and get into school. They could attack anyone, go anywhere. I h-h-h-have to stop them."

Thomas peeled off Andrew's bed and dragged out a cardboard box full of bandages, disinfectant swabs, butterfly tape, even a bottle of mild painkillers. A survival kit.

He ripped open packages with his teeth with the familiarity of routine.

"You do this every night." Andrew sat frozen. "You never told me—" He choked. "We have to tell someone. We have to—"

"*No.*" Thomas looked up, and his eyes blazed with such vehemence that Andrew flinched.

He'd nearly said, *We have to tell Dove,* but maybe they shouldn't. Part of him sat there melting in shameful relief that he had been wrong about Thomas and Dove meeting in the forest, wrong thinking Thomas hated him. He was so relieved that a manic smile tugged at his lips. Sure, monsters were real and wanted to rip out their throats, but at least he still had his best friend.

Thomas slumped back on the bed, swiveling to sit cross-legged. "Take off your shirt."

A ripple went through Andrew's stomach. He obeyed, wincing when fabric stuck to bloodied skin. When he tried to see the damage, Thomas took hold of Andrew's chin and forced him to look away. Then he carefully swabbed Andrew's shoulder with one hand while the other pressed over his collarbone, which lit him up in a horribly beautiful way.

"They'll come after you now," Thomas said. "They've tasted your blood."

"They already did," Andrew said. "Yesterday in the bathrooms. I-I saw the hooves. It was hunting me."

Thomas made a tight, vexed sound. "They grow out of the forest every night, and I used to think they'd disappear when the sun rises. But they don't. If I don't kill them all, they'll go after anyone I hang around. That's why my . . ."

"Your parents," Andrew breathed.

Everything made sense.

Thomas's voice shook so much he kept stopping to swallow. "That day before school started? The fight the neighbors heard? It was a *monster*. I hid. I listened to my parents fight it, but they're always high these days, and I didn't think it was *real*. How could it be goddamn real? I took a knife from the kitchen, but then I saw what it looked like and I ran. I just ran."

His fingers traced the edges of Andrew's cut shoulder before he taped on the bandage. Pain had arrived, white-hot and throbbing, but Andrew still didn't care. Thomas's misery had filled the whole room, and they drowned in it, together.

"I killed my parents," Thomas said, soft and sick and terrified.

"Stop it." Blood roared in Andrew's ears. "These monsters aren't your fault. You didn't ask them to attack—"

"Didn't I?" Thomas went to his desk and dug out a sketchbook. He pulled a loose sheet from between the pages, smoothing out the wreckage of crumpled edges. Then he flung it on the floor. It was the drawing Thomas had snatched away on the roof—the seventh son staring into a wishing well, while a monster with a torn-off wolf's head ate his parents in the background.

Thomas's voice stretched with anguish. "That's what it looked like. The monster in my house. Just like this, down to the stitching at its throat. And this—" He tore a drawing off the wall so hard the corners were left behind.

Andrew yanked it from Thomas's bloodied hands and stared.

Hooves, and corpse skin, and vines exploding from its mouth and ears and eyes.

The monster from the woods.

"When did you—" He stopped.

"I don't know . . . Last year sometime?" Thomas dug fingers through his hair and paced between their beds. "It's not a coincidence. I'm doing this. I'm-I'm *creating them.*"

Andrew couldn't hold the shape of this. He stared at the drawing until it blurred, and then he ripped it up and let the pieces scatter like charcoal confetti.

"I shouldn't tell you this. It'll make it worse." Thomas wrapped arms round his stomach. "They'll kill you like they want to kill me. I can't bear it if they take you from me, too. I need—I need—I'm so *goddamn tired.* It's every night, okay? Every night I go into the woods and fight them so they don't climb the fence, but I can't make them stop. I c-c-can't—"

Thomas would wake up the whole dorm if he kept spiraling

like this. If their counselor burst in here, there'd be no way to explain the blood, their dirt-streaked faces, or why Thomas was ranting about *monsters*.

Andrew grabbed Thomas's shirt and pulled him back down to the bed to cut off the frantic pacing. He cupped a hand over Thomas's mouth, nothing like the bruising way his own face had been gripped in the forest; this was delicate and tentative and full of want.

Thomas went quiet.

Words seemed weak and meaningless when drawings could wake up monsters, so Andrew didn't ask. He peeled Thomas's shirt off and searched for the worst wound—a slash right over his ribs. Blood still oozed sluggishly from torn flesh.

Andrew pushed Thomas's shoulder until he collapsed back onto the pillows. He lay there, chest moving too fast while Andrew cleaned his cuts. Where Thomas had been brusque and efficient, Andrew worked with a featherlight touch. He splayed his fingers over Thomas's heaving stomach until the dry sobs slowed.

They'd never had so much bare skin between them, so much blood.

Andrew's heart felt bruised and weary, but he made his voice steel. "I'll help."

Thomas flung an arm over his eyes. "You know how there's an old boarded-up well in the grove behind my house? I can't even tell the cops to check in there because it's as good as a confession. And if I start raving about monsters, they'll still lock me up."

"I get it, but there has to be an answer. A reason this is

happening. But you can't keep pushing me away." Andrew swabbed the cut harder, and was rewarded with a hiss from Thomas.

"I can't protect you and fight monsters, too."

It stung, but it was true. Andrew had been worse than useless tonight, but he'd been in shock. He'd do better next time.

"You can't figure out why this is happening," Andrew said, steady, "while you're fighting monsters with no sleep. Let me help."

Thomas kept his arm over his eyes and said nothing.

For a vicious moment, Andrew thought about slipping his fingers into Thomas's cut. Taking hold of his rib and *breaking it.* Pulling the soft crumbling bone from his chest and sewing it into his own. They'd be forever together, rib against rib, fused in gore and bone and adoration.

Andrew squeezed his eyes shut.

That wasn't him. He was infected by this night of woken nightmares and ebbing adrenaline—and the starved desperation of wanting Thomas, Thomas, only Thomas.

He taped a bandage over Thomas's wound and disinfected all the other cuts he could find.

"Are you scared of me?" Thomas's voice was small.

"No," Andrew said. "We'll stop this. Everything that starts has a way to end."

Thomas fell asleep in Andrew's bed.

Andrew thought about curling up beside him and seeing if their bodies fit together like they'd been carved from the same oak. Instead, he stared out the window until dawn blushed the sky and let the truth of last night sink into his bones. Horrors always felt less real in the daylight, but this wouldn't go away.

Andrew hadn't asked it in the dark, but the question burned him.

Who was Thomas Rye that he could make monsters?

What was he—

Even though he'd slept for barely two hours, Andrew woke Thomas at the first alarm. They couldn't draw attention to themselves—they had too much to hide.

Somehow Andrew had been shoved into playing the part of the steady one. That should be Dove's place, the one who spoke sense to balance Thomas's fiery impulses and Andrew's panic spirals. She should be the one drawing up a flowchart for how to defeat monsters and still pass their classes. But he was forbidden to tell her.

So it was Andrew who got them dressed and through breakfast where they drank too much black coffee and ate almost nothing before stumbling to their first classes.

It was like Thomas had been holding himself together with string and Scotch tape, and now he'd crumpled. The walls he'd put up had been punched through and he didn't have the energy to rebuild.

All day he hovered around Andrew, stood too close to him, found every excuse to touch him with anxious fingers. It felt like he'd crawl inside Andrew's shirt if he could, sew himself inside Andrew's skin.

Usually Andrew was the one who lay in shattered pieces needing to be put together, so this reversal at least felt fair. He owed it to Thomas.

Because Thomas, beautiful and harrowed and magical, was falling apart.

They sat in calculus when it happened. Andrew had opened his textbook before he noticed Thomas gripping his desk so hard his knuckles had gone white. He hadn't brought a single pencil or notebook into class. He stared straight ahead, his eyes blank as his breathing grew faster and faster.

Panic attack.

Andrew's heartbeat skipped in sympathy, and he leaned over his desk. "Thomas."

Professor Clemens strode in, calling out an enthusiastic greeting. He was white and much younger than their previous teacher and always wore dashing three-piece suits with thick glasses and a charming smile. On day one of school, everyone decided he was hot. On day two, they rearranged their opinion: They all *hated* him.

Clemens demanded perfection. Perfect work, perfect focus, perfect attitudes, perfect respect toward him. Anything less, he mocked. He singled out students with jibes that burned like acid, made people do their work on the whiteboard and ridiculed them the entire time, and cheerfully gave out Fs if anyone so much as spoke back.

It was the power, Andrew knew. Some people could get drunk on it.

"Good morning, students," Clemens said, bright and energetic. He slid off his tweed jacket and rolled his shirtsleeves. "We have a lot to do today, so I'm glad to see everyone in their seats. That pop quiz last week was *fun*, right? Warm congratulations to Mr. Emerson and Miss Obara for full marks. Mr. Murphy got three out of twenty-five, which none of us are surprised about. Miss Sato didn't show her work, so I'll assume she cheated and mark accordingly." His smile grew wider as students shrank. "Ah, Mr. Rye, who loves to nap in my class. Today's question is for you." He picked up a whiteboard marker and wrote fast across the board.

Does Thomas Rye Know How to Read?

A few nervous titters rippled through the class.

Andrew's throat knotted so hard he couldn't swallow. The only reason he didn't get singled out was because Dove did his homework.

Thomas didn't even notice he was today's target. He stared at his desk, each breath low and ragged, still coming too fast.

Clemens tapped the marker on the board. "Judging from your mark of a big fat zero, I'd say the answer to this problem is: No. But we show our work in class, don't we, Mr. Rye? Come to the front and redo question four."

Thomas didn't move.

Clemens had his back to the class, writing briskly across the whiteboard. "Pens out, everyone. Let's play a game. Slowest to find the answer to this problem is next at the whiteboard."

The class buckled down to work without a sound.

"Wake up, Mr. Rye, or you'll be spending the whole class up front with me."

Andrew leaned over and tried to pry Thomas's fingers off his desk. "Hey. You have to slow your breathing."

"I c-can't." His lips hardly moved. "I can't . . . I can't . . ."

Thomas was in pain. Nothing else mattered.

Andrew shoved out of his desk, his chair clattering. Half the class turned to stare.

Andrew framed Thomas's face with his hands to focus his attention. "Look at me."

"This is calculus, not drama, boys," Clemens said in a mocking singsong voice.

Andrew whirled, his cheeks flaming and a *go to hell* stuck in his throat. "He needs some air."

Clemens flicked Thomas a mocking once-over. "Sure. Why not. Why don't we all just skip class today because we don't feel like working? Who cares about grades? Who cares about college?"

Andrew yanked Thomas from his desk and towed him out of the room. He moved like a puppet, strings cut and tangled around Andrew's fists.

Clemens opened the door for them. "You're asking for a failing mark, both of you. Once you've finished your little break, head over to the principal's office and let the secretary know you skipped for fun. Theatrics don't work on me."

The classroom door shut behind them.

In the hall, the world felt still and gray. The air tasted of dust motes and paper, of the muffled weight of being alone.

Thomas started to sink to the floor, but Andrew took fistfuls of his shirt and shoved him against the wall. Hard. Thomas flinched, but he was still hyperventilating.

"Stop it." Andrew pressed against him and dug his fingers into Thomas's collarbone.

"I'm dying." Thomas's mouth trembled.

"It's a panic attack. I have a thousand of them a day, but you *can't*. You're the strong one."

Thomas's whimper came low in his throat, raw and fissured. "I can't keep doing this. Not every night. I can't, I can't—"

"You're not alone anymore, all right? I swear it."

Thomas closed his eyes.

"What if it's your sketchbook?" Andrew said. "It could be cursed. You have to stop drawing."

"I did stop. The only thing I've drawn in ages is a stupid fruit bowl for art class. But I-I have to pass art. It's my *one* thing. Wickwood will expel me if I fail every class. I'll lose you, I'll lose—"

Andrew didn't want to hear him say Dove, didn't want that reminder of who Thomas truly wanted to comfort him in this moment.

"You won't lose me," Andrew said fiercely.

Thomas's tie had come undone, his blazer abandoned, old paint staining his cuffs. He looked a mess, mussy and unhinged. When Andrew let go, Thomas slid down the wall and sat there while Andrew stood over him, his legs a protective wall around Thomas's crumpled body.

"Maybe it's the pens you use?" Andrew's mind powered into a frenzied whirl. "Or you've bled onto the drawings. And the blood, like, maybe it invoked something."

"I didn't." Thomas played with the cuff of Andrew's trousers. "I don't even think while I draw sometimes. I'll listen to music and draw random shit. It doesn't *mean* anything. I just like monsters. Well, I used to."

Back when their teeth were paper, not bone.

Andrew pressed his knuckles to the wall. "Let's destroy your sketchbook in the forest tonight."

"You're not coming."

"I'm coming," Andrew said.

Thomas didn't argue again. He wiped at his face with the back of his hand and let out a shaky breath.

His breathing evened out, but he made no move to get up. Andrew didn't care, not while they still touched. He craved Thomas's affection, with an intensity that left him dizzy. If he never had more, he had this.

It was almost worth being ripped apart by monsters.

TWELVE

They waited till midnight.

Andrew sat in bed, textbook on his lap, but his notebook open over the top as he penned the first lines of a new story. It started with a wicked creature who carved tears off faces to sate his thirst, until he chose a victim who clutched a knife made of antler bone and used it to slash the wicked creature's face instead.

Writing felt selfish, especially when Thomas lay on his own bed, tapping a pencil against his lips and staring at the ceiling, forbidden to draw. This had to be part of why he'd severed himself with such ferocious finality from Andrew over the last few weeks. Andrew would've noticed the lack of charcoal-smudged sleeves and paint in his hair. This had to be a bitter withdrawal.

Thomas sighed for the thousandth time and drummed the pencil against the wall. His old drawings stared back; bone crowns and monster teeth and wicked forests and the curve of a poisonous apple.

"I have till Thanksgiving to decide on my end-of-year art project," Thomas said dully. "Or, you know, I'll fail. I've convinced Ms. Poppy I have *artist block* and she's being nice about it, which just makes me feel even more like shit."

Andrew didn't answer for a long time. "When's the witching hour?"

"I dunno. Two a.m. isn't it? Or three?"

"Do the monsters get worse then? Stronger? It could be . . . witchcraft."

Thomas chewed the end of the pencil. "You believe in that?"

Andrew closed his notebook. "You've kind of warped reality. I'm pretty sure we have to believe in everything now."

Thomas bit the pencil so hard it cracked. He lay there with a mouthful of splinters for so long Andrew nearly shook him, terrified he'd try to swallow them.

Finally Thomas got up, picking splinters from his lips. "I guess they appear around the witching hour every night, but I don't think that's the problem. I think the problem is me."

They walked into the woods side by side, so close their shoulders brushed. When they reached a winding, overgrown track, too thin for two, Thomas went first. He kept glancing over his shoulder, reaching back with a hand to touch Andrew and be sure he was safe.

In the dark, Thomas's eyes turned to pools of black, the fear in them a living thing. The forest should have scared Andrew, too. But it didn't.

Last night, he'd been terrified out of his mind, but he felt different now, solid and firmly inside himself as he walked. This time he'd worn jeans and boots, and tugged on a Wickwood hoodie against the cool September air. Both he and Thomas carried flashlights and spikes they'd dug from the garden, dirt still clumped at the points. The gardener would be pissed to find the new rosebushes robbed, but the boys didn't have much choice.

Andrew carried the sketchbook. Thomas didn't want to touch it.

"We need better weapons." Andrew's voice felt too loud.

"Do you know what would happen if they found so much as a *butter knife* in my room?" Thomas said. "You didn't see how the cops questioned me. They think I'm a murderer."

Andrew stumbled on a knotted root and Thomas spun around to steady him, taking a little too long to let go.

He swallowed and kept walking. "If I get expelled, I'll never see you again. I don't even know who'd take me. My grandparents are in a retirement village. My aunt *hates* my mother and won't have anything to do with me."

"I'd take you." Andrew swung his flashlight around the trees. "I'd pack you into my carry-on."

"Like, okay, I'm short, but not that short."

Andrew snorted.

Thomas narrowed his eyes, but when Andrew smiled, the glower melted off Thomas's face. This was good. Keep him talking. Keep his focus off his all-consuming dread.

"I need to find my phone," Andrew said. "Do the monsters come to you? Or do you have to find them?"

"They find me. It's better not to hide." His voice sounded moth-eaten. "I always want to get it over with. I'm so goddamn tired."

Andrew tucked the sketchbook under his arm and turned in a slow circle. His flashlight carved a groove through the blackness and revealed nothing but trees. No monsters. Night sounds twisted around their bodies as the wind rustled through the trees and crickets thrummed. An owl called to the dark. Thomas jumped, but Andrew took a deep breath of moss and damp leaves, of the vivid green life of the forest pulsing under their feet.

It felt like they'd made the monsters up, a shared fever dream.

Something bit at Andrew's neck and he slapped it. "The only things attacking me are bugs."

"How are you not scared?" Thomas asked softly.

Andrew scuffed leaves around, looking for his phone. "I don't know. I'm crazy?"

Thomas's tone came hard. "Don't say stuff like that."

Andrew sighed. "I think . . . it's because everything wrecks me. *Everything.* I'm so freaked out all the time and there's no reason, just my brain imploding on itself. But monsters are something we can kill, and I think I like that." He let out a flat laugh. "My brain is so broken."

It was easier to make it a joke than close his eyes and think about the hundreds of times he'd been so anxious he'd ended up in tears, vomiting and frantic. Dove would hold him and say, *Tell me what's wrong. How can I help if you won't say what's wrong?*

Andrew didn't know. Life didn't fit against his skin and it never had and sometimes everything was just too much.

Thomas backed up so they stood with spines aligned. "You're not broken."

"I am."

Thomas turned off his flashlight and Andrew did, too. They

stood for a moment in the dark, before Thomas said, "I like how you are. There's an entire world of ink and magic stuffed inside your head, and I think it's beautiful. I just wish everything didn't hurt you so much."

There was an explosion happening in Andrew's chest, a thousand flowered vines growing around his heart. Thomas never talked like this, soft and vulnerable. Maybe it was easier to whisper sweet and aching things in the dark.

Andrew let out a soft, shaky breath, needing to say something back, needing to lean into this gentleness.

But then Thomas flicked his light back on and said, "We're never going to find your phone," and he slouched off down the path.

Andrew followed. He slapped his neck again. It felt like bugs had landed on his back, bloodthirsty little things. "I swear I dropped it near here. I was near some clump of trees—"

"I've got news for you about forests."

Andrew ignored him. "Hey, you know how tomorrow is Saturday? And there's that senior trip to the art gallery in the city?"

"It's not compulsory."

"I put our names down."

Thomas groaned. "I wanted to *sleep*."

Andrew shook the sketchbook. "We can buy new art supplies. If you draw on a brand-new canvas, maybe it'll be different." Another bug dive-bombed his neck and he yelped, using the sketchbook to thwack at it.

"I don't think that's—Andrew. *Andrew.* What the hell—" Thomas ran back toward him. "Holy shit . . . turn around."

Andrew's stomach dropped. Slowly, he turned. He could

feel it then, as Thomas let out a hiss, the way something *skittered* across the back of his hoodie. The weight of a thousand tiny bodies pinned to his back, wings beating in a growing hum.

"Stay really still." But Thomas sounded faint.

Andrew closed his eyes. Something pricked him behind the ear, but this time he didn't slap it. "Please don't say they're wasps."

"I think they're . . . um, thistle fairies."

"Thomas," Andrew said, trying to keep his voice even. "What the hell did you draw?"

"You wrote about them first! I just sketched those stupid little fairies from your story one time. They're the size of thistles, but their teeth are long and sharp, and they drink blood. They're . . . they're all over your back."

Andrew stayed very still. "How many?"

The humming grew louder and his shoulder dipped as more thistle fairies landed. They crawled across his back, his neck, their tiny sharp feet nicking skin as they found his collar and peeled it back. He tried to repress the shudder. Every impulse inside him begged to shake, to scream, *run*. If they burrowed down his shirt—

"Thomas . . ." His voice started to crack.

"There's a lot, okay? I'll get them off you. Just don't . . . move. If all of them bite you at once you'll—just don't move."

Andrew held his breath. His flashlight froze on the pines in front of him while his back grew heavier and heavier. He'd been a fool. He thought monsters came in shapes huge and terrifying, not tiny and insidious with wasp stings and spider teeth. This was somehow worse.

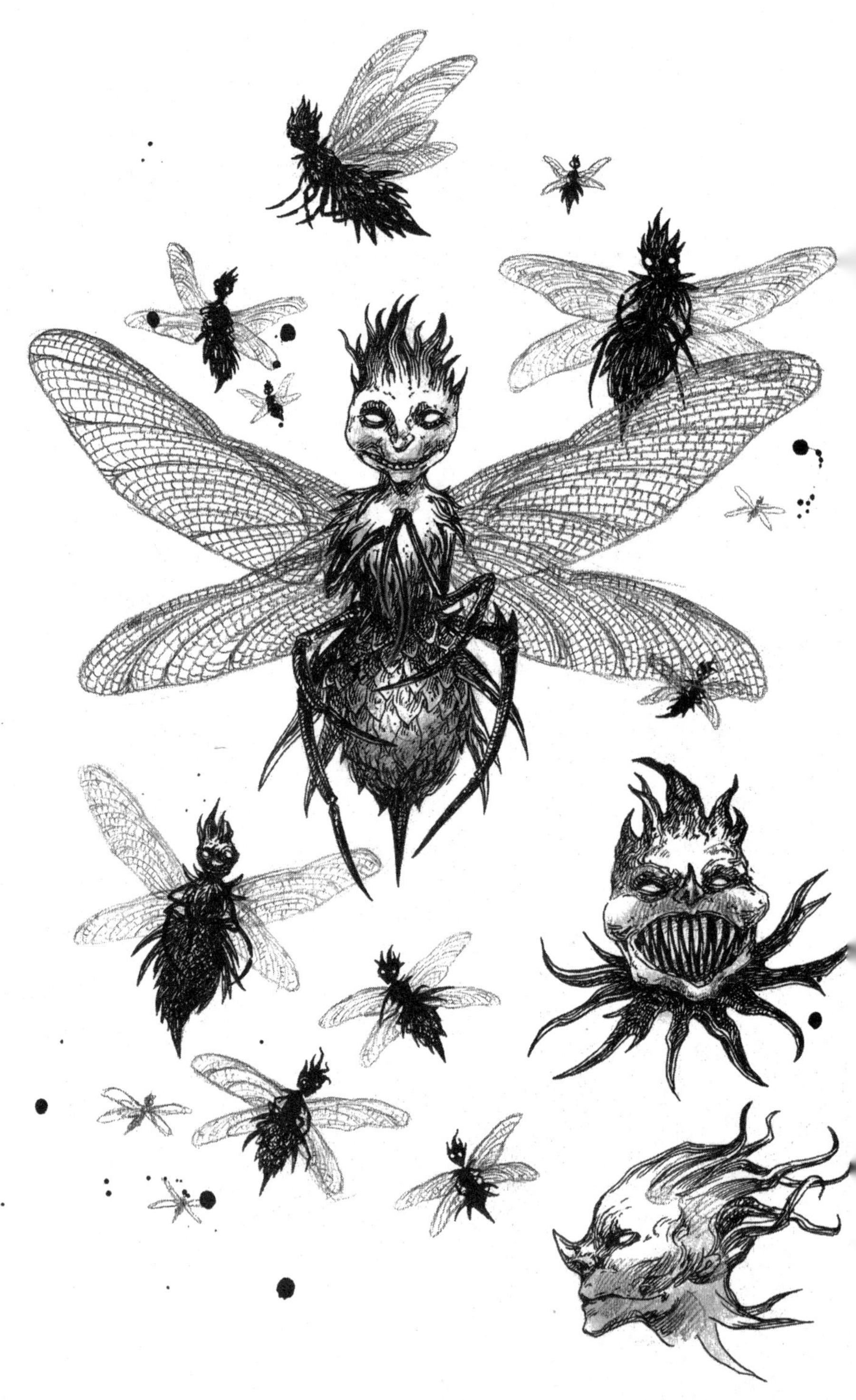

He could feel them at his ears, wings brushing sensitive skin, the first prick of teeth testing flesh. Could they crawl down his ears? Could they sting *inside him*?

Behind him, a spike clunked to the ground.

Andrew tilted his head slightly to see Thomas slip off his shirt and throw it aside. He clawed off some of his bandages from last night and, with a shaky breath, dug his fingers into his own barely healed wounds.

Andrew started to cry out for him to stop, but he was cut off by Thomas's choked sob as he punctured his scabbed cuts and dug his fingers in until blood oozed out, violent and fresh. He smeared the blood across his chest, then took a step back. And another.

"Destroy the sketchbook," he said.

Suddenly the weight on Andrew's back ripped free. The air filled with the humming roar of a thousand wings.

And they all slammed into Thomas.

"GO." Thomas was already running the opposite way, taking them away from Andrew.

Andrew burst forward, his flashlight swinging as he bolted. He shot a glance over his shoulder to see Thomas's bare back covered in thistle fairies. The smell of his blood left no need for further invitation. They shrieked, shrill and victorious and *starving*.

A cry ripped from Thomas.

Andrew ran.

He didn't know where to go, so he flung himself down the path, the woods echoing with Thomas's muffled screams. Their white oak lay ahead. Thickets thinned and the underbrush turned to ground scattered with leaves.

Andrew fell to his knees and skidded in the dirt, flipping pages fast until he found it. Thistle fairies. Thomas had done a study of them, dozens of little green creatures with features honed into sharp points like the tines of forks. One stretched its maw wide to show too-long needle teeth. They could slip right into a throat, veins, reach all the way to a spine—

He ripped up the page and started clawing a hole in the ground near the tree's roots. At least he wasn't seeing blood—rich and vile, turning the ground to sickening mud—this time. But he couldn't dig deep, not as stones and grit tore apart his fingernails, and Thomas's cries grew more desperate behind him. Andrew tore up every page in the sketchbook until there was nothing left but fluffy shreds, and then he buried them all, smoothing leaves over the top of the dirt.

Andrew swallowed. It had to be over now.

He punched to his feet and ran back toward Thomas. Not ran, he *flew*.

Thomas, Thomas, *Thomas*.

It took less than a minute to get back, but Andrew's calm had shattered. It was as if the monsters had noticed him being stoic and factual about this horror, and they'd found the best way to slit him open and make him pay.

Try to kill Thomas, and Andrew would lose his goddamn mind.

The thistle fairies hadn't dropped dead the second the sketchbook had been torn up, but no new ones arrived. They still clawed all over Thomas's bare back, his stomach, his shoulders. They burrowed into his ears and climbed his ribs like ladder rungs and sank their teeth into every bit of soft flesh they could find.

Thomas had dropped his flashlight, and he slammed himself against a tree to kill them. He picked creatures off by their wings and crushed them in his fist. Their tiny bodies exploded in green pus that oozed between his fingers.

He dropped to his knees and let out a broken sob.

Andrew snatched Thomas's abandoned tee shirt off the ground and used it to swipe fairies off his back. He threw the shirt down and stomped on it. Their deaths smelled of cut grass and copper.

"This s-s-s-sucks." Thomas ripped thistle fairies off his throat.

"You shouldn't have done this," Andrew hissed.

"Someone always has to be the sacrifice."

"That someone doesn't have to be you. This isn't your fault." Andrew wrapped his hands in the tee shirt and picked more thistle fairies off Thomas. Each one felt like pulling out a pin buried viciously deep.

Thomas looked at him then, his eyes pooling with tears. "Maybe it *is* my fault. Maybe last year, I made this happen when—"

Andrew didn't want to hear it. He abandoned the shirt and hauled Thomas to his feet. He shoved him against a tree so Thomas could grip the branches as Andrew pried the last fairies out of his skin. His back was a battlefield.

Andrew twisted the last thistle fairy's wings off and dropped it to the ground. He let it writhe around with malevolent, waspish howls before he ground it into the dirt with the heel of his boot.

Thomas crumpled. Every inch of him looked bloodied and

swollen, riddled with puncture marks and lacerations. Andrew felt sick looking at him.

"The sketchbook is destroyed and buried," Andrew said, ragged. "It's over." He knelt slowly, expecting the other boy wouldn't want to be touched, but Thomas flung his arms around Andrew's neck. His sobs came silent, desperate, anguished.

Andrew tried to slow his heartbeat. "Don't ever do that again." He didn't recognize the hard edge to his voice. It felt like black frost had grown all over his tongue. He dug his fingers into Thomas's hair until his breathing hitched at the pain of it.

Thomas didn't answer, maybe he couldn't. It didn't matter anyway. Andrew was busy listening to the echo of monsters cackling among the trees at this pathetic display of bravery.

The monsters knew how weak these boys were and they found it

delightful.

THIRTEEN

The world had no business being this bitterly crisp at 6:00 a.m. The cold stung Andrew's fingertips as he dressed with eyes half-closed, his headache not helped by the feet pounding up and down the dorm halls. Voices clamored and doors slammed. The bus would leave in an hour and no senior wanted to miss the first outing of the year. The art gallery tour would swallow the morning, but they'd been promised the afternoon loose in the city. Senior privileges.

Andrew threw another pillow at Thomas. "Sound off if you're alive."

Thomas gave a muffled groan but didn't get up.

"I'll bribe you." Andrew messed around with his tie and frowned at the place where the mirror used to hang on the inner side of his wardrobe door. It was for the best that he couldn't see the too-sharp cheekbones and dark circles under his eyes. "We're buying art supplies. You can draw again." He paused. "We'll get coffee."

Thomas dragged a pillow over his head. "Kill me."

A fist thumped on their door, their counselor's voice far too cheerful. "Thirty-minute warning!"

Andrew took the edge of Thomas's quilt and flipped it off him. "I refuse to feel sorry for you when you *chose* to be a jackass martyr. Get up." He gently picked at the bandage on Thomas's back to check the wounds. "It's not too bad." He winced only because Thomas had his face buried and wouldn't see.

The bites had turned bright red, some scabbed over and others now swollen bumps, feverishly hot to the touch. He was riddled with them, and the pain had to be excruciating.

Thomas's voice came muffled from the pillows. "I feel like a pincushion."

"That's because you are. But you have to come. I don't know what art stuff to get, and I'll come back with crayons or something." He ran fingers over Thomas's shoulder blades before realizing what he was doing. He snatched his hand away. "Get up." He kept his voice light.

Thomas slithered boneless to the floor, but it was sort of progress.

Andrew left for the bathroom. He desperately needed Dove to tell him what to do. If they told her the truth about the monsters . . . well, she'd explode, furious and frantic. Thomas clearly did not want her to know, and Andrew understood that now. They could give Dove this, protection from things most foul and malevolent. Though he wasn't sure if he most wanted to hide the monsters' existence or how the nights belonged to him and Thomas alone now. He didn't want her to know he liked that.

He missed his phone and their constant stream of texts. He was a rotten brother these days, but Thomas needed him. Andrew hadn't meant to choose between them, but he had.

He checked on Thomas, who had put one leg in his pants with his eyes closed while mumbling something about coffee. Andrew grabbed his backpack and slipped outside.

He hurried down the garden path to the girls' dorm, but couldn't work up the courage to ask the girls lingering out front to get Dove for him. Apparently he could hunt monsters in the woods, but still not talk to people without his words cramping in his mouth.

One of the girls noticed him lurking and started to wave, but her friend knocked her hand down and began whispering. Smiles disappeared. Pity filled their expressions. His breakdown in the bathroom had not helped his reputation of being that highly strung boy who smashed his own hand last year.

Andrew fled.

Students already crowded the marble front steps of Wickwood as the bus pulled in. Andrew hung back, dread gnawing an acidic hole in his stomach. What if Thomas didn't arrive in time? What if he had blood poisoning or an infection or—

Stop. He needed to just—stop.

Bryce Kane and his vultures were harassing the girls boarding the bus, but they cut it out as soon as Ms. Poppy appeared with a huge thermos and a dreamy smile. The art teacher wore a patchwork skirt the size of a small country and golden bangles against her dark skin. Every year the student council unanimously awarded her Most Lovely Teacher. Andrew started to relax knowing she'd be in charge of this trip, until he saw Professor Clemens stroll off the bus with his smarmy smile. He'd ensured both boys served a lengthy detention after Andrew had yanked Thomas from class to quell his panic attack, and even the sight of the professor made anxiety ripple through Andrew's stomach.

"Why do you look like you swallowed a frog?"

Andrew's heart punched into his throat as he whirled, but only Thomas stood there, yawning and scrubbing a hand through his matted curls. He looked like a cat that had been put through the dryer—pants wrinkled, collar popped, tie draped like a scarf, blazer missing, shirt untucked and flecked with old paint. He had sleepy eyes and a disgruntled mouth, and he kept scowling at the growing crowd of boisterous seniors like they existed just to spite him.

"Clemens is driving the bus," Andrew whispered.

Thomas made a face. "He can eat nails. What's in your backpack? Snacks? I need snacks. Sugar, specifically."

"What you need is to be ironed."

Thomas slumped his forehead against Andrew's shoulder. "I need to be treated softly, like a delicate egg."

Andrew gave a wry smile, but it slipped as soon as he saw Lana Lang thundering toward them. Her boots seemed to grow more violently purple every time he saw her.

Lana halted before them, her glare hard on Thomas. "Are you *hungover*? Because, wow."

Thomas jerked his head off Andrew's shoulder and put space between them. Andrew tried not to read anything into that.

"I am *not*," he muttered. "Take your judgmental self somewhere else."

"Right, well, once Mister Bad Decisions gets kicked off the trip"—Lana turned to Andrew—"feel free to come sit with us."

"He's not hungover," Andrew said quickly.

A muscle ticked in Thomas's jaw. "And he doesn't need you fussing over him."

Lana crossed her arms, attitude simmering toward a boil. "Dove asked me to watch out for him, so I am. She told me everything about you, Thomas Rye, and I mean *everything*. Especially about you and—"

"You know what? I don't need this." Thomas turned, tugging Andrew after him.

But Andrew stayed rooted. How had these two gone from zero to war in a matter of seconds? And did this mean Dove wasn't coming on the trip? Now that he knew she and Thomas hadn't made up and weren't having clandestine make-out sessions in the forest, he'd reverted back to guessing they were still in a fight.

He needed to talk to her. He always needed Dove.

"Tell Andrew the truth, then," Lana snapped. "Dove said you were a coward and she was right."

Panic crept into Andrew's voice. "What truth?"

Thomas whirled back and got in Lana's face, but she didn't move an inch. The way her eyebrows rose was equal parts scathing and condescending, and Thomas's attempt at looking formidable was lost due to them being the same height.

"You don't know anything about me," he said, low and venomous. "And you know less about Andrew if you think he's some delicate wallflower that you need to ball up in cotton wool. He could cut me to bloody pieces if he wanted. I couldn't stop him even if I tried. So can you stop pretending he needs saving from me? Back up and *leave us alone*."

There was something so raw about being known this intimately, being understood down to his darkest parts. Andrew's heart felt swollen to twice its normal size.

Lana looked like she wanted to eviscerate Thomas. Instead, she gave him the finger. Then she turned to Andrew and eyed him with a ferocity that seemed more concerned than anything else. "Invitation to hang out with me always stands. Have fun with this toothache incarnate." She stormed off.

Andrew stared at Thomas. "What was that?"

"Forget it. She has a problem with me."

"Is this about your fight with Dove?" Andrew said.

Thomas's teeth clenched. "Leave it alone."

Andrew did not know how to swallow all of this. He hadn't realized Thomas and Lana hated each other this much—or maybe both only meant to protect another. Lana on Dove's side, Thomas on Andrew's.

Andrew didn't have time to gather his scattered thoughts before Clemens's voice boomed through a megaphone telling everyone to board the bus. But then he looked straight at Andrew and Thomas and added, "This is a public event, and students are to conduct themselves with the respect and decorum befitting Wickwood Academy. Anyone not in full uniform will be left behind. Anyone with an attitude problem will be left behind. Anyone unable to comply to the rules will be left behind."

Andrew winced as he looked at Thomas, who had already failed that entire checklist. Thomas glanced down at his missing tie and blazer, and red flushed across his freckled cheeks.

"He's doing this to stop me coming," Thomas said. "Because failing us in class wasn't enough."

"I can't go alone." Andrew tried to keep the growing anxiety out of his voice. "Turn your shirt inside out. It'll hide the paint stains."

"But the buttons—"

"Button it inside out. Just do it."

Everyone else began filing onto the bus.

Thomas started unbuttoning his shirt. Students behind them started whispering and made a wide arc around their disaster zone. Thomas stripped his shirt and fought with the tangled sleeves.

Ahead, Bryce Kane wolf-whistled. "God, Rye. No one asked for a striptease."

His friends jeered, and Andrew quickly stood in front of Thomas to hide all the bandages and tape covering his torso while he wrestled his shirt back on and fumbled with the backward buttons. He still had no blazer, but Andrew snatched the limp tie and redid it, jerking the knot a little too tight. The collar wouldn't sit flat inside out, but it had to do. Thomas tucked in his shirt, agitated and frenetic, as they lined up to board.

His eyes locked on Clemens. "I'm dead without the blazer. He'll ban me."

Lana, about to board the bus, had turned to watch their disorganized wardrobe shuffle. Her eyes met Andrew's for half a second before she turned and bumped into Ms. Poppy, who in turn spilled her thermos on Clemens's shoes. He leaped backward with a barely stifled curse while Ms. Poppy twirled around in a flurry of apologies, her enormous skirt only adding to the confusion.

Andrew grabbed Thomas's wrist and dragged him aboard the bus while no one was watching.

It didn't make sense, Lana gifting them this distraction after her vehement verbal collision with Thomas earlier, but maybe Dove had put her up to it.

Andrew followed Thomas down the aisle. "That was way too close."

They packed themselves into seats, Thomas wincing as his abused skin pressed against the bus upholstery.

"Are you okay?" Andrew whispered.

"All I care about right now is you and dealing with the"—Thomas's voice dropped low—"*monsters*. Nothing else matters."

Andrew looked out the window until he'd forced his expression neutral. A strange heat blossomed in his chest, and it was taking too long to pack it back into a manageable corner. *All I care about right now is you.* He was liked by the boy who liked no one at all, and he wanted it to stay that way so much it hurt.

Thomas's face darkened as he watched Clemens settling into the driver's seat. "I'd drag Clemens into the forest and let the monsters have him if I could. I'd sit back and watch." He slouched in his seat with a glower.

Andrew didn't disagree.

The bus pulled out of Wickwood and the world blurred through all shades of dark green as the forests whipped past their windows. Thomas fell asleep on Andrew's shoulder, his mouth open and the angry lines of his face softening in a way that made Andrew ache.

He put in earbuds, but didn't listen to anything.

Everyone was rowdy and talkative, and a few kids kept swapping seats with whispered giggles until Clemens ordered an end to it. But Dove slid into the empty row in front of Andrew and he felt breathless with relief that she had come after all. He had this odd, suffocating need to be sure she was all right, never hurt, never in danger. This time, *he* would be the twin made protector.

Thomas was still asleep, so Andrew leaned forward so his chin rested on the back of her seat before he tapped her shoulder. "Why aren't you sitting with Lana?"

"Checking up on you." Dove lightly flicked his nose, so his face wrinkled. "Also I called you, but you didn't answer?"

An image of the forest devouring his phone flashed in Andrew's mind. "I need to charge my phone." He needed to *find* it. Fast.

"Well, you have to answer when I'm calling you. I need to know you're coping." She said it in a fussy way, as if he were a child who would wander off and get lost before starting to cry.

It burrowed between his ribs, the frustration of it. Everyone saw Andrew as shattered and fragile, and maybe he was to them. But when Thomas looked at Andrew's sharp edges, he thought them dangerous and beautiful—not weak.

He could cut me to bloody pieces if he wanted.

Andrew hated the way he loved those words.

FOURTEEN

Traffic delayed their arrival in the city, and then the stop by a coffee shop lost them another half hour, so the bus reached the art gallery late enough to make Andrew antsy. The tour started and the class dribbled through the immaculate building with their notebooks and sketchbooks out. Ms. Poppy glowed seven times brighter as she floated between paintings. When she passed Thomas, she squeezed his shoulder and chatted to him about pushing through artist blocks by refilling his "creative well." Thomas twitched, but nodded.

His face darkened to thunderclouds as the morning wore on and he couldn't do a single sketch. He picked at his bite scabs and stayed close to Andrew.

When the morning finally ended and the class was to be released for their precious hours of free time, they assembled at the bus for a lecture about boundaries. Everyone wanted to hit the closest mall and cinema, anyway. Deprive rich kids of ways to spend their parents' money and they go all out once released.

Andrew and Thomas went the opposite way.

"I don't have my phone to look up the nearest art store," Andrew said.

"We'll do it the good ol' fashioned way." Thomas power-walked across the street and Andrew had to run to keep up.

"Ask directions?" he said.

"What? No. Walk around until we find one."

They wasted fifteen minutes before Thomas gave in and asked for directions. Then they tumbled into a cozy arts-and-crafts store, its walls lined with rainbow tubes of paint and white canvases. The second they entered, Thomas's whole body relaxed, his eyes brightening as if, for the first time in weeks, he had a chance to breathe. He touched everything. Tested Copic markers and inspected oil paints. Hovered in the background while a man conducted a paint-mixing tutorial. He almost kissed the shelves of pencils and charcoals until Andrew had to cough to hide his laugh.

They stocked up on everything. "You should throw your old stuff out," Andrew said.

"Yeah, I guess." Thomas didn't meet his eyes. "Maybe just that one sketchbook was cursed."

"No, get rid of it all—"

"You know I can't afford to." Thomas kept his back to Andrew as he inspected stacks of boxed charcoals. He rapped the edge of the shelf in a poor display of nonchalance, but his shoulders had tensed, knuckles white with the effort of clenching back some twisting emotion. "I have nothing now, Andrew. My parents barely gave me money before, and now . . . well, obviously they can't." His voice had gone tight. "No one's even told me what's happening with the investigation. I guess the cops contacted my aunt . . . She'll probably deal with the house and, like, the finance stuff. I don't know. Not like she's talking to me."

Andrew frowned, but didn't answer. It felt like finding a

paper cut in the corner of his month, a sting both sharp and surprising. Thomas had him. He would never have nothing.

Andrew reached over Thomas's shoulder and collected a few boxes of charcoals, and the silent weight of the declaration that he would pay, that he would take care of this, made Thomas seem smaller than before. But he didn't have to make it a *thing*. Money barely felt real to Andrew anyway, what with its sudden appearance in his life and the inevitability that someday it would vanish as fast as it had come. Good things didn't last; they felt like a daydream he'd lose sight of if he shook himself fully awake.

"You haven't lost anything with them gone." Andrew said it with such softness that his mouth barely moved, not sure if Thomas would lash out, but unable to cage the words.

Thomas snatched a few new drawing pads and boxes of Derwent pencils and then stormed away. Andrew trailed behind, but he wasn't sorry. If he could stop Thomas from ever being hurt again, he would. He'd do anything.

At the cash register, a woman with tattooed arms rang everything up while Thomas glared at Andrew until he finally sighed and held out his arms to take the unwieldy canvases. Thomas stacked up his supplies in Andrew's grasp so that every corner dug into his ribs and jabbed at his collarbone. Thomas tucked the last box of pencils under Andrew's chin with a somewhat snaky look of satisfaction. Fine, if this was payback, they were even now.

Andrew's mouth made a thin line. "My wallet's in my back pocket."

Thomas flashed a wicked smile like a feral changeling, a creature you'd bargain your heart to and not even mind. He slipped a hand into Andrew's back pocket, and for a second they stood too close, lungs moving in sync, Thomas's touch easy and familiar, like this moment meant nothing and they'd replay it a thousand times for the rest of their lives.

Then it was over. Thomas swiped Andrew's credit card.

"You know what we need?" Thomas said, as they exited the shop with Andrew still struggling to carry all the art supplies alone. "Sugar. Since you're burdened with the need to pay for everything right now, let's get food."

His glib tone sounded a little too forced, but Andrew wouldn't comment. Let Thomas make it a joke if it made him feel better.

"I'm not hungry." Andrew shoved a bag at Thomas. "Can you take your stuff?"

"Okay, okay." They redistributed the bags while Thomas gave him a careful look. "When was the last time you ate? I feel like you never go to the dining hall anymore."

Andrew did not need this right now. Eating felt like a sickening concept when the forest was filling him with nightmares.

"Let's get milkshakes and fries," Thomas said.

"Chips," Andrew mumbled.

"You know they're fries and you're wrong. Stop correcting me with your Australianisms." Thomas walked backward to give him a raised eyebrow. "There's still time to become American, you know."

"Er, no thanks. I only like one thing about this country." It slipped out before Andrew's brain caught up. Why did he say *that*? He backpedaled madly. "Your bookstore prices, I mean. Way, *way* cheaper than ours."

"Sure, that's what you meant." Thomas patted him on the shoulder. "Nothing to do with me and my . . ." He trailed off as he looked over Andrew's shoulder. "I have an idea."

He ducked across the road, and it took Andrew a few seconds to catch up and follow him into a store.

Carson's Camping & Hunting.

Inside smelled of cardboard boxes and metal, tenting canvas and boot polish. The shelves stood so tight together that only a single person could walk between them. Camping supplies spilled into hunting gear, and a bearskin on the wall watched them with empty glass eyes. Andrew's stomach turned over. He saw the entire wall dedicated to guns and he wanted *out*.

When he stumbled around a corner, he found Thomas standing on tiptoes in the next aisle.

"I hate this," Andrew said.

Thomas turned around. He held a hatchet with a red blade, the tip under a protective cover. The handle fit sturdy against his palm, and it looked so violent and cold and final that it made Thomas seem lost under the weight of it. It was the last one on the shelf, and it felt like a sign.

Andrew chewed his lip. "We'll never get that into Wickwood."

"I can't survive this." Thomas sounded hollow. "I pretend it's fine, but every time I look at you, I think about monsters ripping open your stomach and feasting. And . . . and you just lying there. Torn to nothing because of me. It's stuck in my head, Andrew, it *lives* there. I can't win this with a goddamn garden spike."

"Okay." Andrew took a survival first aid kit off the shelf. "But this, too."

They paid and stuffed everything in the bottom of Andrew's backpack, receiving no dubious looks from the man in a red flannel with a huge beard. As if teenage boys buying weapons wasn't something to question.

Andrew's backpack clinked as they walked back to the bus. He kept it hooked between his legs during the trip back so nothing clattered and drew attention. Thomas crammed in the seat next to him and sketched frantically—trees and forests, willows and twisted oaks. It was painful to see how much he'd missed this, craved it with a ravenous ferocity—being able to draw again where he was a god of paper and ink, and his monsters bent to his commands. Andrew loved watching him like this, the unguarded intensity.

Thomas's knee kept bumping Andrew's. Between them everything felt electric.

But when they pulled into Wickwood and everyone filed off the bus, Clemens put out an arm to cut off Andrew's escape.

"I see Mr. Rye has either lost his blazer on the trip or never had it in the first place. Yearning for another detention, are we?" His smile was aggressive in its politeness. "What's in the backpack?"

Andrew's chest caved in.

"Snacks," Thomas said from behind Andrew. "We're allowed to stock up, Mr. Clemens."

Clemens gave Thomas a cool look at the omission of *professor*. "Nice. Unzip it and show me what you bought, boys."

Andrew froze with his eyes on the ground, and a thousand thoughts blazed in terrified circles through his brain. But Ms. Poppy swept past in her patchwork skirt. She smiled when she saw Thomas's new sketch pad under his arm.

"Let the boys out, Chris," she said. "Wickwood isn't a prison. We don't pat them down."

Andrew stumbled off the bus before Clemens could argue with a senior teacher. Thomas catapulted after him and they bolted for the dorms.

"We're going to get caught and expelled." Andrew's heartbeat roared in his ears. "Maybe the monsters won't even be there tonight."

Thomas gave him a dry smile, but there was something empty behind his eyes. Something hopeless.

The night was a living thing, breathing with them as they stood in the forest. Moss thickened in their lungs and they could taste autumn leaves.

Thomas held the hatchet, flashlight glancing off the red blade until it looked dipped in blood. Andrew carried a garden spike and his anxiety knotted around his throat like it meant to strangle him.

Thomas had pulled his hood up and kept his eyes on the ground to hide his dread. But Andrew could feel Thomas's fear, the exhaustion—but also his loss.

First his art, now the woods. They used to belong to Thomas. This was the place where he roared and grew taller, where his smile could make flowers bloom and his energy could flow endless and untamed.

Monsters had eaten that out of him. The trick would be to stop them before there was nothing left of Thomas to save.

Thomas's hand trembled around the hatchet, and he couldn't stop twitching and snatching glances at the forest as Andrew made a half-hearted attempt to find his phone again. If he had to confess its loss to his dad and ask for a new one, he'd have to lie about what had happened. No way could he say where he'd lost it.

"It could be anything tonight," Thomas said. "Once it was an elven queen with a moon sickle blade, and I only survived because she got bored."

"Maybe we should set a trap," Andrew said. "Find something for bait."

Thomas's smile had a hard edge. Humorless.

Andrew understood it then. *They* were the bait.

The wind picked up and scattered leaves over the path as they set off to hunt. No use waiting for the monsters. The night pressed close to Andrew's spine, cool hands sliding up his sweater and over his ribs. It seemed fascinated with the concept of his beating pulse, and it left inky fingerprints along his collarbone. If it asked to kiss him, he thought he would say yes.

If the trees belonged to Thomas, midnight was in love with Andrew. It made him braver somehow, invisible, hiding his delicate edges and leaving behind a lean and hungry shadow. In the dark, no one could see his hollow and empty places. Instead he looked like he could have teeth.

They felt, more than saw, the monsters wake.

Things pulled out of trees. Breathing came, hot and heavy, so close but out of sight.

Andrew could smell it: rotting leaves and earth left to

molder for a thousand years. It was diseased trees and putrefied sap and that disgusting sweetness of decaying meat.

The monsters could be anything tonight—except they didn't attack. They just watched and nipped at the boys as they passed.

"Right, so it's not the sketchbook," Andrew said. "But something's different. Do you feel it?"

Thomas adjusted his grip on the hatchet. "I guess destroying the sketchbook and getting a real weapon has threatened them?"

The boys waited, but dawn drew soft pink lines in the sky before they realized nothing would come for them that night. They returned to bed exhausted, because it turned out that not fighting monsters was just as harrowing as fighting them.

The next night was the same.

And the next.

They heard snickering among the trees, or maybe it was their boots crunching leaves. They found claw marks in the bark and a half-eaten deer with its belly ripped open and splattering the roots of the Wildwood tree. Andrew remembered when his boots had sunk into bloodied mud here, but that hadn't been real. This was real. At least, he thought so.

But nothing attacked them.

"I hate this," Thomas said, his voice cracking. "They're waiting."

Andrew tilted his face to the black-painted sky. "So something else is coming."

"Something worse," Thomas said.

FIFTEEN

October arrived with cold teeth sharp enough to split bone. It was early in autumn to be shivering this much, but Andrew never had stamina for the cold. He was too thin these days, he knew, but he couldn't eat. If he layered up with sweaters and avoided Dove with her sharp perception, he thought he'd get away with it. He figured Thomas wouldn't notice how much weight he'd lost, not if he was careful to never take his shirt off and show the way the bones seemed ready to cut free of skin.

Thomas was distracted anyway. The first of October had rattled him, and Andrew didn't want to ask why. They'd stacked themselves into a study nook in the library that afternoon, textbooks and class notes spread across the table. Thomas chewed pencils and drummed on his books and kept accidentally kicking him under the table until Andrew lost patience and stomped on his foot. Thomas settled down with a petulant frown, propped a textbook in front of his face, and started writing.

He needed to focus. Both of them did. They were failing classes, but they didn't *sleep*, so how could they survive hours of lectures and assignments? Even without the monsters attacking, they had to check the forest every night and show the trees the sharp edge of the hatchet. Whispers of mocking laughter filtered through the forest and hot breath licked their necks. But nothing attacked.

Nothing.

Maybe it was the sleep deprivation, but Thomas had become a string drawn so tight it took nothing to snap him into a rage or a panic spiral. A classroom door would slam and he'd jump out of his skin. His chest was a broken cage for his emotions, and they spilled out of him like paint.

But Andrew was calm. Maybe it was because he'd grown used to packing his own anxiety into boxes and pasting on wan smiles while on the inside he imploded. Maybe he'd been freaking out for so long it felt normal.

Andrew finished with his revision notes before he noticed Thomas's pen wasn't moving from left to right. Andrew sighed and slammed down the textbook Thomas had hidden behind.

"Interesting idea of calculus homework," Andrew said.

Thomas looked guilty. Inky roses and thorns grew over his workbook page, vicious and cruel and lovely. The thorns curved like hooked scythes, and it looked as if whoever touched that paper would bleed.

"They're not technically monsters," Thomas said.

"They're not helping, either." Andrew gestured to their mounds of work.

Dove would have had them organized by now. Color-coded schedules. Binders of prioritized assignments. Practice quizzes corrected with her purple gel pens. She never used red because she said it was demoralizing. Andrew tried to explain it was *still* demoralizing when she wrote *Nothing You've Written Here Even Remotely Makes Sense* in the margins.

"Schoolwork seems pointless when it's, you know, October." Thomas rested his cheek on a fist and kept drawing. "Halloween month."

"Halloween is one day. Your country has a weird obsession with it."

"I just have a bad feeling."

Andrew slapped his notes over the top of Thomas's drawing. He received a glare in return, but he didn't care. "I have a bad feeling about us failing senior year."

"Who cares." Thomas started doodling on Andrew's notes instead. "After this, we should take a gap year. Drive around Australia and surf every beach."

"You can't drive," Andrew said. "Or surf. And if you stand in the sun for five minutes, you scorch like a little tomato."

"All things I can overcome," Thomas said in earnest. "I can duct-tape myself to a surfboard and I'll work on my tan."

"Isn't it raining right now?"

"That doesn't matter. I'll stand under a big sunlamp."

"You don't need a big sunlamp, a short one will do," Andrew muttered, taking out his laptop.

Thomas gave him a deeply offended look. "That's enough out of you, or you're uninvited. I'll thrive in Australia *alone*. Eating Vegemite by the *spoonful*. I'll live at your house and go see that big rock you're famous for."

Andrew choked. "That's not how you eat Vegemite. And my dad's house is in Byron Bay. Uluru is like three thousand kilometers away from there. Have you ever, *ever* looked at a map of Australia?"

"Stop bringing logic into this . . ." Thomas trailed off as he frowned at Andrew's history notes. He stopped doodling and flipped the page around a few times. "Hey."

"Hmm?" Andrew started an email with a very solid lie to his dad—or probably his secretary—about why he'd lost his phone and needed a new one. It wouldn't involve forests. Or breaking rules. And definitely not monsters.

"Did you mean"—Thomas sounded quiet—"to write your notes . . . in mirror reverse?"

Andrew looked up.

Thomas slid the pages back to him, but his expression had gone carefully blank, a useless precaution against Andrew, who knew him well enough to dissect it.

He didn't even know how to write in mirror reverse. He hadn't . . . he didn't know—

He scrunched the papers and stuffed them in his satchel.

Silence sat between them: Andrew frozen while his brain spun in dizzying spirals, Thomas chewing his pen and watching Andrew from the corner of his eye.

Then he yawned and peeled from his seat. "I can't work under these conditions. I need a sandwich. Let's get sandwiches."

Relief melted Andrew. Good, they'd ignore this. "It's an hour till dinner."

"Well, I'm hungry now. C'mon, the dorm kitchenette always has bread and fruit and stuff. Wait, you guard our study spot and I'll bring it back. Peanut butter and jelly sound good?"

Andrew hunched over his laptop. "I'm not hungry."

"Irrelevant." Thomas stretched, cracking his neck and making a huge effort to act unconcerned. "Let's eat now and skip the dining hall. Okay?"

It was manipulation. Andrew would've skipped dinner anyway, and this meant Thomas would get to oversee him eating—which meant Thomas had, in fact, noticed Andrew avoiding meals. He should be annoyed, but he only had energy for a small frown, which Thomas returned with a grin so mischievous it was impossible to stay mad at him. He took off, humming to himself.

His absence felt like an electrical surge turned off, as if Andrew didn't exist without Thomas in the room. He couldn't focus on his essay, and his skin felt too tight, his neck prickling like someone watched him from between the shelves. Plenty of students packed the library this rainy afternoon, but everyone was focused on their own work. No one was looking at him, right?

He twisted suddenly to catch them out.

Yellow eyes blinked behind the stacks.

Then vanished.

Andrew rubbed his face. He knew he was overtired. But still, it had been . . .

Nothing. Monsters only escaped the dark if Thomas failed to catch and kill them, and there had been nothing in the forest for days.

He forced himself to stare at his laptop screen before he heard familiar footsteps. He brightened, turning to greet Dove—but she swept past with an armful of books and hurried for the upstairs studios.

"Dove?"

She didn't pause. Maybe she had earbuds in.

Andrew scrabbled after her. He should convince her to study with them. Avoiding her because he and Thomas held too many secrets felt like working with a punctured lung, and he didn't want to grow used to the pain.

Andrew turned a corner of shelves and stumbled into the librarian. She gave a startled laugh as he grabbed her arms to steady her and stammered an apology.

"That's all right, darling," she said. "While you're here, I have a book you would like."

"Oh, thanks . . . um, thanks, Ms. Ye. I'll come back?"

Not waiting for an answer, Andrew took the stairs two at a time, but when he reached the halls, all the studio doors were shut. He hesitated, chewing his lip, not wanting to knock and have strangers' eyes boring into him, pitying or annoyed or mocking. He hated being looked at, asked questions. He hated figuring out what to say.

Only one door lay ajar at the end of the hall, so he slipped toward it—Ms. Poppy's art classroom. Dove never took art, but he could snoop on Thomas's new projects since he'd started drawing again.

Andrew didn't see anyone inside, so he pushed the door a little wider and crept between rows of art tables before he heard voices. He went still.

Two people sat cross-legged on the carpet ahead, tables pushed back to make room for the mess they'd tumbled all over the floor. It looked like a rainbow had vomited across their laps. Shredded and knotted fabrics tangled with a huge box of embroidery thread and sewing supplies. Two girls bent their heads together as they sorted the fabrics. Andrew was about to fling himself out of there, but they looked up and caught him.

Lana raised an eyebrow. "If you're looking for Thomas, he's

not here." She had her hair in her usual spiky ponytail, blazer discarded and sleeves rolled up to work.

"I wasn't." Andrew stuffed his hands in his pockets. "I mean. I was looking . . . for his art."

"In the corner. He's got the window because he's Ms. Poppy's favorite. All that dark artist angst." Lana rolled her eyes. "So glad I switched to drama this year because I can't stand all his monsters."

Andrew's heart tripped over itself before he realized she meant his old drawings. Not his *real* monsters.

He made a wide arc around Lana and her friend and found Thomas's workspace. Tall wooden tables with drawers took the places of desks, the stools tucked in and art supplies piled everywhere. Begonias stood in mason jars all over Ms. Poppy's desk, and she'd propped a tiny hand-painted sign on her laptop to say: OUT TO GET TEA! BACK IN 5 MINUTES!

With the walls covered in paintings and the huge windows overlooking the forest, the room felt alive with creativity. No wonder it was the only class Thomas thrived in.

Andrew flicked through a few sketchbooks, but Thomas had only been doing exercises. His canvases still lay blank. Oil pastels unopened. The new charcoals had been worn to nubs already, but Andrew had to dig through the trash to find what they'd been used on.

The paper had been slashed, but it looked like a face framed in soft gray feathers. Dove feathers.

He dropped the mess back in the trash.

He shouldn't have come. Even if Dove had cut ties with Thomas, he was still tangled up in her, and it made Andrew's pained heart stretch in pathetic ways.

He started to leave, but slowed to watch the girls sorting their fabric scraps.

"Oh," he said, "those are your Pride flags?"

"Yup." Lana sounded terse. "Someone slashed them. A hate crime. Wickwood wouldn't bother to track down the culprits even if we reported it. Useless."

The girl beside her piped up, "It might've been a senior prank?"

"Hate. Crime." Lana slapped a piece of shredded green and gray into a pile. "Chloe, stop thinking all people are nice. They are either inherently annoying or downright oxygen wasters." She narrowed her eyes at Andrew. "Want to help? We're seeing if all the pieces are still here and then we're sewing them back together. Ms. Poppy said she'd buy new ones, but I think this sends a stronger statement. We will *not* be cut down."

"Well, I'm sewing," Chloe said. "Lana needs to practice her running stitch."

Lana wrinkled her nose, and Chloe stifled a laugh. Andrew thought she might be a junior, because he knew her name but didn't recognize her from class. Chloe Nguyen had light brown skin and hid behind incredibly long hair. Bright motivational bracelets covered her wrists, saying things like: YOUR WORTH IS INFINITE! And HAPPINESS IS A CHOICE! That much positivity went against his entire nature and stressed him out.

He wanted to ask if they'd seen Dove come upstairs, but the words pooled like tar on his tongue. Maybe if he lingered, they'd talk about her and he'd have pieces for the puzzle of her strange behavior this year.

He knelt and pulled a handful of torn fabric into his lap. Lana looked pleased and then hid it with her trademark scowl, while Chloe gave him a shy but encouraging smile.

The flags felt soft and silky in his hands. "Why do you even want people to know you're . . . you know? It's not their business." Had he just said that out loud? What was he thinking? He glanced up, mortification flushing his cheeks hot. "Sorry. I-I didn't mean to—be offensive—"

"You can talk, Andrew. I won't bite your head off," Lana, known-head-biter, said. "And you're right, it isn't anyone's business. But some of us don't want to hide. I don't care if people know I'm a lesbian. It's just part of me."

"And it's nice to find other people like you?" Chloe sent Andrew a cautious smile. "No one understands what it's like to be bisexual like other bisexuals."

"Not that anyone *has* to come out," Lana said so close to Andrew's ear that he jumped. "You don't owe them, and people suck anyway. All of them. Well," she added, grumpy, "you two are okay. For now."

Chloe nudged Lana in the ribs until she batted her off with a begrudging smile. "You're so not as crabby as you pretend to be."

Lana sniffed. "I am, actually."

"Thomas isn't as mean as he pretends to be, either," Andrew said in a quiet voice.

Lana snorted and untwisted more pieces of flags. "Thomas is a menace."

"Wait, Thomas Rye?" Chloe said. "Half the girls in my year have a crush on him."

This time both Andrew and Lana shot her alarmed looks. Having a crush on Thomas would be a little like putting a blade to your mouth and then being surprised when it cut you.

"He's a genuine bad boy," Chloe went on. "Not the 'I got drunk and totaled my dad's Mercedes' bad boy, but the kind that has dark secrets and is so beautiful and talented and unknowable." She noticed their matching horrified expressions and looked embarrassed, fussing with the flags again. "That's just what the girls say."

"Thomas is such a bad idea," Lana said. "Plus, he's already way in love with . . ." She darted a glance at Andrew and then looked away. "Someone already."

Stones settled in Andrew's stomach. *Dove.*

They sorted flag pieces in silence for a few minutes before Chloe started talking about types of embroidery stitches and Lana blustered that she could learn to sew within the next half hour. Andrew wanted to fumble an excuse to leave, but he also felt tied to this moment with thin cords of defiance. Of *want.* Just once, Andrew wanted to step outside of his skin and be someone who could talk easily, fit next to other people and not want to take himself apart and analyze everything he'd done wrong. He wanted to know if anyone at GSA was asexual too, if they packed it down inside their chest because it hurt them the way it hurt him.

He should ask.

He *couldn't ask.*

He hadn't meant to make the girls come out to him just now, but it felt like they'd held out a tentative gift. Opened a door in case he wanted to slip inside, too.

"I think I'm asexual, but not like—" He stopped and tried to collect himself. "I could fall in love once, I think, but I don't want the . . . physical stuff. I know this isn't, um . . . normal. I just—" Why had he even started talking? He burned from the inside out, and his cheeks must be flaming by now. He'd all but said *sex* without saying it, and they were probably confused because he was being unclear, and talking in circles and—

Lana gave him a careful look as if she was fully aware of his inner meltdown, and she spoke with all her sharpness filed back. "There are plenty of people like that. But strike 'normal' out of this conversation—it's the most obtuse word and I hate it. There are asexual people who don't want sex or they hate it or are indifferent about it. It's a spectrum."

The knot in Andrew's chest gave. He had never talked about this because he couldn't afford to take his feelings for Thomas out of their battered box and ask if he was broken to fall in love and not want sex.

"Okay." Andrew barely got the word out. He'd said it, he'd confessed out loud, and now he needed to disappear inside himself and breathe for a second. Maybe they sensed this because the conversation tumbled into how long it would take to sew all these flags, and they let him sit in silence.

He kind of liked Lana and Chloe.

Footsteps scuffed at the classroom door, and they looked up expecting Ms. Poppy's return—but Thomas stood there. Since classes had finished for the day, he'd changed into jeans and a green striped tee shirt with a frayed hem. Without his uniform, he went from disreputable private school bad boy to mussed and distracted artist who wore half his paint on himself. He held a paper bag of the dreaded sandwiches and chewed his lip. Maybe he'd been watching them for a while.

Andrew wasn't sure if he wanted Thomas to have heard or not. He scrambled to his feet, careful not to mess up any of the fabric piles.

"Thanks for helping." Chloe waved at him, black hair falling over her face to hide her quiet smile.

Lana grunted, giving Thomas a sour glare, but she tugged at Andrew's pants as he started to step around her, so he looked down. "If you're lonely, you can talk to us whenever."

He nodded, because speaking felt too much right then. She let go.

Andrew followed Thomas downstairs, their footsteps in sync. Part of Andrew wanted to blurt it all out, but most of him didn't. It was irrelevant to start obsessing over how he felt when the truth was this: Thomas liked girls. Specifically, Dove.

"What were you all talking about?" Thomas said, too casual.

Have you ever thought about kissing me? "Just how their flags got destroyed."

"Probably Bryce Kane and his vultures." Thomas led them back to their homework table and surveyed the mess. "Let's eat outside. Rain sort of stopped. Unless you don't want to?"

"I'm not the one scared of October," Andrew said, as if he wasn't scared of everything else.

SIXTEEN

Andrew followed Thomas into the garden with the weariness of a boy facing a briar noose. If this was one of his stories, he'd write about a cornered fox chewing its own leg off to escape until the wound bloomed with flowers.

The sharp hunger inside him was never for food these days, not when he already felt crowded with monsters and panic and anticipation that everything might grow so much worse.

Thomas plunged deep into the gardens that wrapped around the Wickwood manor and dorms. When the sun shone, the gardens sprawled like a fairy tale, with hedges and lawns the color of emeralds and jade, all trimmed and precise. Brick paths nipped around rosebushes and ivy trellises and led to cherubic stone benches and an ivy-smothered gazebo. Now everything shimmered under a layer of silver rain and the garden didn't look whimsical. It looked like it had been crying.

"You said it wasn't raining. I'm literally getting wet." Andrew knew he sounded petulant, but he didn't want to be here. He didn't need to be fed and monitored like a baby bird.

"The gazebo will be dry." Thomas hopped over a puddle.

The air felt damp enough to drink; Andrew's lungs were already having trouble. He pinched the bridge of his nose and crushed his eyes closed for a second before he realized it wasn't the heavy air wrecking him—he was sliding toward a panic attack. He hated being like this.

"Thomas, can we just go—"

The path curved toward the gazebo, and Thomas pulled up short. Bryce Kane and his friends were already there, shoving each other with bullish laughter. They'd stomped mud all over the white wood floors and littered chip bags everywhere. The second they saw Andrew and Thomas, they started howling.

"Hey, there's Tommy and his girlfriend!"

"Shut up, dude, remember he killed his parents. Want to be next?"

They broke into wheezing laughter.

Thomas speed-walked in the opposite direction. The paper bag smacked against his leg with an unappealing *squish*.

"Someday I'm running away to a dessert island," Thomas said. "I will never speak to another person again."

Andrew sighed as he followed. "It's *desert* island."

"I said what I said, Perrault."

They sat on a low stone wall at the very edge of the gardens. Ahead, the sports fields stretched and ended against the sharp line of the fence. The forest watched them. They stared back, unblinking. The air felt even grayer here, and they could taste the soaked leaves and mud and moss of the forest on their tongues.

A lonesome shadow crossed Thomas's face as he stared at the woods. He must miss it, those days where he sneaked out there for the pure enjoyment of it, returning with mud stains and pockets crammed with interesting rocks and leaves. Dove would go off on him about risking expulsion, and he'd look her dead in the eye and lie. *What? I haven't been in the forest.*

He used to kiss trees. Now they made him flinch.

Andrew picked at his sandwich. The peanut butter felt like glue in his mouth.

"I'll fight Bryce Kane if it'll help," Thomas offered.

Andrew shot him a flat look. "Help you get kicked out? Ignore him."

Thomas rummaged in the paper bag. "So, my aunt finally contacted me. Apparently she's been sorting out affairs and stuff even though the case isn't closed yet. But she . . . she knows about our well." He bit savagely into another sandwich. "It's overgrown with ivy, so the cops would've missed it. But she might look in there."

"If she does," Andrew said, picking his words like shards of glass, "the cops will have answers and they'll close the case. Nothing ties it to you."

"But I don't want—" He stopped. "They might have escaped, you know?"

Andrew didn't point out it had been weeks since his parents "vanished," because he could hear the tentative wish in Thomas's voice.

"They probably escaped," Andrew said.

"But my aunt might pull me out of Wickwood. It's the kind of vindictive thing she'd do."

That couldn't happen, not to Andrew. If he lost Thomas, and Dove kept this strange new distance from him, how impossible would it be to hold on to himself?

Thomas sighed and then cast a careful glance at Andrew. "Are you okay?"

Andrew gripped the sandwich. He'd taken two bites and he

already felt stuffed all the way up to his throat, but he didn't want Thomas to baby him, so he took another huge mouthful and tried to chew.

It tasted of mud. He had to be imagining it, what with the air smelling so thickly of forest and him already being on edge. But mud was all through his mouth, cloying and suffocating, bits of gravel grinding into his molars. He choked and bent double, spitting out the sandwich.

Thomas leaped up and grabbed Andrew's shoulders as he gagged. "Hey, what? What's wrong?"

When Andrew peeled apart the bread, the peanut butter was mixed with black, wormy soil, grubs wriggling with their guts pulsing out their severed edges where Andrew had bitten in.

Andrew dropped it and dry-heaved.

"What the hell—" Thomas stared. "I didn't—that peanut butter was fresh out of the jar! Shit, I'm so sorry—"

Andrew's mouth tasted of leaves and muck and worms. He was breathing too fast. He'd *eaten* that. He'd put filth in his mouth and—

Thomas crushed himself down on the wall next to Andrew, close and tight, his hand sliding over Andrew's stomach and up his chest. Feeling him hyperventilate. Holding his ribs together so they didn't burst apart. It was so intimate and he leaned into it, *needing* the way Thomas bent his head until his mouth nearly brushed Andrew's neck.

"See, this is what I mean." Thomas's voice came low and urgent. "They're watching us. They're *here*. The dark doesn't hold them back, and it's like they're all over us, all the time."

Andrew felt sick. He'd wanted to get out of eating and so he

had. As if he'd *asked for it*. He scraped dirt out of his mouth and spat.

"Let's go back and get water." Thomas stood, but Andrew grabbed his elbow.

Mud stained his mouth. "Do you hear that?"

Thomas's eyes flicked around the dripping garden. The sky looked ready to crack open again, and it had grown darker.

"It's probably Bryce coming to mess with us." But his body felt stiff under Andrew's touch.

"I think," Andrew said, "you were right about October."

Something moved behind the hedges—thick, tarred, malevolent.

They both shot away from the wall, backing toward the path. It had to be Bryce. They hadn't found monsters in the forest to kill last night, so there couldn't have been any, right? This wasn't—

fair

Thunder rumbled above them, light rain kissing the tops of their heads. A musk crept up the path, decaying leaves and damp earth and the ugly fester of rot.

A hiss sounded behind them and they spun as a shadow shifted. It left a claw mark dug into the grass.

Andrew's pulse picked up, fast as hummingbird wings. Maybe they'd done this by taking solace in each other. Their soft touches, their bodies magnetized closer and closer—it must enrage the monsters, who wanted nothing more than their bare throats and pale wrists offered up as sacrifice.

From the corner of his eye, Andrew saw the tips of antlers jutting out of bleeding skin, a body smeared in the muck of the forest.

Thomas grabbed Andrew's arm. "We have to go. *Now.*"

The creature unfolded itself from the rosebushes, tall, so tall, with clumps of earth and torn flesh clinging to its antlers. It grew from the wicked deep; it belonged there.

And it had come for them.

When it opened its mouth to show rows of pointed teeth, tarred saliva dripped down to splatter on the grass. Green shriveled. Black roses bloomed across the ground instead, their leaves corroding even as they grew.

Whatever this monster touched died and grew back *wrong*.

It reached for Andrew.

Thomas shoved him. "RUN!"

They shot for the school, tripping on each other's heels with no air to breathe between them. They vaulted a low stone wall and threw themselves at the side entrance. Locked. How could it be *locked*? This late in the afternoon, students should be trickling from the dorms and library to the dining hall and the school should be full of people—

Which meant they were leading the monster toward a feast.

"Thomas, we can't—" Andrew said, but Thomas grabbed his wrist and wrenched him forward.

The monster came fast, hooves and claws cutting up the path and murdering the garden as it came. It snarled a roar that tipped into a scream that felt like thin pins driving into their eardrums.

Andrew clapped a hand over one ear, but he felt blood trickle down his cheek. It was as if the monster wanted nothing more than to find a way inside him, to curl between flesh and bone and flourish there.

"Just *come on*!" Thomas dragged them around the back of

the school, but everything was bricks and ivy, closed windows and locked doors.

They skidded around the corner just as the monster lunged. It hooked a claw into Andrew's shirt and yanked him backward toward that cavernous mouth, its tongue exploding with maggots. This close, its antlers looked sharp enough to cut anything, curved into a mockery of a crown.

He remembered this drawing. It was tacked to Thomas's bedroom wall.

The Antler King. Who carved off faces with knives made of its own horns.

A cry escaped Andrew. He dropped to his knees as Thomas whipped around and flung himself with fists flying at the monster. He punched it in the chest and it stumbled backward.

"GO!" Thomas shouted.

Andrew scrambled to his feet, slipping on the rain-slick path, and bolted for one of the narrow staff doors. This time, the knob turned. He shoved inside, Thomas on his heels. They both slammed the door a second before the monster snatched for them. It roared and punched the wood so hard the hinges rattled. Thomas braced himself against it and Andrew fumbled to fasten the lock.

They stood there in a disused, darkened service corridor, shaking as their eyes met.

"I need the hatchet," Thomas whispered.

Something crashed into the door with a boom. The wood splintered.

Andrew flinched back, but not before he heard it: a voice of foul, rancid blood.

you shall not leave the Antler King without a tithe . . .

cut it from your chest—

come back come back bACKKK BACCCCKKK—

Andrew could hardly stand, he was trembling so hard. His fingertips had unconsciously crept to rest over his heart.

"Hide," Thomas hissed. "I'll come find you."

"No-no-no we have to stay together—"

"It wants me." Thomas's eyes were too bright. "I'm the one bringing this on you, okay? Hide and let it follow me."

Then he shoved away and ran down the hallway.

Andrew stood there a second, shaking. His mouth moving in silent, unheard words. *Please don't leave me.*

A fist splintered through the wood, claws slashing out. Andrew bit back his cry and fled.

He went left, since he knew Thomas would've gone right, toward the front of the school. But Thomas was leading the monster to a dining hall full of kids, and how was that safer?

It hit Andrew then, how Thomas would sacrifice the world for him without even thinking.

How terrible that was.

How part of Andrew's chest caved in with the relief of knowing it.

For a second, he hated himself—or maybe he hated Thomas.

"Monsters aren't real," Andrew whispered as he ran toward the downstairs classrooms.

This late, they should be empty. All he had to do was stay away from the student lounge and rec rooms. He slipped down the hallway with his arms wrapped around his aching stomach, dirt in his mouth and blood sticky in one ear. Windows lined one wall, classroom doors the other. In the deep afternoon gloom, the wallpaper looked black.

No, it looked . . . like it was moving.

Andrew paused. A faint scratching ticked across the walls. He let out a long, shuddering breath and tried to center himself. The monster hadn't followed, and it wanted Thomas, not Andrew. It wanted its creator.

The wallpaper exploded.

Andrew threw his arms over his head, wrenching his body away as he cried out. Everything was lost to the sound of wallpaper tearing and glass shattering as the windows smashed inward. He didn't understand what he was seeing, couldn't make his brain accept it.

Vines grew out of the wallpaper. They shot across the floor, growing and writhing like fat green snakes. Roses blossomed as he watched, each petal the red of pooled blood. They didn't stop. Ivy punched through the broken windows, and brambles unfurled over the carpet. Everything took a breath together, loud and wet and rasping.

And they *grew*.

Leafy tendrils shot for Andrew's ankles. He tripped backward, kicking them away.

They kept coming, feeling their way across the carpets.

Hunting.

And if Thomas wasn't here, it meant they wanted *Andrew*.

SEVENTEEN

Blood curled in a soft line from Andrew's ear down to his jaw. Metallic and hot and *furious*. The vines smelled it. He knew they did.

Andrew flung himself down the hall and crashed around a corner. Someone would see, someone would help him.

Unless, a tiny malevolent voice whispered in his ear, *only you can see it. It's all in your head, Andrew. It's all in your—*

He cast a glance over his shoulder at the floor covered in vines. They tangled in each other and grew with every pulsing heartbeat. More wallpaper shredded as brambles grew up to the ceiling. Roses cut free and wept blood up the walls.

Andrew backed up, terror shredding his chest until he couldn't breathe. He turned to run around a corner—and he slammed into a body.

He flinched away, hands fluttering uselessly to cover his face, but there were no antlers and claws and bone knives snicking toward him.

Instead a hand clapped onto his shoulder and Clemens stared down mockingly, his lips quirked, as if finding Andrew sweaty and trembling was the highlight of his day.

"Ah, the exact person I wanted to see," Clemens said.

Andrew stared in numb shock. If Clemens turned the corner, he'd see the vines unspooling from the walls. But instead he pulled something from his pocket and gave it a jaunty shake in Andrew's face.

"Look what I happened to find in the forest today. Lost something, did we, Mr. Perrault?"

Clemens held up Andrew's phone. Moss and mud caked the back of it, dirt ground into the case and beads of rainwater collected on the glass. He tried to stammer that it wasn't his, but Clemens tapped it and the screen lit up.

That was impossible. It had been lying out in the forest for *weeks*. Even if the weather hadn't killed it, the battery should be dead.

But with the screen glowing in his face, the evidence hit him like a brick to the jaw. Andrew's lock screen was an old photo of him and Dove, their cheeks squished together to fit in the narrow frame. Dove had her hand on his chin, dragging him into the photo, and her smile was all mischief while his was wry reluctance. It was a rare moment of undiluted joy. No exam stress. No piles of homework. Just them together, twins and best friends.

A thousand emotions punched through his stomach. He felt dizzy. The forest was literally eating the school and Thomas had gone to get a *goddamn ax* to stop the Antler King ripping out their hearts—and all Andrew wanted in that moment was for Dove to appear and talk him out of this mess.

"Considering the forest is strictly prohibited," Clemens was saying, "I have to wonder how your phone ended up there."

"But why were you out there?" Andrew's chest moved raggedly, his voice too pitchy, and as soon as he said it, he wished he hadn't. It only made him sound more guilty.

Clemens let out a cold laugh. "I know what you seniors get

up to in the forest, as if that fence means anything. Beer cans and cigarette stubs galore out there. I thought I'd gather evidence."

He wanted to get back at Andrew and Thomas for walking out of his class. It was a typical bully move—defy them once in front of an audience, and they'd circle back with hooked knives ready to exact revenge.

But Andrew knew the phone was all Clemens would have found. No seniors had been messing around in the forest this year. If they had, they'd be dead.

"You don't understand." Andrew tried to worm free. "There's s-something in the hall. I need to get help—"

"What you need is a little trip up to the principal's office." Clemens dug his fingers into Andrew's neck and propelled him forward. "I know boys like you. The soft, spoiled little brats who hide their manipulation under all these politically correct *mental health* woes to get out of studying. You want out of my class? Then you can leave this entire school."

He frog-marched Andrew toward the stairs to the staff offices. Andrew glanced frantically over his shoulder, but vines hadn't started exploding from other walls. Not yet. Outside the rain grew stronger, and it tapped on the windows loud enough to drown out everything else. But someone would see that hallway soon. Someone would see the Antler King prowling the halls.

Andrew tripped on the first step, and Clemens yanked him forward.

"You won't wriggle out of this, Perrault," he said. "But do tell me who you were with, or else I'll name Rye anyway. I've seen his record."

"Please, you don't understand," Andrew choked.

A scream cut through the thunder of rain.

Andrew closed his eyes, a tremor stabbing up his spine. Real. This was real and people were going to get hurt.

Clemens frowned, but kept directing Andrew up the stairs.

Another scream came, then shouts followed by pounding feet.

Anger flashed in Clemens's eyes. All the suave young teacher charm had flattened, as if without an audience, he felt no need to wear that mask. "Let me guess, more senior pranks. The discipline in this school isn't just pitiful, it's negligent. Is your friend Rye behind this?" He gave Andrew's shoulder a sharp shake. "Snap out of it. Hysterics will do nothing for you, you entitled little shit."

They reached the top of the stairs and Clemens shoved Andrew toward the principal's office. Every door lay shut, the storm outside rendering the halls dark and close. A thick, wet smell spooled from the carpet, and Andrew felt fungi and damp dirt stuffing up his throat. He reached out to steady himself against the wall.

His fingers sank into spongy moss.

No . . .

He shied away as Clemens looked down and swore in confusion.

"What is . . . are those leaves on the floor?"

The lights flickered off, on.

Off.

They stood still in the dark, the walls too close as the paper seemed to breathe in and out. Clemens peered up at the lights, annoyance knotting his brow. Only Andrew saw the

vines slithering out of the wallpaper, bloated and green, poisonous leaves unfurling as they reached toward his ankles.

Andrew jerked away.

Clemens's expression went hard. He snapped his fingers, as if Andrew were a dog meant to heel, and started to snark a new threat.

A vine snatched at Clemens's leg and yanked.

He went down with a garbled shout, slamming onto the carpet. Vines snapped over his legs, his wrists, and his confusion turned to panic. He yelled. But Andrew backed up. A small terrible part of him didn't care if the forest attacked Clemens. He should hate himself. He should hate Thomas for leaving him when they should have stayed together. He had to run, he had to get out, get to Thomas—

Brambles caught against Andrew's pants, and one lashed across his forearm, pinning him to the wall. He tore at it, but his fingers only shredded fleshy vegetation. Maggots burst out and scattered across his sleeves. Andrew yanked at it uselessly, frantic now, as the lights flickered on and off faster and faster. His heartbeat pounded against his ribs, and the broken pieces of a scream lodged in his throat.

Clemens's swearing turned vicious as he unhooked vines from his clothes and flung them away. But more grew. And more.

The stairs creaked.

As one, Andrew and Clemens turned toward a shape growing from the dark, pushing its bulk between the spasming lights and swelling vines devouring the walls.

Then every bulb blew with a shriek.

Andrew choked on a cry. He needed this to stop.

The Antler King stepped out of the shadows. It came toward Clemens, one heavy step at a time, its skin waxy underneath the smeared grime of the forest. Spidery arms shot forward, too long for its broad shoulders. The weight of its antler crown buckled its neck and, as Andrew stared with bile rising up his throat, this close he could see the way crown had been driven in upside down. The tips splintered into the monster's skull, blood running pitch-black from its eyes.

It was a nightmare and it was alive and there was nowhere to go.

The monster snatched Clemens by the throat and hauled him upright. His feet dangled midair, his scream a terrified wheeze.

Andrew tried to melt out of sight, but his back only hit the wall as more vines closed around him. One wrapped around his middle, another slithered over his collarbone and tightened around his throat. Tendrils crept toward his bloodied ear. Soft green leaves brushed skin and began to push—*push*—toward the hot pulse of his eardrum. He shook his head madly, but the vines slithered with insidious persistence. He'd die pinned to the wall.

He wanted to scream for Thomas.

Instead, he mouthed a frenzied chant. *Take Clemens as the tithe. Take him, take him, take him. Please—*

The Antler King reached up slow and methodical and broke off a piece of its own horns. It still held Clemens by the throat, its claws puncturing into skin so blood oozed from Clemens's neck. The monster twisted the piece of antler as if to inspect it. Then it rested the tip between Clemens's wide eyes.

Clemens burbled a throttled cry. He was begging. Weeping.

tithe tithe tithe

The Antler King grinned, all teeth.

Then it drove the bone shard right through Clemens's face.

Andrew didn't look away.

Clemens screamed. Blood exploded across the Antler King's chest as Clemens's body spasmed like a butterfly hooked by its wings. His screams drowned in his throat as his head lolled. Slowly, the Antler King dragged the shard from between Clemens's eyes. He licked it. Then he began carving the skin off Clemens's face.

Andrew lost feeling in his legs. He sagged against the wall while the soft green shoot dug gleefully into his ear. He didn't even care anymore. He could only stare in numb horror as Clemens's body stopped twitching while the Antler King peeled skin off his face. It hit the floor in soft slaps like pieces of wet leather.

Then the Antler King looked up and its eyes locked on Andrew.

there you are

prince

"Stop. S-s-s-stop." Andrew tried to jerk away, but the vines had him bound to the wall. He had to wake up from this nightmare. Wake up. This wasn't real. *Wake up.*

The Antler King dropped Clemens into a bloody pile. Vines surged over his body and twisted inside his face to feast.

Andrew tried to struggle, but he had nothing left. He could only make each breath shallower than the last, pain growing in his ear as the vine dug deeper.

The Antler King reached

down

and down

and down

to caress Andrew's tearstained face.

Its claws stretched out and the tips began puncturing Andrew's skin, gently first, but in a second his face would match Clemens on the floor. Andrew's cries turned to stammering, sheer nonsense and undiluted panic. He would die here. He was going to die, he was going to—

The Antler King's arm spasmed suddenly, and its head tipped back in a roar.

The sharp edge of a hatchet sank into its shoulder.

The Antler King reared, claws scrabbling to grab the blade, but Thomas wrenched it free and swung again—this time crashing into the monster's spine.

Its scream could curdle marrow.

Andrew ripped one hand free of the vines and fought, terrified and feral. He might have been screaming, too, but everything was drowned out by the Antler King's roars. It whipped around and slammed a fist into Thomas. His body was flung backward, limp as he slammed into the wall. But he sprang to his feet.

Thomas planted his boots among the festering vines, his chin tilted up in defiance as the monster bore down on him. Blood flecked his tee shirt, and his freckles stood out against his bone-pale skin.

He bared his teeth and swung the hatchet with two hands.

He was mad and brutal beauty in that moment. Andrew forgot how to breathe.

Thomas swung the hatchet again and again. The monster reeled, but not before slashing claws across Thomas's shoulder. Blood sprayed. Thomas leaped for the Antler King and brought the hatchet down on its skull. It sagged to its knees, clawing at its face.

Thomas swung again, again, again*againagain*—

The monster's head caved in as it hit the floor. Its skin exploded like it had been built of nothing more than leaves and packed dirt. Thomas heaved the hatchet into the air and brought it down as if he were chopping wood. Bones splintered, but he kept going.

The Antler King had long ago stopped breathing.

"Thomas." Andrew's voice cracked. "*THOMAS.*"

Thomas hovered for a heartbeat longer, his hatchet raised and his chest moving ragged and fast. Then he let his arm fall dully to his side.

He turned, slow and hesitant, blood beading on his face, in his hair, a glossy coating on his lips. He wiped his mouth and smeared crimson in a vicious arc.

Silence settled, thick enough to step in. The vines had stopped growing—they turned brittle and gray. Bloody roses disintegrated to ash.

Andrew let out the smallest sob and sagged down the wall.

Thomas forced himself away from the ruin he'd made of the monster. It crumbled to autumn leaves, ribs like old sticks. Thomas crouched by Andrew and used the hatchet to cut him free. He went slow, his fingers light on Andrew's wrists and even more careful as he peeled the vine from Andrew's ear. The vine came free in a clump of blood. Thomas tossed it behind him.

Then he tilted Andrew's chin up.

They stared into each other's eyes. Thomas was breathing hard, his bloody shirt stuck sloppily to his chest, but he felt solid and firm. He'd break down over this later, Andrew knew—but right now he was the glorious fairy-tale prince come to save them all, while Andrew was nothing more than a thing made of skeleton leaves needing to be cupped between safe hands before he blew away.

Deep within the school, more shouts rose. The fire alarm went off.

Andrew's world spun slowly, sick and sticky. "Clemens . . ."

"He's dead."

"N-n-n-no, you don't understand." Andrew's voice scraped over each raw word. "You're the one covered in blood. Holding a weapon."

Understanding bloomed in Thomas's eyes, wretched and terrible.

EIGHTEEN

They didn't speak. Words had turned to mud in their mouths, and if lips parted, who knew what would come out. All they could focus on was this:

disappear

Andrew dragged his sweater off, and Thomas copied. He wrapped up the hatchet, while Thomas used his bloodied shirt to mop his face and arms. The feral blaze of war faded from his eyes and he started to tremble. He was all unsteady fingers, fumbling movements, his eyes darting to the leafy remains of the monster as if it might rise again.

Neither of them looked at Clemens's skinless face.

But Andrew did spend a few seconds scuffing about under the vines for his phone and pocketing it. No evidence could be left.

They had to know nothing about this. They had to have *not been here.*

Andrew slipped downstairs first, the hatchet bundled to his chest so tightly he could feel the bite of the blade against his skin. He deserved that, though. Pain. Punishment.

What . . . what had he *done*?

A group of teachers ran past, and the boys ducked into an empty classroom. Somewhere, screaming had reached a crescendo. Thomas jimmied a window and they climbed down into the garden. Rain beat in a steady rhythm, and they'd never been so grateful for the way it washed the blood from Thomas's bare skin and kissed away evidence of Andrew's tearstained cheeks.

It was chaos outside. Half the students had dashed through the rain for the sports field like this was a normal fire drill. Others tangled in the garden in confusion while teachers yelled at everyone to go back to their dorms.

"Please calmly make your way to your dormitory!" A professor had snatched a megaphone. "Remain in your room until otherwise instructed!"

Andrew looked for Dove, terror leaving claw marks in his guts until he saw her filing toward the girls' dorms. She was safe—*breathe, Andrew, goddammit.*

Thomas sneaked them around the back of the boys' dorm so they wouldn't have to explain his lack of shirt or the bundled hatchet. As soon as they'd climbed the trellis and tumbled into their bedroom, Andrew slammed the window shut and Thomas started pacing.

"Shit shit *shit,* they're going to blame me. They're g-g-going to—I'm not a murderer. I'm not—" Thomas jammed fists against his head. "I'm not, I'm not—"

"Shut up." Andrew snatched towels and clothes, and wrenched their bedroom door open. "We have to get rid of the blood. Shut up, *shut up.*"

With everyone bottlenecked downstairs, they still had the second floor to themselves. They sprinted for the communal bathroom and locked the door. Thomas peeled off his clothes

and left a trail of muddy footprints as he stumbled into a shower stall. Tiny green shoots bloomed from his jeans, soft and delicate. Andrew smashed each with his fist and flushed them down the drain.

The forest had left its teeth marks all over them, and it would never leave them alone.

Carefully, Andrew unbuttoned his shirt and used a towel to scrub out his swollen ear. It pulsed with terrific pain, as if someone had hooked their fingers into his eardrum and *twisted*, but he could still hear. He was fine. Unscathed.

He stared at the mirror with bloodshot eyes.

The Antler King stared back.

Blood dripped down the crown as its skin flaked into burnished autumn leaves.

take Clemens as the tithe take him take him take him

Andrew was the murderer.

He'd done this.

The monsters had grown bored of biting Thomas and cutting Andrew. Their tithe wasn't big enough. They wanted *more and more and more—*

Andrew's chest heaved. His fingers tightened into a fist, scars stretching. "Get out of my head. Get out. Get out, GET OUT GET—"

He raised his fist and he didn't know what he was doing or how to stop seeing skin slough from Clemens's face or how to stop the monsters stop them stop them stop—

He swung.

A hand caught his elbow and wrenched him backward.

Andrew slipped on the steam-slicked bathroom tiles, but Thomas wrapped wet arms around his chest and held him up. Andrew closed his eyes.

"Don't do that again." Thomas's voice came so quiet. "Please."

Andrew forced his fingers to uncurl. The spiderweb of scars stared back at him like a map of lost control.

The bathroom door rattled and they both jumped apart. Andrew spun away, burying his face in his hands while Thomas knotted a towel around his waist. Which meant he had been very naked when he held Andrew a second before, but that had to mean nothing. They were slashed to the core right now; it had to mean nothing.

Andrew tried to remember how to fit back inside his skin.

"Why is this locked?"

"Who's in there! Hey!"

"You aren't allowed to lock the main bathroom doors. Open up."

The doorknob rattled.

Andrew pressed his forehead to the door. "Just give me a minute."

Voice turned to low mumbles.

Then Bryce Kane said, clear and bright, "Nah, that's not Eckers. It's totally Perrault."

"Why's he need the whole bathroom?"

"He's probably vomiting. Did you see how skinny he is?"

They scuffled, hushing each other. Someone laughed.

Blood scorched across Andrew's face, and for a second his fury narrowed to a startling point. He would wrench open the

door and snatch Bryce Kane by the throat and slam him into the wall just as vines exploded outward and wrapped around the thrashing body to—

A fist banged on the door again.

Andrew flinched. His ear hurt so much it was hard to think.

Thomas finished pulling on the hoodie and bundling his trashed clothes inside a towel. The stink of sap and blood twirled down the drain, but even slathered and washed off with soap, he still smelled of fresh earth from an overturned grave.

Andrew unlocked the door.

Thomas shot out like a bullet, breezing past the boys without a glance. Bryce's smirk grew as he tracked Andrew slinking out next, and when he turned to his friend, they both burst out laughing before the snide comments started. Their words blistered against Andrew's back all the way down the hall, but he forced himself not to react, not to turn around.

It was only after he'd slipped back into his room and slammed the door that he realized he'd been so dizzy with the horror of the Antler King in his reflection that he hadn't put his shirt back on. He'd walked out in the open with skin stretched so tight over his chest that his bones looked like knobbed roots pressing against his skin. Embarrassment roared in his ears as he pulled on a sweater with shaking hands.

Thomas had returned to his frenzied pacing, his fingers clawing through his soaked hair, his breathing quick and unsteady. Outside, voices and footsteps flooded their floor. Questions and complaints clamored over the top of each other. No one wanted to be shut in their rooms.

Andrew needed to breathe, sit down, think—or maybe he

didn't want to think. He couldn't close his eyes and see Clemens again.

He sank to the floor, the bed too far away, but as his knees hit the ground, Thomas grabbed Andrew's arms so hard he winced.

Thomas's eyes looked liquid green, violent and wild and bright. "Are you hurt? I'll kill anything that touches you. I *swear*."

"We have to . . . have to . . ." Every word came out strangled. "We have to make them stop."

Thomas looked away, his throat working. "I'll kill them all. I don't know what else to do. I-I-I don't know, Andrew. I don't know what to do."

Everyone was told to stay in their dorms for the rest of the evening.

Supervisors went to every room and gave the official statement: A rotten root system had collapsed some of the school walls. Mishap of an old estate, but maintenance would have it fixed directly. Wickwood clearly didn't want the truth getting out about how Clemens died and freaked-out parents withdrawing their kids, so they simply said:

Everything would be fine.

Please stay calm.

You're safe.

Thomas ripped all his drawings off the wall, lit a match, and burned them in a trash can while Andrew opened a window and tried to fan the smoke out into the thickening twilight. He wished he could stuff the ashy remains in his mouth, inked

monsters and matches and wicked flames and all. It would burn him to the core but not before he spent a bright, searing moment feeling full. Emptiness banished.

take Clemens as the tithe take him take him take him

Andrew fell asleep and only woke because rain drifted in the open window to wet his clammy skin. Thomas was midway through climbing out into the witching hour.

Andrew could've rolled over and let him go alone, but he didn't deserve to feel safe.

They saw the first monster before they'd even made it to the fence, a hulking shadow on the other side of the chain links. A wolf, but not. Its head looked sewn onto a different body, fur bloodied and matted until it disintegrated around its chest to show its rib cage and spine white and bare. Branches and briars burst from its pulsing organs and wound out past the stark bones. When Thomas tried to climb the fence, it lunged, white frothing from its snarling jaws.

Andrew caught Thomas's sleeve. "Don't."

"I made this." Thomas's voice came thin and broken. "I have to stop them."

He climbed the fence and killed the forest wolf. Then another, and another. He made Andrew stay behind the fence, claiming it was because they only had one hatchet, but it felt like punishment for being so useless, so thin and weak.

When dawn came, they crawled back into their room, Andrew frozen and Thomas with claw marks gouging his arms and chest, palms blistered. He'd have to wear layers and long sleeves tomorrow to cover it all from questioning eyes. Thomas fell asleep with one hand dangling over his bed, whimpering as his eyes moved restlessly behind closed lids to the beat of his nightmares.

Andrew couldn't take it. He lay on his back on the cold floorboards under Thomas's limp hand. Carefully, not daring to breathe, Andrew brushed his mouth over Thomas's raw red palms.

Kisses, but not.

Apologies, but useless.

The fever in his hands burned Andrew's mouth.

NINETEEN

An uncanny hush had fallen over Wickwood Academy. Students crowded in the foyer, the mood sober and tentative, rumors growing like weeds down throats as they swapped stories about what they'd seen. First period had been canceled and everyone was meant to file into the assembly hall after breakfast for announcements, but it was impossible not to notice which hallways had been blocked off or how there was a barricade in front of the faculty stairs.

It was said there had been police here last night. A body bag had been packed into an ambulance and whisked away.

Andrew chewed his lip and looked for Dove among the students trickling into the auditorium. Thomas had slipped off to the bathroom again to check he hadn't bled through his bandages, and Andrew had forced himself not to follow. At least everyone was preoccupied with the fact that vines were growing out of the school's walls and less interested in gossiping about which boys had locked themselves in the bathroom together yesterday, but he didn't doubt Bryce would be foul about it soon.

Andrew had charged his phone and texted Dove a million times last night, but she still hadn't replied. She was the one who'd told him off on the bus for missing her calls, and now he deserved a cold shoulder? He hadn't done anything. Moths ate holes in his mind and their wings beat a frantic migraine behind his eyes. It was all he could do to stand up straight and keep his face blank and guiltless.

He finally saw her standing at the farthest end of the foyer and hurried over. She still wore her summer uniform of a short-sleeve blouse and perfectly straight tie. No stockings or even a blazer. Not usual for someone who always worshipped cozy things like cardigans and hot chocolate, but maybe she was preoccupied with the unsettling chaos.

"Hey." Andrew slid beside her and blinked as she leaned away. "Are you . . . mad at me?"

"Why is everything always about you?" The frosted steel in her voice said, yes, in fact, she was mad at him.

Annoyance ticked in his jaw, but he swallowed it back. "I'm not the one ignoring you. I look for you all the time and you always disappear. You don't study with us—"

"Study *for* you."

"—and you don't hang out with us—"

"I have my own homework, believe it or not."

"—or eat with us in the dining hall."

Dove shot him a sideways glance sharper than a scalpel. "As if you eat."

He forced himself to take slow breaths. They bickered sometimes, but not like this.

"What do you want me to say?" His jaw clenched. "I know you fought with Thomas, but he's my roommate. I can't pick you over him. Stop—stop making me. And stop being like this."

"Being like what? Being honest? One of us has to be."

Andrew turned on her sharply. "Okay, what is your problem with me?"

She sniffed and looked away.

"Dove, stop it." His voice rose, all animal panic. "I don't understand. We didn't have a fight? I-I don't know what I've done. I don't even know what you and Thomas fought about."

"You do. If you really thought about it." Her eyes shone, amber and glossy. "You should've chosen me."

"What?" Andrew had lost all control of this conversation. "I'm not"—he hated how uneven he sounded—"choosing anyone. He's your best friend, too. He's both of ours."

Dove's mouth twisted, jealousy maybe, or frustration that he missed her point.

But he had no idea what she wanted him to say. Unless it was *I'll give up Thomas for you.*

He couldn't say that.

He let numbness steal his heartbeat instead.

The foyer was almost empty as everyone found seats in the auditorium, and the urge to see if Thomas had already gone in ate at him, but he wanted Dove to come, too. He wanted—no, *needed*—the three of them to be okay.

"I have to go." Dove gave him one last look, steady and scathing, before she stalked off. She didn't look back.

He checked no one was looking before wiping at his stinging eyes. *Get a grip, Perrault.* They were siblings, they fought, they'd get over it.

He busied himself with his phone so he wouldn't look pathetic trailing directly behind his sister, but holding it made the world spin in sick circles beneath him. All he could think of was Clemens dangling the phone in front of him with that condescending smirk. How the battery should be ruined. How none of this made sense. It was password protected, but he hadn't checked his apps yet for tampering. When he opened his photo gallery, his stomach bottomed out.

All his old photos had been deleted. Instead, the reel had been crammed with black shots. Hundreds of them. He scrolled down the endless black squares, dread leaving malignant fingerprints down his throat. None of this was possible. Only Thomas and Dove knew his password, and they wouldn't do this.

Cold air touched the back of his neck then, an autumn chill laced with the thick scent of the forest. Moss and decaying leaves and *rot*.

Andrew brightened one of the photos and stared at the grainy, murky shot.

It was him.

He had his back to the camera, flashlight clutched to his chest. Ferns bunched around his legs and the trees rose ominously behind him.

He brightened the next photo, then the next. Him again, his head tilted back to see the stars through the trees, his white throat exposed like an invitation to monsters.

In the next one he stood slender and smudged, while behind him loomed a shape big enough to blot out the stars. Teeth gleamed. Antlers curved from a skull. A monster grew behind Andrew and he had no idea.

He squeezed his eyes shut and swallowed back the bile. Who had taken these photos? Who *watched him*? Thomas was right there, half in the frame, and more than one photo showed them curved toward each other or standing with limbs entwined.

If Dove saw these pictures, she'd tell herself a sour story. Maybe this was why she was furious at him? What if she'd taken the photos—

Okay, no. He had to gouge that idea from his mind. She'd never do this. If she saw the monsters, she would have run for help.

Unless she couldn't see the monsters and had only seen them, together, their intimacy clear. No wonder she was furious at him.

He deleted everything and stuffed the phone in his pocket before hurrying to find a seat in the auditorium with Thomas. All he had to do was sit still and listen to the principal calmly lie about how, tragically, a wall had collapsed and resulted in the death of a beloved teacher, Christopher Clemens. There were counselors available for anyone who needed to talk. A freak accident. But the walls would be fixed by tomorrow and no one was in danger.

Andrew tried to catch Thomas's eye, but he sat hunched, chewing his thumbnail.

Maybe he could put on a brave face when he fought monsters, but afterward he was always this: a panicked ruin, barely keeping himself together. He needed someone to hold him up, and hadn't Andrew been doing just that? He was the only person in the world who understood.

They had to stay together.

They should never be apart.

That night, their dorm felt bare without any of Thomas's art watching them get ready for bed. With classes a disjointed mess due to half the school being blocked off and swarming with maintenance workers, their teachers assigned a criminal amount of extra reading to be done in the library or their dorms. Andrew and Thomas chose the safety of their room, wanting a locked door between them and the prying eyes, the whispers, the settling realization that they had let monsters attack the school and somehow gotten away with it.

Although as Andrew sat on the floor surrounded by textbooks and cupping a hand over his hot, throbbing ear, Clemens's screams echoing in the back of his head, he didn't feel like he got away with much at all.

Thomas struggled into his pajama shirt, toothbrush hanging from his mouth. "Back in a sec." He wrenched the door open and strode out like he was marching to war.

It was fair to feel that way when all the rules had changed: Their monsters weren't bound by forest or night or the fence, and they weren't scared of their pathetic little hatchet. Andrew pulled his legs up and pressed his face to his knees, needing to block out the entire world for a second and just *breathe*. They couldn't keep surviving this.

Even with the window shut, he smelled the forest, felt it pulsing like a moldering second heartbeat beneath his skin. He touched the swollen lump behind his ear, now grown to a boil the size of a grape, a gorge of blood and pus. Just an ear infection. It depressed when he dug his thumbnail in.

He suddenly couldn't stand it.

Rummaging around in Thomas's art supplies produced a paper clip. He uncurled it and bent his ear with one hand, resting the sharp tip against the lump.

Don't, a small part of him whispered.

He stabbed the paper clip in, hard.

Pain shot through his ear in a dazzling explosion. He gasped as the lump burst, liquid sliding down the back of his neck as agony slashed red across his vision.

The thick smell of the forest seized his throat. When he peeled his hand away from his ear, mud smeared his fingertips in clotted clumps. Milky sap instead of pus. A single seed coated in blood.

Everything inside Andrew twisted in shuddering repulsion, and he wanted to close his eyes and fall out of this entire universe.

The bedroom door creaked open and Thomas came in with a wet face, midway through muttering something hateful about an annoying freshman when he saw Andrew hunched up and shuddering, his hands as filthy as if he'd dug around in garden soil.

Thomas ran over, his eyes gone wide with panic. "What the—wait, why is your ear bleeding? Is that . . ."

"When Clemens died"—Andrew's voice sounded thick and distended—"a vine went into my—my ear."

"But I got it out. I swear I did." Thomas grabbed for a towel and crushed it against Andrew's bleeding ear.

"I need this all to stop," Andrew whispered.

"I know. Shit. I'll fix it. Whatever it takes."

"We have to give the forest what it wants," he said. "More blood for a tithe?"

"No." Thomas's mouth made a grim line. "It wants a better sacrifice."

They ended up sitting on Andrew's bed, trying to come up with a plan, though every idea felt thin and insubstantial, doomed to fail before they'd even tried it. There had to be an answer, something about the drawings, but both of them were too exhausted and wrung out to reach for it. Andrew pressed his palms hard against his eyes to distract from the sickening pain in his ear, but when he opened them, he realized Thomas had fallen asleep. He still lay in Andrew's bed, his face snuffled into the pillows and his breathing already evening out. A shove didn't wake him. There had been too many bitterly sleepless nights.

The obvious answer was to cross the room and sleep in Thomas's bed instead, but everything seemed too far away, required too much effort. So what if Andrew stayed where he was? Friends shared beds all the time, and they didn't have to touch. He lay down, his body pressed close to the wall, and let his eyes drift shut to the soothing lullaby of Thomas's breathing. A few minutes, then they'd go out and fight monsters.

But it was the witching hour that woke him. The sound of a howl pulled from a ravenous throat filled the night beyond their safe little room. Andrew startled upright, his heart hammering and his stomach a seasick riot, and he climbed over an unmoving Thomas and collapsed onto the floor just in time to vomit leaves and bloody nubs of violets in the trash can. They were late to leave for the forest, but he shook with a foul cold, too nauseous to see straight, and the idea of facing the dark, the monsters, turned him inside out with despair. Thomas slept on, oblivious. Andrew didn't wake him.

He touched his ear and felt it swollen afresh, stretching as if something had regrown while he slept. But this time it wasn't pushing against skin and trying to escape. It was growing the other way. Going in deeper.

It was inside him, he knew.

The forest.

Once there was a boy who slept in an enchanted tower, his back flecked with whip marks from battles lost and monsters who'd won. He wore a crown of cherrywood and firebird bones, gifted to him by his sisters who were trees in the forest. But they had not been able to protect him, and his capture meant endless years of torture.

The boy whimpered in his sleep, waiting for the whips to return.

Instead, a witch climbed through his tower window. She wore a cloak covered in the gold dust of wishes, and she promised to save him. For a price.

"Take this ax," she said with a coy smile, "and cut down every tree in the forest. Then nothing will ever harm you again."

"But the trees are my sisters," he said, his bones already filled with dread.

"Why do you care for them?" the witch asked. "They do not love you. They did not come for you. Take the ax."

He began to cry, but he took the ax.

TWENTY

Soft warmth pressed against Andrew's side. Sleep left him too muzzy to investigate, so he merely let his fingers trail through thick curls before a very faraway part of him understood this was Thomas.

They must have rolled into each other during the night. Thomas's head lay burrowed under the blankets, his face against Andrew's ribs. He breathed slow and even, and he smelled of soap and sleep and boy.

It was nice, this warmth nested beside Andrew, no expectations that their touch had to turn into anything else. He let his fingers tangle lazily in Thomas's curls and pretended vomiting leaves during the witching hour had been a crumpled dream.

He might've fallen asleep again if the pounding of feet outside their door hadn't reminded them it was a school day and they were already late. Thomas sighed, stretching out with a yawn, before he suddenly bolted upright and flung himself from Andrew's bed. The way Andrew's stomach turned inside out, his mind already racing for an excuse, for a denial of how he'd barely noticed they'd fallen asleep together, hit with such sickening brutality that he almost couldn't breathe until Thomas said, "Shit, *shit*, we didn't kill monsters last night. We slept? How did—we're in so much goddamn trouble."

He flew around the room, stripping off pajamas and

yanking on his pants before shoving feet into unlaced shoes. Andrew kept very still and very quiet.

There. It hadn't meant anything. It was fine. They were fine. They didn't need to acknowledge that skin and curls and limbs had been entwined, or how they'd fallen to an unrepentant craving for closeness and stolen a comfort they could never deserve.

While Thomas fought with his tie, Andrew emptied the trash with covert swiftness—the mess of smeared mud and seeds and bruised petals looking more like an overturned compost pile than something that had been down his throat—and he did his best not to touch his ear. But a headache flourished behind his eyes.

As if small, green vines had grown into a tight knot while he slept and now pushed up at the confines of his skull, hungry for more room to stretch.

Stop. Worry about it later.

The thing to focus on was the sin of their laziness and the monsters that could be around a corner or folded into a wall, breath hot and rancid, tongues craving the wet blood of the two boys they hungered for relentlessly. The anticipation of it, the dread of not knowing, had both Andrew and Thomas flinching at every shadow, every movement, skittering away from windows and double-checking classrooms before they slunk to their desks. It made them look on edge. Paranoid. *Unhinged.* When they had to separate for the classes they didn't share—Andrew to Classic Literature and Thomas to Art—neither of them felt like they'd make it out the other side.

Andrew found a swollen line of fungi growing on the underside of his desk. When he brushed up against it, the fungi clung

to his pants, feasting on the fibers as he desperately tried to rub them off while Dr. Reul lectured. He could feel dirt inside his shoes, though that was impossible. The splitting headache was the worst part, still growing from his ear up behind his eyes. He had the sudden urge to grab a compass out from his pencil case and shove it into his ear, dig hard and deep and gouge out every green, growing thing before it slid roots deeper into his brain.

Except he'd look absolutely mad massacring his own eardrum with blood exploding down the side of his face. He had to sit still. He had to get through this.

Lunch hour meant the torments of the dining hall, but at least he'd be back with Thomas. Andrew fell in behind a few students talking loudly about the vine infestation and if their parents should be paying the school's hefty tuition when "all these accidents keep happening." He decided to slip down a shadowy side hallway and wait for them to pass—except there were two students lingering at the far end, close enough for clandestine whispers. Or kisses. Wickwood had many narrow little hallways like this, relics from the days when servants needed swift access where they wouldn't disturb the lord of the manor. Art hung on the walls in tarnished gold frames, each piece darker than the last. Apples with dull black skin, bowls of grapes furred with mold, plums split open and oozing soft, spoiled innards. He could almost smell it, the sweet decay of fruit dripping from ancient canvas.

An uncanny crawling sensation prickled up his neck, and he started to back away from the narrow hall when one of the students raised their voice in an unmistakable razor-sharp snap.

". . . take a freaking second to think about what you're doing to him."

Andrew pressed himself against the art frames and went still as he listened. Lana stood with fists clenched and body taut as she bore down on the slouched figure of Thomas leaning against the wall. He had his arms folded, his mouth at a sour angle, but for once he wasn't trying to escape her. That was the confusing part.

"I'm not doing anything to him." Thomas's voice held less of the usual acid he leveled at Lana, and instead he just sounded annoyed. And tired.

"Well, doesn't look like it from here. Looks like you made your move when he's clearly a vulnerable mess. He's not even eating, is he?"

For some reason, it didn't shock Andrew to realize they'd talk about him behind his back. He stared at another painting: brown-speckled pears next to cheese veined with rot, tiny white worms dangling from the perforated edges. It was unrepentantly gross, but somehow easier to focus on.

"I'm not . . ." Thomas trailed off and sighed. "You don't understand anything."

Lana huffed. "Dove told me enough. If you hadn't hurt her—"

This made him shove away from the wall. "I *didn't* hurt Dove. I'd never hurt her. And I'll protect Andrew with my life."

"Seems like you need to with all the creepy stuff going on in this school. Guess you don't know anything about that?"

"No," he snapped. "Sorry I don't control the goddamn building and can't stop it falling apart for Your Majesty's convenience."

There was a terse silence, both of them with dagger-expressions and tight jaws.

"The school," Lana said, stiff and low, "isn't the only thing falling apart. Don't use him as a distraction from your nasty little inner monsters."

Andrew slipped quietly away, his breath held, and he hoped they didn't hear his footfalls on the carpet. He wanted to have never heard any of that, and he wanted to not think about what it meant.

He hid out next to the bathrooms until he saw Lana storm out of the narrow hallway, each step a staccato beat of righteous fury. A minute passed, then two, and when Thomas still didn't emerge, Andrew backtracked and wound his way between the walls of putrefied paintings until he found Thomas sitting cross-legged under a gilt frame of a fruit bowl infested with beetles and spider eggs. He could almost taste the corruption under his tongue, the mold like a carpet of poison. Surely Wickwood hadn't hung paintings like this on purpose, but he wasn't sure if he was imagining their corruption or if this was an effect of what had escaped the forest last night.

A monster shaped like decay was crawling into the very bones of the school.

"Hey." He kicked Thomas's shoe lightly.

Thomas stayed where he was, glowering at the floor. Without any windows, the dusty light tarnished his hair to the color of old blood.

"If getting rid of my artwork doesn't stop them," he said, "the next step is obvious. I'm the creator. I'm the problem."

A panicky feeling took hold of Andrew's lungs, and he

already didn't want to hear the rest. "Maybe that *is* the answer. You are the artist. You drew them to life, so can't you, like, I don't know, draw their deaths?"

Thomas looked pained. "And while I'm doing that, you're swinging the ax? I'm meant to fight the battles, not you."

"Does it matter?" Andrew said softly.

"I have to protect you." Thomas scrunched up his brow and scrubbed tiredly at his face. "That's always how I've drawn us. Me, the prince with the sword, you the valiant storyteller."

"We can't kill monsters every night until we graduate. They're getting worse. The Antler King was a freaking lot more to handle than thistle fairies."

"I know."

"What if," Andrew said, "we killed them with ink?" He was rewarded with a blank stare, so he hurried on. "I mean, it makes sense, right? Control your art and then you control the monsters."

"Maybe I can't control them."

"You have to try. We . . . I need you to try."

Thomas finally pushed to his feet with a barely concealed wince, a hand going to his side where the wolf monsters had bitten. He took a step closer to Andrew, then another, only light filling the aching space between them.

"I won't let my monsters hurt you." His hand reached out, tentative at first, and then he took hold of Andrew's Wickwood sweater and twisted his fingers into the soft fabric so hard Andrew felt the shape of Thomas's finger bones against his heartbeat. "If I lose control, you'd stop me, right? If I'm the true monster, you'd fight me."

"You're not the monster." But all Andrew could think was if

he could crack open Thomas's ribs right then and fit his whole self inside him, he would.

"But if I am"—Thomas's teeth clenched—"you have to swear you'd stop me."

"I can't," Andrew whispered.

"Yes, you can." Thomas's eyes were on him then, wretched and dark and mossy. "Prove to me that you can. Hit me."

Andrew stared.

"I need to know you can do it." Thomas let go and took a step back. "That you can defend yourself from me."

They stood an arm's length apart, both breathing too fast as if they'd run a thousand miles and still not outpaced the dark. Between them the world crumbled into a cavernous black void.

"No," Andrew said.

Thomas shoved him. Andrew's shoulders hit the wall and air burst from his lungs with a gasp.

"Hit me." Thomas's eyes blazed. "Or I swear I will fucking leave you in case that's the only way to save you. I will leave you and never, never come back. I'll—"

Andrew hit him.

His fist met flesh with a thick and terrible sound, and he felt the moment blood slid across his knuckles like a crimson tithe to the woods.

His second punch made Thomas stumble backward, hand to his mouth as his fingers came away red.

Everything felt vicious and electric between them. Sweat ran down the back of Andrew's neck and raw, red heat ravaged his eyes. He wanted to kiss Thomas. He wanted to press their bloody mouths together with a hunger he thought would kill him.

He hadn't needed to hit Thomas twice.

But he had.

Thomas wiped his mouth. "Okay." He sounded calmer. "Okay, good."

This is all they were, at the end of it all, boys with stomachs empty and concave, waiting to be filled by Wickwood and forests and rot.

TWENTY-ONE

It was impossible he'd gotten away with it.

He kept waiting for Thomas to bring it up, or a teacher to pull him into a dark room where a detective would step out of the shadows, handcuffs ready, the accusation written cold in their eyes: *Murderer.*

Andrew couldn't stop thinking about it as he slipped into one of the halls dedicated to independent study, textbooks crowded in his arms and a sweater on under his blazer because he was cold, always cold. His hair was swept back in a deep, honey wave, and he looked a shy and lovely boy, not one to sacrifice a teacher.

take Clemens as the tithe take him take him take him

He had to stop thinking about it. He should think, instead, of Thomas's scabbed-over lip, how he kept worrying it in class until it split afresh and lined his chin with a perfect paint stroke of vermilion.

Yesterday's violence felt like a fever dream, but a bruise ghosted Andrew's knuckles in the soft shape of Thomas's mouth.

He should stop thinking about Thomas's mouth.

Finding a free table in the study hall proved harder than he anticipated, especially since most of the seniors had clustered in groups of two or three, their books and laptops taking over whole tables. Tall mahogany bookshelves divided the room, desks and students sequestered between them, and with the dark wallpaper and ornate carved cornices and bronze chandeliers, the whole room felt oppressive and airless. But he couldn't keep hovering, awkward and alone, while he waited for Thomas to be released from art class. Not to mention how much work he had to catch up on.

He was failing classes; they both were. Sleepless nights full of monsters weren't conducive to Wickwood's rigorous academic schedule, apparently.

Hiding in a corner was about to be his best plan, when he rounded a shelf and pulled up short. Dove stood at the end, dust motes dancing above her head in the light like a crown of feathers as her long, elegant fingers trailed over book spines. The pain of their last conversation—their *fight*—came back with the brutal swiftness of a knife sliding into his lungs. He wanted to go to her. He wanted to walk away.

She looked up as if she could sense him hovering, anxious and jittery, and the dismissive way she turned away to continue searching for a book made heat flare in his chest.

He hurried over, trying to balance his armful of slipping textbooks and still look stern. In control. But when he opened his mouth to speak, she got in first.

"Do you hear what they're saying about Thomas?"

Andrew blinked. "No? Who's saying what?"

Dove gave a dismissive snort, as if of course he couldn't be relied on to know what was happening around him. "That he killed his parents." She pulled out a book, inspected it, then slid it back into the shelf. "And Clemens. It's all over the school."

A wave of nausea turned over Andrew's stomach, the pain in his ear suddenly spiking as if the vine had sprouted a fresh tendril to worm deeper into the soft tissue behind his eyes. He pressed a thumb to his temple.

"Maybe you could talk to Thomas . . ." But he trailed off, ashamed of the feeble attempt.

"Also, here. I went over your story for you. I would suggest rewriting the whole thing." She unfolded a paper from her pocket and smacked it atop his pile of books.

He flinched in surprise and then frowned as he glanced over the page soaked in red strikes and circled spelling errors. It was unmistakably torn from his notebook, but more than that, he recognized the story. The woodcutter who'd stolen an enchanted tree to burn for his fire and had then been encircled by the rest of the walking forest to be punished for his sins.

But he'd wedged this page in the window for Thomas to find. How could Dove—

"I—" he started, but Dove cut him off.

"I can't just keep correcting your work again and again," she said. "Especially when you make the same mistakes. Use a dictionary or, like, your brain."

Tears rose hot and wild in his eyes, and the battle to hold them in, to hold his voice steady, was nearly lost. She was never like this with him, abrupt and curt, going heavy with a red pen—she *always* used purple—and she never corrected his stories. These were part of him, sacred and personal and quiet, and to strike out whole lines with a little penned-in comment of *cliché and melodramatic* felt like the cruelest blow she could deliver.

With an abrupt jerk, he twisted away from her and strode

off between the shelves. Dove had the gall to look annoyed, her arms folding and her mouth pursed in a tense line.

"You're seriously leaving me again?" she said. "Are you about to *cry*? You have no right to be—"

He whirled on her. "Just *shut up*."

Hurt flashed in her eyes, and he couldn't take it. He—a coward, not a prince like Thomas—fled around the shelves until he couldn't see her anymore.

He must have yelled a lot louder than he meant to, because several students looked up as he rushed past their tables, their expressions ranging from annoyed to bewildered. He probably looked unraveled and wild, one of those students already cracking under the weight of senior year.

He was saved when he caught sight of a table at the far end of the hall, shoved tight in a corner and ruled by the vehement presence of Lana Lang stabbing at a laptop while Chloe sat next to her underlining notes with pastel highlighters. Perfect. If Dove followed, she wouldn't continue the fight in front of a junior she barely knew—though she was acting so erratic and vindictive, maybe she would. Maybe she *wanted* him to cry where people could see and snicker and roll their eyes at his uncontrollable emotions.

Punishment for a crime he still didn't know he'd committed.

He dumped his books on the table and dropped into a chair across from Chloe before remembering he hadn't asked if they wanted him here, if he was taking someone else's seat. Chloe looked up in surprise, her highlighter dashing an unintentional line across her page, while Lana paused her argument with the laptop to eye Andrew suspiciously. He busied himself arranging his books and then quickly swiped his sleeve over his eyes.

"Are you okay?" Lana said, cautious.

"Yup." He snatched for his biology notepad, flipped to a random page, and stared at it. "I'm just waiting on Thomas, then I'll go." What else would he say? *My sister was mean to me*... Sure, and sound like a whining baby.

"You can stay." Lana exchanged a quick glance with Chloe, who shrugged. "It's just that someone yelled two seconds ago and it sounded like . . . you."

He decided not to answer and then wondered if that made him seem more guilty.

"Also." Lana dragged out the word as she slowly shut her laptop. "Did Thomas get into a *fight*? Because his face is totally busted. I haven't noticed anyone else looking like a lowlife brawler, but I can't imagine he took a punch without swinging back."

Andrew's bruised knuckles tightened into a fist under the table, the cut of Thomas's teeth on his skin hidden from her perceptive eyes. "He didn't."

Lana raised one eyebrow, but Andrew didn't have a lie prepared, his pounding headache liquefying all common sense. He shouldn't have sat here, he should've hidden in the bathrooms or gone to the nurse's office for painkillers or—

Chloe's fingers appeared at the top of his biology notepad and she carefully tugged it out of his grip, flipped it, and then slid it back. When he looked up, she gave him a reassuring smile.

Shame flushed his cheeks. He'd been staring at it upside down.

He was losing it.

He needed Thomas, needed their lungs sewn inside each other so he could remember how to breathe. He needed to take words from Thomas's mouth and put them in his own so he had something to say.

Laughter burst from around a row of shelves and he stiffened as a group of seniors strolled into view. Of course it had to be Bryce Kane, flocked by his vultures. Andrew squeezed the edge of the table so hard his knuckles went bloodless, hoping they'd walk past, but their exaggerated whispers were hard to ignore.

Thomas Rye killed his parents.

He has a temper, have you seen it?

Did you know he hated Clemens?

Suspicious, right?

Especially after what happened with him and Dove Perrault.

Bryce's eyes lit on Andrew's table, and it was like he could taste vulnerable meat, ready for mincing. A wide grin spread across his face as he sauntered over, his shirtsleeves cuffed and hair swooped back at a rakish angle.

"Hello, girlies." He grabbed the back of Andrew's chair and leaned in, his weight heavy and suffocating as he hovered way too close. "Getting in some hard work before the next attack?"

Andrew could feel himself being squeezed thin as paper, panic tapping the insides of his teeth as Bryce kept getting closer and closer.

"What 'attack' are you talking about?" Lana snapped. "Get a life and get out, Bryce."

Chloe gave Andrew a sympathetic look of misery, but even she was shrinking beside Lana. Apparently only one of them had any guts, and they were both going to leave Lana to do the dirty work.

Until Thomas chose that moment to show up.

He materialized like flame struck from a match, his scowl already monstrous as he adjusted his grip on his notebooks, as if he was considering using them to rearrange Bryce Kane's face.

Lana rolled her eyes to the ceiling. "Here we go."

"Hey, President Asshole," Thomas said, all teeth, "how about you get off Andrew before I throw you off."

Bryce straightened with a magnanimous smile, spreading his arms wide as if about to greet an incoming friend. His vultures sidled closer and Andrew was suddenly aware of how few teachers were in this room.

"Tommy," Bryce said. "Want me to get off him so you can get on? We were just talking about you. Wanted to check in and see if you're all cut up about Professor Clemens . . . unless you were the one who cut him up in the first place."

Lana smacked her palm on the table. "That's so inappropriate. Clemens's death was an accident."

Bryce gave a dramatic shrug, clearly playing it up for his audience. "Was it, though? I saw Perrault with Clemens that day. Looked like they were headed to the principal's office. So like, it makes sense." He swept a hand through his perfect hair and shrugged. "Perrault gets in trouble, Rye takes revenge. But I mean, what did you even do, Andy? Offer to blow the professor for better grades now that Dove's not doing your homework? Poor Rye was getting jealous about being left out."

His vultures smirked, a few holding back laughs, feeling safe behind their leader with his dashing smile and his rich boy family name. He was as tall as he was untouchable, and they thrived under his daring.

"You know what?" Thomas's face burned. "Shut the fuck up."

Bryce whistled. "There's that temper. Keep it up, Rye. Confirm what we know you're capable of . . . Murderer."

Thomas moved.

Panic seared Andrew's vision, and he thought the world would invert and he'd fall over the edge of oblivion. He tried to get out of his chair, fumbled, his limbs suddenly too long and slick and unwieldy as he grappled against gravity. Chloe made a small noise of distress, but it was Lana who rose like a phoenix lit in bold flame. She must've started moving before Thomas did, and she grabbed the back of his shirt and dug her heels in, holding on like she'd just wrapped her fists around a hurricane.

"This is for Dove," she muttered. "You're not getting your ass expelled for fighting on my watch."

It gave Andrew time to stumble out of his chair and slide between Thomas and Bryce.

"Kinda surprised with this threesome." Bryce waggled his eyebrows. "But I guess if Lang only does girls and Andy's pretty much one—"

Lana's fury rolled over her face in a tidal wave. "It's incredible how you think being a bigot is still trendy or that no one will report your asinine comments. Because I will. There's zero tolerance for bullying in this school."

Bryce smirked. "Zero tolerance for murder, too."

Thomas tried to lunge, but Lana grunted as she held on while Andrew put both hands on his shoulders and pedaled him backward.

"That's your comeback?" Lana's serrated smile could have

flayed skin. "No defense for how you're obsessed with talking about the supposed sex life of minors? Aren't you already eighteen, Bryce? It's looking a bit predatory now."

His smile dropped. An ugly purple flushed over his face and he moved toward her. "Slander me again, Lang, and I'll—"

Chloe popped out of her chair, voice artificially cheerful. "Oh, I think Ms. Bevan is coming over."

The threat of anyone with authority seeing the ugly side of the school's golden boy had Bryce rearranging his simmering rage into a sneering smile. He swept past, pausing only to pat Thomas on the head, each thump harder than the last, then he took off with his vultures in tow. Andrew's bones felt like dust, his lungs full of feathers, and he was sure Lana had done the true work of holding Thomas back. He was a wisp of cloud barely gripping a comet.

With the coast clear and no teacher appearing, Lana released Thomas's shirt and he stumbled forward only to be caught by Andrew.

Lana gave Thomas a scathing once-over. "You need to cool it."

A muscle flexed in Thomas's jaw. "If he touches Andrew again, I'm killing him."

"Or maybe don't talk like that?" Chloe said, small and timid. "After everything . . ."

Thomas didn't even spare her a glance. "I hate this school. I hate *all* of them. Everyone pretends to be so perfect and clever, so bursting with 'potential,' and all they do is layer money over their shit. This school grows foul, poisonous spores and calls them roses."

Andrew plucked at Thomas's sleeve. "It's okay." It barely made it out of his mouth, the words breathless, too thin to offer comfort.

But Lana watched Thomas with something almost curious behind her glower. "I mean, you're not wrong. Who hit you, by the way?"

Andrew shoved his hands in his pockets, but her eyes tracked his quick movement and he wished he'd done nothing.

"I'll tell them you said thank you," Thomas said, cold.

Lana rolled her eyes. "Whatever. I'm reporting Bryce Kane. Some people get high off making other people feel worthless. They're monsters."

Something flickered behind Andrew's ribs.

They knew how to deal with monsters.

TWENTY-TWO

The forest came alive that night as they slipped between the trees. Leaves skittered in their footsteps on a breeze they couldn't feel, and something crawled through the underbrush with a form they couldn't see. It was the witching hour and Thomas held a sketchbook and Andrew gripped the hatchet.

The prince and his poet climbed over fallen logs, soft with moss and fungi, and the shadows made it look as if they wore crowns of holly berries and thorns.

Andrew would write them as a story someday. He'd make the blackest parts beautiful and he'd write the kisses bloody and the vengeance sweet.

It was going to work tonight. They'd win, they had to. They had the answer.

Ink already stained Thomas's fingers as he put his back to a shadowed pine and sank into a crouch. He balanced the sketchbook on his knees and propped his flashlight up beside him.

"I finished drawing the monster in study hall," he said. "As soon as it appears, I'll draw a noose of vines around its throat."

Blood crusted behind Andrew's ear. He rubbed his head against his shoulder and tried to reassure himself the wound was only oozing pus now, not mud. An improvement . . . sort of.

He adjusted his grip on the hatchet and zipped his fleecy jacket up to his throat. "How do we know that's the one that will come out?"

"I've destroyed everything else." Thomas sounded strained. "It doesn't even make sense how they're still appearing. If I'm not drawing monsters, why haven't we won?"

"What about art class?"

"Those are portraits. I mean, I have birds and mountains bursting out of heads, but"—he spoke louder to cut off Andrew's protests—"that's different. No monsters."

"Are you drawing forests? Trees?"

Darkness shrouded most of Thomas's face, but a small corner of light touched his resentful mouth. He'd always hated being told what to do.

"I think," Andrew said, "the problem is everything you draw."

"If I can make monsters, do you . . . do you think about what this makes me?" Thomas uncapped a Sharpie, but the sideways glance he shot Andrew was wary.

Trapped between monsters and the waking dark for so long, Andrew was focused on only one thing: Make the monsters stop.

Not who had started it.

Not why.

His stomach flipped as he looked at Thomas's unsure face, the way his chin tilted up as if he was starved for any reassurance Andrew could place on his tongue. This vulnerability made him look younger, softer.

"Magic," Andrew said. "I think it makes you magic."

Inside him, what he really thought beat against his pulse,

dark and fervent and cruel. *You are a nightmare, you are a god of wicked places, to stop your horror maybe we have to stop you—*

Thomas allowed himself the smallest smile before turning back to his drawing. But some of the tension had left his shoulders, and it made Andrew's lie worth it. He wished he could fit his face into the crook of Thomas's throat and hold on until his anxiety thinned and they both felt warm again.

A stick cracked behind them.

Andrew turned slowly, his grip firm on the hatchet. He refused to fall apart this time like a boy made of glass.

Thomas drew faster. "It will be a devil with a terrible face and flowers in its horns. The tree roots will strangle it. If this works, we won't have to do much."

"What does this devil want?" Andrew said.

Thomas flicked a puzzled glance at him. "I don't know, to eat us? It's a monster."

Something turned over in Andrew's mind, a puzzle piece, toppling into his outstretched hand. Everyone wanted something. Everyone yearned or searched or hungered—even monsters. Clemens had wanted to feel clever by making others feel stupid, and Bryce Kane wanted to feel powerful by making others small.

So what did the monsters in the forest want?

Thomas drew them fierce and wicked, but he put no story behind his drawings—his monsters began and stopped on paper. Andrew knew Thomas drew how he felt, but did he ever understand his own feelings? He never seemed to know why he was angry or scared or lonely—this was obvious in all his wild moods and his bewilderment when Dove called him out for being loathsome and in the desperate way he held on to Andrew.

Maybe, this whole time, they'd been fighting the monsters wrong.

"What do *you* want?" Andrew said, and watched Thomas frown in confusion.

He stared at Andrew with the night pooled black in his eyes, and when his mouth shaped a word, Andrew so desperately wanted it to be:

You.

But Thomas didn't say that. He didn't have a chance to say anything.

Behind him a claw shot out of the darkness and snatched him by the throat.

Andrew cried out and vaulted forward, but Thomas had already been dragged backward into the brush. He kicked with a frantic, animal fury, sketchbook torn from his hand and papers ripping and scattering across the forest floor. The page with the monster he'd designed whipped up and caught on Andrew's leg before flying away.

The monster who had Thomas now was all wrong.

Its body twisted in the vulgar imitation of a human. Arms too long, spine mangled. Its torso was naked but for twine wrapped around and around its chest and neck and head. Dirt and rotten fruit and twigs oozed between the bindings. No eyes, no ears. Only its mouth showed in a red, lipless slash, and when its jaws parted, a tongue slithered out, long and forked like a snake's.

It was nothing like Thomas's drawing.

Everything in Andrew's head started screaming.

He swung the ax but the creature ducked. It slammed its head into Andrew's chest and he flew backward, landing hard with a wheeze.

The hatchet clattered down between Andrew and the monster.

Thomas scrabbled toward it, but the monster screamed and flung itself over him, pinning him bodily to the ground. Thomas landed a good punch at its face and the monster hissed, rearing back.

Then its tongue shot out.

"Thomas!" Andrew's fingers closed on the hatchet, but his sweaty hand slipped. He was too slow, too shaky. He slammed the hatchet into the monster's back, but it bounced off as if its skin was impenetrable.

Andrew staggered backward just as he realized the monster's tongue had never been forked. It was an arrow tip.

It plunged into Thomas's stomach.

Thomas screamed. He writhed beneath the monster, kicking so madly it had to fight to keep his limbs down.

No, *no no no*—Andrew was failing. He was *failing him.*

He flung himself on the monster's back, but it flicked him off like he weighed no more than a butterfly. It hunkered over Thomas and rocked, slow and languorous, as it sucked on its tongue like a straw. Lisping smacks of pleasure came from its mouth.

Thomas stopped screaming, but his whimper alone could have murdered Andrew. He suddenly sounded so small, so full of pain. His mud-slick fingers grabbed at the tongue, but it was too slippery to hold.

Andrew dropped the hatchet.

A wildness grew in his head, thorns and fury and poisonous berries. If this was a story, he would have written himself strong enough to kill the monster.

So he'd make it a story.

He snatched Thomas's Sharpie from the dirt.

Then he ran.

Thomas's cry broke behind him, a thousand shattered pieces taken by the wind. His thrashing body churned the leaves, but he couldn't get away. He was prey, impaled.

And Andrew had left him.

He didn't look back even as Thomas sobbed for him.

Andrew vaulted the mossy log and flung himself at a smooth-skinned birch. He braced one hand on the trunk, forcing his other hand to steady as he rested the Sharpie to the bark. Think, *think*. He was static electricity; he was full of Thomas's screams.

Then he began to write.

The dark hid each word as it bled out over the birch, but Andrew kept writing. The pen tripped over grooves and whorls, but the story tore out of him.

Deep in the hollow woods, a witch liked to catch boys and soak her tongue in their blood.

Thomas's whimpers turned to another sobbing scream that left holes in the night. Andrew wrote faster, his heart pounding.

But when she dipped her tongue inside a boy with hair of stoked flames, she burned to ash from the inside out and everything left of her blew away.

Andrew shoved away from the birch, chest heaving as if he'd

been the one running, fighting, screaming. He spun, his mind full of hatchets and blood, and this clawing terror for Thomas Thomas Thomas—

He saw the moment the monster's body spasmed and curved backward as if its spine were made of rubber. Then, with a shrill scream, it exploded into ash.

Gray flakes swirled over Thomas's body before the wind took them.

Andrew ran back, slipping and tearing the knees of his jeans on sharp rocks before collapsing at Thomas's side. His hands were all over Thomas, feeling across his stomach, his chest, pressing a palm to his beating heart before cupping his face.

Thomas's sobs came thick and low. With trembling hands, he pulled up his shirt.

Even in the dark they could see the hole, a perfectly round burrow straight into his stomach. It didn't bleed. It was a black tunnel to another world.

Andrew flattened his fingers over it. "You're okay. The monster's dead."

"What did you do?" Thomas choked on each word. "H-h-how—"

"I told a story." Andrew gripped Thomas like he'd never let go. "I killed them with ink."

They had to try it again, to be sure it hadn't been a coincidence.

They stuffed Andrew's pockets with thick black markers, and this time Thomas held the hatchet. His eyes were hollowed and bruised with exhaustion, and he held himself gingerly. They'd cleaned and bandaged his wound, but the hole didn't close. It stayed there, round as a coin and pitch black. Andrew thought if he slid fingers into it, he'd find no blood, just a tunnel all the way to Thomas's spine.

It was freaking Thomas out in a way nothing else had yet. He kept one hand around his stomach as they walked into the forest, and whenever the bushes rustled, he looked ready to fall apart.

As Andrew stood before the birch he'd written on last night, Thomas rested his back against Andrew's and matched their breaths. His came ragged and damp, Andrew's steady.

He shone his flashlight over the bark and picked an empty space.

"I don't want them to touch me," Thomas said. "I can't . . . not again. I—"

"I'll write it different." Andrew bit the Sharpie cap off and put pen to the bark, ready. He curled his other hand around Thomas's wrist.

Thomas curved into him then, and Andrew's breath caught, a riot of butterflies behind his ribs. They were so close, cheek to cheek. He thought if he tilted his head sideways, Thomas might kiss him right then, and it would be wonderful and terrible.

It would answer one thing and ruin everything else.

Or maybe it wouldn't ruin anything. He didn't know. It ate at him, how he didn't know and was too scared to find out.

"Andrew . . ." Thomas said his name with such careful softness. "Do you . . ." He stopped. "When we slept—"

They couldn't talk about this, not now. Andrew didn't have

words lined up to justify why they'd curled against each other in his bed, saying nothing like it meant nothing—

Andrew must have stiffened slightly, or maybe they both sensed the weight of monsters shifting in the dark, because Thomas pulled away.

"What?" Andrew said, mouth dry.

"I'll ask you later." Thomas's voice was low and rough.

Then the monsters were there.

Andrew knew them from one of the drawings Thomas used to have tacked above his bed. Creatures slim as poplar trees and so tall Andrew's neck ached to look up at them. They wore cloaks of mottled black, and their bones rattled as they walked.

Their heads were ram skulls, twisted and grotesque monsters with flesh rotted away and teeth full of worms. Lichen and mushrooms grew up their cloaks, and they didn't so much walk as sweep forward.

Thomas smashed the hatchet through one and the bones exploded apart and clattered to the forest floor. But when he stepped back, the creature simply reformed behind its cloak and rose again.

This time it gnashed its teeth and Thomas stumbled backward into Andrew to get away.

The monsters came forward with jaws clicking, heads tilting as bits of dead flesh dripped from their skulls.

"Andrew . . ." Thomas dug fingers into the back of Andrew's sweater. "They're bone shrikes. When they scream—"

One of the shrikes tilted back its head and screamed as if on request. The sound whipped like a lash across their eardrums, and both of them bent double as they cried out. Blood ran from

their ears, their noses. It dripped wet and metallic over Andrew's lips as he pressed himself to the birch and began to write.

On a night of velvet black, the bone shrikes walked their favored forest paths to call for secrets. If they screamed into an ear, their prey had no choice but to bare their soul.

Thomas clapped hands over his ears, hatchet abandoned. Andrew thought Thomas seemed more desperate than usual to protect himself, as if he owned too many secrets he couldn't let slip.

But when the bone shrikes screamed before the marrow prince and his poet, their enchantment happened in reverse. It was the bone shrikes' secrets that spilled. The shock and shame of losing their own secrets caused their own words to devour them whole.

Andrew wore the Sharpie tip ragged on the rough bark, but as soon as he finished and turned to watch Thomas take another swing with his hatchet, the story began to come true.

The bone shrikes' jaws creaked open, but their screams unwound before they started and punctured backward into the shrikes' chests. They swayed with the force of it.

"Don't attack," Andrew said. "I swear it'll be okay, Thomas. J-just don't attack."

Panic twisted Thomas's face—it was clearly taking everything he had to stand still. But Andrew wanted to hear the shrikes' secrets. He didn't know how they'd speak from skeleton throats, but he let them come closer, closer, and the rattling of their bones filled the forest.

One loomed over Andrew, its horns gleaming like daggers in the moonlight and its arms stretching out like endless tree limbs. It ran fingers through Andrew's hair, and he bit his tongue so hard copper blossomed in his mouth.

Don't fight. Don't run. Don't fight.

"Tell me your secret," Andrew whispered.

It opened its mouth and clumps of dirt and worms tumbled out. Fungi grew on its jaw hinge. It dragged a finger down Andrew's face, toward his eye, and he squeezed them shut as an agonizing, bone-deep cold filled him.

"Why are you doing this?" Andrew's mouth barely moved. "What do you want?"

. . . sacrificeeeeee . . .

every good story ends with a wishbone snapped . . .

a bloodied kiss—

the prince's sacrifice.

—cut out a heart—

and bury it in the woods.

but you already

knew that, prince.

The bone shrike drew back as one of its own kind came up behind and broke pieces off its skull and began to eat them. They all stood there, devouring each other, while Andrew watched in horrified awe as his story came true.

He backed up and knelt beside Thomas, who sat trembling in the leaves, hands clasped around his legs and knees up to his chin.

"Did they say something to you?" Andrew said.

Thomas shook his head, but his face was white, and an unnatural frost coated his cheeks. Maybe he was lying, but it didn't matter. Andrew had the answers he wanted. He dragged Thomas to his feet.

When there was nothing left of the shrikes but their jaws

still working on the ground, trying to chew themselves to death, Andrew and Thomas escaped back to the school.

Neither could get warm. Secrets apparently stole all the heat from your body. Andrew put on another sweater over his flannel pajamas and crawled into bed. He flicked off the lights so they could steal those slim dawn hours for sleep, but before he could close his eyes, his mattress depressed at the edge. He could feel more than see Thomas hovering, one knee already on the comforter, questioning.

Andrew rolled over, and Thomas folded himself into the bed.

They couldn't pretend it was an accident this time, so they said nothing, just curled into each other until they stopped shivering.

"You can control them," Thomas said. "All this time and you could've saved our asses with your stories. Can we stop them now? Forever?"

Andrew pressed his face into Thomas's curls and thought of princes with their hearts cut out. "I don't know."

Liar. But he'd always been one.

Instead, he whispered, "Would you die for me?"

Thomas sounded warm and cottony with sleep. "Of course I would."

TWENTY-THREE

They sat together on the stairs, working through a package of Oreos between them. Rain had left the garden glossy, hedges beaded with diamond drops and the air thick with that dense, clean smell of a freshly washed world. It was a relief to breathe in something that wasn't the forest—suffocating, cloying, all-consuming. These stairs led to a side entrance into Wickwood and were only used by staff heading to the parking lot, so the boys felt safe in their aloneness. Unwatched.

They should've been in the dining hall for lunch, but this was Thomas's compromise: They'd avoid everyone if Andrew would eat.

He tried. He wasn't doing this on purpose. He just never felt hungry anymore, and the flood of anxiety about food tasting of mud, of leaves, of the forest made it impossible to even force it into his mouth. It helped that right now he sat on the top step while Thomas was a few steps down from him. Thomas kept his back to Andrew as he bit into an Oreo, inspected it, and then passed it over his shoulder. No eye contact. No confrontation about this anxious, needy habit Andrew had developed. He couldn't bite into food until Thomas had first.

Even now, Andrew's tongue searched for the grooves Thomas's teeth had left behind.

"They keep saying it," Thomas said.

Andrew looked up from the notebook cradled in his lap. He had a routine: Bite an Oreo, think, then write a line. He was cold, October crawling into his blazer to leave frosty lingering kisses, but he didn't mind. "Saying what?"

"That I'm a murderer." He glowered and then twisted to pass back another Oreo, and Andrew leaned forward to accept. "I know Bryce Kane is spreading shit to rile me up, but it feels like . . . so many people *want* to think it. Some guys I've never even spoken to were talking about me and they didn't even stop when I walked past. They smirked. They were like, 'If he's not guilty then why's he so twitchy?' I just—" He stopped abruptly and let the pause stretch for a long minute before he said bitterly, "Maybe we should let monsters eat them. I do *not* look guilty."

Andrew didn't point out that they did, both of them. A frenetic energy chewed Thomas through every waking moment—he was stretched and harrowed, attention split a thousand ways, always flinching as if he expected a blow, a scream, a knife through his side. Meanwhile Andrew was faded halfway to invisible.

"And Halloween is tomorrow. The monsters are bad enough now, but they'll be worse then. I know it." Thomas bit savagely into the next Oreo. "Why can't you write a story that says 'and no more monsters manifested out of my goddamn drawings and we all lived happily ever after'?"

"I tried," Andrew said. "I wrote 'and all the monsters died' last night and they *didn't*. I have to tell some sort of twisted, macabre fairy tale. I have to write . . . suffering. For them, but also for us. I'm not making up the rules, okay? It is what it is."

Thomas glowered at the crumbs in his lap and said nothing. From this angle, Andrew had a perfect view of the softest curls at the nape of his freckled neck, the way his shirt tags stuck out at odd angles, the old smear of turquoise paint on his rumpled collar. Thomas, the beautiful wreck. It took Andrew's mind off the pulsing headache that never, never left. Or how he felt so full that cramming the Oreos into his mouth left his stomach distended.

How he needed to tell someone that something was wrong with him.

See the school nurse.

Call his father.

Get help.

But he didn't.

He crumbled Oreos into lavender bushes where Thomas wouldn't see.

Thomas started to say something, stopped with a sigh, and went back to eating.

Silence pulled over them, companionable if a little morose, and Andrew wrote a few more lines of a new fairy tale. Making up stories in the dark with monsters breathing down his neck was the kind of high-pressured environment he hated, so he jotted down a few ideas in the daylight. His phone lay open beside him, unanswered messages to Dove on his screen.

He should give in, let her win, but if this truly was a war over Thomas, Andrew couldn't just let go and—

"Hey, can we talk?" Thomas still had his back to Andrew, but his shoulders had tensed.

Andrew's stomach tightened. "We *are* talking."

Thomas let his head drop and dug fingers through his hair. Andrew was acutely reminded of how many times Thomas had

started to speak only to pack everything back inside himself and deflect.

His next words hit Andrew like a fist to the mouth.

"Do you like me?" Thomas said.

No, they couldn't do this. They had an unspoken agreement to *never do this*. Panic clawed up Andrew's throat and his heartbeat seemed too fast, too loud. What would it even look like, to cut their feelings out, bloody and aching and raw, and compare them? To find they didn't match. To be left with guts vivisected and no way to sew themselves back up so they looked the same as before.

Thomas would ruin everything. What if he asked for more from Andrew, asked for *everything*?

Or what if he asked for it all to stop?

Andrew had this desperate, shaky urge to flatten his hands over Thomas's mouth and press until he lost his breath and forgot he wanted to speak.

Thomas still didn't turn. "I know you don't like to talk about stuff, like *really* talk, but—"

"We talk all the time, all day." Andrew snapped his notebook shut, heart galloping. "I was thinking, are you sure we haven't missed some of your sketchbooks? Any lost under your bed? In the art room?"

For a long moment, Thomas said nothing. He picked at moss between the bricked cracks in the stairs. "I gave one to Dove. Ages ago. She probably got rid of it."

"I'll find out," Andrew said. "Maybe Lana will look for us."

"I don't think it's the problem," Thomas said, voice low. "We're erasing everything I ever created and it hasn't *helped*.

Maybe we should talk about that, too. We don't talk about why the monsters won't stop. Why they even started. We don't talk about Dove. We don't talk about what will happen after we graduate." His words scraped against each other, as if he struggled to even pull them out of his throat. "We sleep in the same bed nearly every night now and we don't freaking talk about that, either."

Andrew shoved to his feet. His body felt like an unwieldy colt, limbs detached, and he nearly fell as he stepped over Thomas and hit the damp path. It would start raining again soon. Sodden air pressed against his cheeks, but it did nothing to cool him. He was burning up; he was made of fever.

Thomas said, "It's ruining me."

And Andrew couldn't look at him.

"You could cut me open and devour everything that I am," Thomas said, ragged and thin. "I would let you. I'd *ask* you to. But I have no idea what it means to you. What . . . what I mean to you."

"Of course I like you." It came out rougher than Andrew meant.

"But do you want me?" Thomas stood then, too, crumbs on his pants and his shirt half untucked. "*How* do you want me?"

Andrew closed his eyes. "Stop."

"Because I watch you, okay? I have for years." Thomas ran a hand over his face, but he was already blushing his trademark red. "You don't look at boys. I mean, we've been in locker rooms, in our bedroom, and you've seen me naked. It's like you look away fast because you don't want to see. Not . . . not that you're embarrassed to be caught."

Andrew couldn't do this. A muscle in his jaw clenched. "You like girls. What is this even—"

"Not just girls." Thomas's ears had gone beet red. "But you know that."

"I don't know anything."

"Damn it, Andrew." His voice had gone uneven. "Can't you tell that I'm in . . . that I like you? Because I-I like you a lot, okay?"

Andrew had heard the slip, the save. *I'm in love with you.* His blood roared so loud he couldn't think and all he could focus on was the tight nub of pain in his ear. Burrowing, searching, *hungry*. Just like him. He starved—for this confession, for the raw, helpless look on Thomas's face. Hadn't Andrew wanted this all along?

It shouldn't be so hard to whisper, *I'm in love with you, too, but—*

But.

That word was too huge.

But what about Dove? But what if she loved him first? But what if Thomas wanted more than Andrew could give? *But—*

The world felt ready to spin away, and he couldn't swallow properly. In his chest, his heart beat itself bloody against his ribs. He was losing control.

"Everything inside me is in ruins," Thomas said. "For you."

A fine misty rain started, and it tasted of the forest. Andrew stared at his knuckles gone white against the spine of his notebook. He could tear out a dozen stories and shove them in Thomas's face. Each said, in bloody and beautiful ways, *I love you I love you I love you.*

Instead, his voice felt like it came from someone else, distant and mechanical.

"I'm asexual," Andrew said.

It sat between them, echoing. Mist coated Thomas's eyelashes as he blinked. His face was still full of aching questions and want—but a furrow dug between his brows.

The pause went too long.

"Okay." Thomas sounded hoarse. "I don't know . . . I mean, I kind of know, but I don't . . ."

"I don't have crushes," Andrew said. "I don't want—I don't think about . . . about . . . sleeping with people. I don't want it. With anyone." He was blinking fast. He didn't know why. "Sometimes it's different for other asexual people. But for me it's . . . this."

"You don't like boys." Thomas's voice sounded stripped.

"That's not what I said."

Thomas turned in a jagged circle, hands in his hair again as he paced to the stairs and back. Andrew could almost feel the heat churning from Thomas's spinning mind.

"I like you," Andrew said, his mouth dry. "But not . . . not how you need."

Thomas stopped sharply. "Wait, what are you assuming I need?"

"Don't pretend." Andrew's skin felt too tight. "You would want . . . you w-would want to sleep with me. Someday." He couldn't look at him.

"Well, obviously? Andrew, you're beautiful. Of course I . . . I *told you*. I am in ruins for you. I'd give you anything."

Andrew was going to cry. This was worse than anything, worse than the monsters sinking teeth into his skin.

He wanted to say, *You are my everything, too.*

He wanted to say, *I don't exist without you.*

He wanted to say, *Kiss me.*

But he had to step back, because he couldn't be what Thomas wanted, and for that he was going to lose him completely.

This was why they should have left it. Been whatever they were without words. He knew there was nothing wrong with intimate, platonic affection—but for him, under all his rotted and tremulous layers, there was nothing platonic about what he felt for Thomas. Andrew loved this boy so deep and whole and obsessively that he couldn't breathe, and the weight of it terrified him.

"I can't." Andrew tucked his shaking hands behind his back.

"I'm not saying right now." Thomas jerked at his tie until it loosened, and he looked everywhere but at Andrew. "I know you're anxious. I'd never pressure—"

"It's not *anxiety*. It's . . . I can't. I won't. I—Just forget it, okay?" The notebook slipped from his shaking fingers and thwapped on the path between them. Andrew's hands shook as he scooped it up. "What about Dove?"

It was a cruel thing to throw. He knew it as soon as Thomas's face shuttered.

"I was never in love with Dove." His voice came low.

"Did you two kiss?" Andrew said.

Say no. *Say no.*

But Thomas said nothing. He pulled at his bottom lip and

then suddenly dropped down to sit on the stairs again. He scrubbed at his hair, curls so damp they plastered his forehead.

"What else did you do together?" Andrew had stepped outside himself. "Is this why you fought? Last year after school ended? The big fight that made her cut you out."

Thomas looked up, surprise warring with confusion. "Sort of, but it's complicated."

But Andrew took a step forward, and he sounded so terrible he knew his face must match. "How many times did you kiss?"

"When we kissed it felt wrong, it was . . . a mistake. We both agreed." Thomas struggled to keep his mouth straight, but his eyes were far too bright, the agony there brutal to behold. "Why are you doing this?"

To protect myself. To keep you away.

Because I can't stop.

"Do you even like me," Andrew said, "or do you just miss Dove?"

It was like Thomas had taken a lash to the face. He physically turned away, curled in on himself after the invisible blow. His mouth looked too red, eyes glossy in the rain.

"You know that time when we were twelve and hiking in the forest for class?" Thomas's voice was uneven, and it took Andrew a second to realize it was with anger. "We decided to race, Dove and me. And the whole time, I was thinking, *I want Andrew to look at me. I want Andrew to see me.* I've loved you since then. So you know what? Fuck you. I think you do love me back, you're just—you're too much a coward to admit it."

Andrew shoved away and took off down the garden path. He couldn't see, couldn't hear past the world ending. He wiped furiously at his eyes, but what he needed was to curl into a ball and stop existing for a second before he completely lost it. *Panic attack.* But he couldn't force words out to warn anyone. Not that there was anyone to go to for help. He hadn't just pushed Thomas away, he'd made sure to cut his throat on the way out.

Why had he done that—

The remains of a battlefield lay in his wake, broken swords and hollyhock crowns left to decay among piles of bones. But the sword plunged through his stomach was his fault. All Thomas had done was ask to love a boy lost in fairy tales, and the boy had ordered him punished.

"Andrew."

Then again, anguished and breathless, as if he regretted what he'd said.

"Andrew, *wait.*"

He ran.

TWENTY-FOUR

Andrew couldn't remember the shape of himself, if he'd ever had one.

He felt nothing, saw nothing, as the forgotten garden fell away and he ran toward the dorms. A cool autumn breeze licked at his corners, and he'd never felt more like paper about to be swept into the sky. He wanted this to stop. He wanted to *not be here*. In his skin. In his head.

He was goddamn *done*.

He collided with a group of students exiting the library, knocking books and folders from their hands while they yelled after him. He kept running. Nothing mattered but the name tearing from his lips.

"Dove. *DOVE*."

A pathetic boy made of glass and delicate things, running to his sister for help; it was an embarrassing picture, but he didn't care.

Ahead, a ponytail of honey gold disappeared around the corner, and he plunged after her. But the path ended at the girls' dorm—one place he couldn't follow. She'd done that on purpose.

Everything inside him boiled over, a wave of something foul and black and malignant gushing up his throat to coat his tongue. They were twins, she his other half. She could not abandon him when he needed her most.

"DOVE. *Please.*" He tore forward, the world blurring around him.

He pushed through a group of girls hanging out in front of their dorm, and their voices rose, surprised and indignant. Words hit his back and slid off, meaningless. Someone said his name.

He shoved through their front door. "I have to find my sister. Dove? DOVE."

A person blocked his path. He was so far underwater, drowning in ink, that he couldn't make out her face or expression, could barely feel the timid hands on his shoulders, pushing him backward.

"Andrew, go back outside. Please, listen to me. Our supervisor will hear. Just—please?"

A dull part of his brain registered Chloe's face before she propelled him outside with a surprising amount of force. Her brow scrunched up in anxious lines and she kept petting his arm as if to apologize for pushing him so hard.

As soon as they stumbled onto the grass, several of the other girls stormed over, arms folded.

"I'm so telling a teacher. No boys in our dorms."

Chloe kept a firm grip on Andrew's arm. "And I'll tell Lana that you snitched. Do you want to deal with that?"

That shut them up. They backed off, but Andrew could still feel their suspicion and curiosity drilling holes in his back. He had fallen halfway through time before realizing Chloe had left him and then returned with Lana. He should be grateful, but he couldn't feel anything. He was numb, blinded with rage, and he didn't know which way was up.

Lana stalked toward him, half in her drama costume with heavy eye makeup and an unreadable expression. "Andrew, what the hell?"

Whispers beat against his back.

". . . that's Andrew Perrault."

"Do you hear what he did to his hand last year?"

". . . I heard—"

"Oh my God, as in *Dove's* brother?"

In his mouth, the forest flourished. Mud ground between his teeth, and he could feel damp leaves pasted to the back of his throat.

All he could see was Thomas, expression raw and hopeful.

Andrew, you're beautiful.

The boy who loved no one loved *him*.

His explanation about being asexual had been a mess. But it wasn't fair how he had one shot at coming out, at explaining himself, and if he tangled the words, then it was somehow his fault.

"Andrew? Hey? *Hey.* Look at me."

Fingers snapped in front of his face and he inhaled so sharp it hurt. He hadn't been breathing.

"I need Dove." His voice shook with the effort to keep his voice level, to not sound like he was having a panic attack. "I need to talk to her. I-I-I have to."

Lana exchanged a look with Chloe, both their expressions pinched. He was not theirs to deal with, and they owed him nothing, but the people he depended on had left him. They'd left him and they didn't care and he needed someone.

His vision blurred.

"Do you want to call your dad?" Lana said slowly.

He swallowed. "No. It's—I'm fine. It doesn't matter. Did Thomas leave a sketchbook in Dove's stuff?"

She looked startled. "Actually, yes. I was going to throw it out, but hadn't gotten around to it."

"Can I have it?"

"Sure . . . Are you okay?"

Andrew couldn't look at her. "I'm fine."

"Because you're totally not having a panic attack right now." Lana glanced over his shoulder for the familiar shadow that should be tethered to Andrew's heels but wasn't there. "Was Thomas being a prick?"

He said he loved me and then he called me a coward.

"Did they kiss?" Andrew had no idea how he was forcing the words out. "Thomas and Dove? He said it's *complicated.*"

Lana hesitated. "I hate agreeing with him, but yeah, it is complicated. They were disasters about a lot of stuff. I shouldn't say this, but also what the hell—Dove told me she used to think Thomas fought with people he liked because that's how he knew to get attention. But not with you. She told me, 'Andrew is his safe space. He is forever gentle for Andrew.'" Her eyes narrowed. "Is he pressuring you about anything? Because I will beat him up."

"I think," Andrew whispered, "it sucks to be ace."

"I think," Lana said, "the world sucks for making you feel that way."

"I need to talk to her." He pressed his palms against his eyes so hard that white stars burned behind his lids. "She was so angry at me, and I-I-I don't understand. And now she's abandoned me when I need her. Why is she doing this? We're twins. I *need* her."

He started toward the girls' dorms again, but Lana shoved him back. He was taller, but she felt stronger.

"Getting expelled won't help," Lana said. "You need to calm down. Now, listen. Chloe and I are late for GSA, but we're not leaving you alone like this, so guess what? You're coming, too. You can sit in the back, you don't have to participate." He started to shake his head, but she cut him off. "Or I'll take you to the nurse and she calls your dad. You are clearly not okay."

"I'm sorry." His voice still sounded wrong. Inside out. *Drowned.* He was drowning in front of everyone. "This is stupid and I'm messing up your plans. I'll go—"

"Wrong. You're with us. We can talk about what happened later. Also," she added, "you're allowed to be around people who aren't Thomas."

But he didn't know how.

If a monster climbed out of the rosebushes right now with teeth as long as knives, Andrew would let it bite deep into his ribs and tear him in half like a rotted plum.

He just wanted everything to

stop.

TWENTY-FIVE

He had a beast caged behind his ribs and it took all his energy to keep it there.

He needed a distraction. Focus on something else. He sat hunched in the back of the studio above the library, both hands spread on the carpet with the rough fibers scratching his skin.

Last time he'd felt like this, he put his hand through a mirror.

Around him, the studio thrummed with giddy chaos. Chairs and desks had been pushed back, and kids trickled in for the GSA club. Nothing seemed organized. Everyone was everywhere, talking and joking and gushing over the person who'd brought in delicately frosted cookies from culinary class. Ms. Poppy wore a huge scarf she'd either splattered with paint or had purposely used as her paintbrush—the latter seeming more likely since her brown skin was also smeared by turquoise and lavender. Instead of leading a discussion, she'd said, "Halloween has us, I think. Let's discuss gender expression in clothing and you can all tell me about your costumes."

Andrew kept waiting for someone to bulldoze over and ask why he was here. No one did. Apart from a few curious glances, he generated no response. Maybe Lana had warned them off, or maybe the entire school had always assumed he was gay.

Two deep purple Converse boots halted in front of him, and he squinted up at Lana.

She gave him a knotted frown. "I need to welcome some newbies. Are you okay here?"

"I'd rather leave," Andrew said, voice low.

"Too bad. You're stuck with me until we have a chance for a good long talk. Sit tight and wait." She patted his head, but it felt like being affectionately thumped instead of consoled. Then she charged off to bark at the timid freshmen clustered by the door.

"Lana refuses to let anyone feel alone."

Andrew pulled his legs to his chest as Chloe sat down beside him. She held two of the frosted cookies decorated with snowflakes so detailed they looked like they'd fallen fresh from the sky. He accepted one because he didn't know how to say *There's a forest growing in my stomach, so I'm never hungry.*

"She has resting murder face," Chloe said, "but she's aggressively friendly. This is my first year at Wickwood and she took one look at me and said, 'We're friends now. Keep up.' She won't let anyone get away with asking if we're sisters, either, which they do all the time since we're both Asian. As if we look anything alike. But I guess this is how she deals with everything? This school is intense and she puts up with a lot. When she's upset, she cares for people in, like, angry revenge at the world for being crap."

"She doesn't have to keep scraping me off the floor." He sounded washed-out. "You're all busy and she doesn't owe me anything . . ."

Chloe gave a sad smile. "She looks out for you because, well . . . you're Dove's brother."

He thought *and clearly falling apart* might be the unsaid conclusion. "You don't have to sit with me if you don't want . . ."

He trailed off, finishing sentences having become an exhausting task.

"Um, please pretend you need me." Chloe gave him a sheepish look. "I'm so, *so* shy, and if I sit in the circle, they'll try to include me. They're all nice, but I prefer to listen."

"I get it." He risked a sideways glance at her. "But shy people don't make good friends. Neither of them can keep the conversation going."

"Silence is okay with me," Chloe said.

She ate her cookie and the quiet between them was companionable as they watched everyone descend into a passionate discussion about gender and clothing. Not everyone dressed up for Halloween, but most of the drama kids did. Lana had corralled the newcomers into the circle and made sure they had a place to sit. She already had her phone out to exchange numbers with them. When she glared over at Andrew and Chloe, he realized it wasn't a reproach at them for being antisocial. She was just checking they were all right.

Crumbs from the uneaten cookie stuck to his cuff. He sighed and then noticed Chloe twisting her rubber bracelets. She wore six on each arm, the colors candy bright against her light brown skin.

She noticed him watching. "My therapist suggested wearing something I can fiddle with. I have, um . . . social anxiety? Probably obvious, I guess, but this helps."

Andrew slowly flexed his bruised fist, the small cuts on his knuckles left by Thomas's teeth. "When I get anxious, I hurt myself. Or other people." He had no idea why he said it. He was never this honest.

"Do you want to talk about it?" she asked gently.

"Have you ever wanted to be something else so . . . so someone would still want you?"

Chloe considered this, and he liked how she didn't rush her answers. "Sometimes? Like I'm anxious and queer and Vietnamese, and I just think . . . wow, no one could be bothered with me if I'm too *much*. But it isn't true. You just have to find the people who love you for you. I'm lucky to have those."

"It's shitty that it has to be *luck* to be loved as you are," Andrew said.

Chloe looked serious. "Agreed."

"Sorry, I'm . . . sorry." Andrew squeezed his eyes shut. "I know how whiny I sound compared to what you deal with."

She gave him a small smile. "Did Thomas do something to you?"

He loves me and I put a knife through his ribs. Andrew fumbled for words through the haze of anguish still smoldering in his mouth, but Lana stomped toward them and dropped cross-legged on the floor. She demolished the last of a cookie and then eyed Andrew's.

"Are you going to eat that? I'm starved. Rehearsals flattened me. Also, Chloe, are you dressing up tomorrow?"

"No." Chloe looked mortified. "They said *optional.* I'll just wear a nice dress."

"I'm going as a witch. I bought a hat." Lana sneaked a hand toward Andrew's cookie, but he passed it over to Chloe.

Chloe bit into it, smiling demurely at Lana.

Lana narrowed her eyes. "Leaving you two to bond was a mistake."

Chloe beamed.

Andrew hugged his legs tighter to his chest. "Aren't you a junior, Chloe? How did you and Lana get close?"

"I tell you," she said, "Lana hunts for lonely people. *Hunts.* But we're also roommates, so that helped."

Something heavy thumped in Andrew's stomach. He shot a glance at Lana, but she busied herself retying her shoelaces. He couldn't jump to conclusions. Tons of the dorm rooms slept three. Lana said she had the sketchbook Thomas had given to Dove, so clearly they were still in the same room, but why did he never see her around Chloe?

Dove had isolated herself from everyone.

But *why*?

He thought of Lana and Thomas in that dim hallway, how she accused Thomas of hurting Dove. She would know, wouldn't she? But Thomas wouldn't *hurt* . . .

"After we wrap up here, let's go for dinner," Lana said. "It's meat loaf night, isn't it? Freaking fantastic. They better serve Halloween cake tomorrow. Remember that time Dove had lemon cake in a Tupperware box and was eating it under her desk all through class? She never even got caught."

Andrew huffed a laugh. "Thomas caught her. He followed her around all day begging for some."

"Typical needy boy." Lana rolled her eyes, but she didn't sound as barbed as usual.

Andrew couldn't stop himself. "Why do you hate him so much?"

Lana abruptly went still. She shot a glance at the teens hanging out around the room, surrounded by queer flags draped over desks and unequivocal acceptance as they chattered. It was a happy moment, and he'd dragged war into it. He should never speak.

Lana pushed to her feet. "If they hadn't had that fight, maybe this year would've been amazing. We could've all been friends."

Andrew could see it, unwrap it like a story: all of them together, an unwieldy group with sharp elbows and sharper tongues, but with enough laughter and teasing to smooth it over. Dove would soften Lana and Thomas. Andrew and Chloe would share wry smiles and retreat to watch the more energetic explosions from the others. Thomas would always reach a hand back for Andrew. Dove would quietly stick them all together.

He missed it in a deep, aching way, even though it had never happened and it never would.

"I get that you forgave him." Lana looked away. "But he was the reason you put your hand through that mirror."

Andrew said nothing; it was easier that way. But a yawning emptiness opened in his mind, an endless black nothing where a memory should be.

He had no idea what she was talking about.

TWENTY-SIX

The Wickwood manor's foyer had been decorated with pumpkins covered in spiderwebs and unsettling skeletons with button eyes holding trick-or-treat buckets. Their grins followed Andrew as he trailed behind the girls toward the dining hall. This year's theme was simple: Fall. Walking on a carpet scattered with velvety golden autumn leaves creeped Andrew out. It felt like the forest had reached twiggy fingers into the school again. He cupped his palm over his throbbing ear. They were plastic decorations, it was fine, none of this was real.

Before the bell had rung for dinner, Lana had fetched the sketchbook from her dorm and given it to Andrew without question. He'd torn it up, every last ink-smeared page, until not a single monster was left whole. This had to be the last of Thomas's drawings, it *had* to be.

Ahead of him, Lana was arguing that pumpkin cake was better than pumpkin pie, and Chloe wasn't having it. Neither noticed Andrew getting farther behind. He needed to vanish before he had to make an excuse why he didn't want to eat.

But he couldn't go back to his dorm. Thomas might be there.

Andrew needed to find words before he saw Thomas again. He needed to pull himself back together and figure out how to explain himself in a way that made sense without his ribs snapping one by one. He was suffocating in a vortex of his own darkness. He needed Thomas to pin him to the floor, fingers tight around his wrists, hips against hips, their mouths inches apart, so Thomas could breathe two words into Andrew's lungs—

Calm down.

Andrew couldn't calm down.

He walked into the dining hall and lined up for food he couldn't eat. The servers piled his plate as if he were an average teenage boy with an appetite, not this gaunt ghost of a creature. Lana strode off to snag them seats, leaving Chloe to expertly manage both of their plates—another sign these two were close friends in a way that didn't need Dove. Someone moved in behind him and a few people complained about cutting the line.

Andrew didn't need to turn. He could feel who it was by the shape of his breath, how he leaned forward in a way that spoke of deep familiarity, as if any part of Andrew he touched would instantly respond to him.

Andrew's heartbeat picked up, but he focused on accepting his overfilled plate of meat loaf and mashed potatoes. He swept a glance across the long tables crowded with green Wickwood uniforms until he saw Lana wave.

"I should never have called you a coward." Thomas's voice sounded wrecked. "Talk to me. Leave the plate and come outside."

Make him beg. The thought came slick with tar, insidious and bitter, and Andrew hated the way it fed the monster gnawing behind his rib bones. He didn't want to be this.

But his jaw felt wired shut, and he gave Thomas nothing, not even a glance, as he strode toward the tables.

Thomas swore and ran after him.

Lana had saved a spot at the end, and Andrew slid onto the bench across from her and Chloe. The noise was worse than usual, because everyone had been into the Halloween candy already and their sugar highs tipped them to Noise Level: Extreme. Seniors hyped each other up, playing viral videos on their phones and singing along. Bryce Kane seemed to be at the head of it, a lord overseeing his court. No teachers had called for quiet yet. Or maybe they'd given up.

Too much noise, too many bodies. Even the smell of the soggy meat loaf congealing in gravy turned his stomach. He wanted to run, but Thomas could corner him in a quiet hall and Andrew wasn't ready for that. He forced himself to fork up mashed potatoes.

Thomas straddled the bench beside him, no uniform jacket, no plate, no interest in anything but Andrew. His face looked shattered.

"I'm sorry," Thomas said, low. "I lost my temper and it was shitty to call you a coward when you were just . . . telling me who you are."

The chaos around them did an effective job of hiding their conversation, but Lana glared as she leaned forward in an unsubtle attempt at eavesdropping. She gripped her knife and fork in a threatening way, but Andrew gave her the tiniest shake of his head.

If he wanted Thomas gone, he could deal with it himself. He knew how to ruin Thomas the same way Thomas knew how to ruin him.

They could be so beautiful to each other. They could be so cruel.

Andrew stabbed at his peas. "It doesn't matter."

"It does." Thomas's eyes looked bright as daggers. "Do you want to hit me again? You can. I'll ask for it, I'll—"

Andrew slammed his fork down and turned on him. "Shut up. Can you even hear yourself? You screw up and you want to be punished. You want to be absolved in violence. Do you realize how incredibly fucked up that is?"

Thomas's face looked stripped, and it hurt to stare at him. Andrew turned away, his jaw so tight his teeth felt about to crack.

"I want . . . I *need* you." Thomas's voice came so thin it was nearly lost under a wave of laughter from the other end of the table. "We can just be what we were. I swear I won't ask for anything else. It's just—I make monsters. I *am* a monster. I lost my mind for a second and freaked out that you could never love someone this wicked."

Andrew's mouth tasted of moss and metal, of trees and blood-soaked bark. He had this boy in pieces, had him carved down to a desperate, trembling nub. He'd sliced into Thomas's heart with brutal precision and found no trace of Dove, so shouldn't it feel like he'd won? Thomas couldn't exist without him and he wouldn't ask for things Andrew couldn't give.

But he felt frozen, too sick to move. The food on his plate oozed brown liquid and . . . blood. It looked undercooked and roiling on his plate, a heartbeat still throbbing.

Another burst of laughter boomed across the hall, and Bryce Kane climbed onto the bench to take a bow. A teacher finally went over and demanded they settle down.

Lana had both elbows on the table, and she looked pissed that Thomas had run out of words before she'd heard everything. She pointed her fork at him. “Give Andrew space. Pretty sure you’ve caused enough damage for one day.”

Thomas whirled on her, his broken softness for Andrew suddenly packed up. Now he was all feral wolf with a mouthful of broken glass. “Shut the hell up, Lana. Do you ever ask for two sides of a story? Or is the whole point to hate me as much as you can?”

Sparks snapped in Lana’s eyes. “Excuse me for trying to step in before you hurt another Perrault.”

Thomas shoved to his feet and slammed both fists so hard on the table that their plates jumped. “I did not HURT DOVE.”

Heads had swiveled their way. Interest piqued. Dinner made more interesting by a fresh, juicy drama. It would bring a teacher and detention slips soon, but Thomas and Lana didn’t seem to care.

“Um, should you lower your voices?” Chloe said meekly.

“You left her.” Lana rose from her seat, too, and Chloe shrank. “It’s your fault—”

“I did nothing to her!” Thomas was halfway to yelling. “You have no idea what happened.”

“You’re such a manipulative liar,” Lana hissed. “And a bully. And a—”

“Stop,” Andrew said, but he was too quiet to be heard.

“—a *monster*.” Lana spat the word.

“Yeah, maybe I am.” Thomas’s voice went deathly cold. “Maybe I’m to blame for everything that’s gone wrong at this school. Will that satisfy you?”

Lana laughed, but it was a harsh sound. She looked about to cry. “Oh, go to hell, Thomas Rye. Murderer.”

He shoved away from the table and Andrew lunged for him. He caught Thomas's wrist and twisted it hard enough for him to cry out. A teacher stormed toward them, but the entire world had been eclipsed except for Thomas.

Thomas.

Thomas.

In pain, hurt, falling apart.

Lana's level of vitriol didn't even make sense. Maybe Thomas broke Dove's heart, but Dove didn't have to ice them all out over it. They could make up. Andrew could still make her listen.

"Don't talk to him like that," he said to Lana. "I can fix it with Dove."

She stared at him.

Whatever. He knew Dove best, not her.

Right now all he could do was tug Thomas into him so their bodies collided and their anger pooled in each other's heaving lungs.

Andrew took Thomas's face and turned it toward him, his heart ripping in half when he met Thomas's eyes. Green and glossy, a forest in a storm. He was furiously trying to hide how close he was to tears.

Andrew tried to say, *It's okay.*

But someone screamed.

They whirled around at the same time, the very moment a monster pulled out of the wallpaper.

A boy crept softly through the forest, looking for a white stag that legend said could grant three wishes. From his back grew gossamer moth wings that dragged on the ground and tore at a touch, and words had been cut into his skin that wept indigo blood. A wish would cure him of these peculiar miseries.

But he grew tired as he searched, and his feet bled and his tears left tracks of salt down his weary cheeks. He did not find the stag.

He did find a fairy prince, though, with a sharp smile and roses blooming from his wrists.

"You should come with me," the boy said. "A wish from the white stag will fix me and it could fix you, too."

The fairy prince looked at him quizzically. He bit a rosebud off his wrist and twirled it before handing it to the boy with a shy smile.

"Why?" he said. "You're beautiful just as you are."

TWENTY-SEVEN

They had fallen into a nightmare, eyes open and heartbeats stopped because this couldn't be happening. Not in front of everyone. But their monsters had no rules anymore; they didn't stay in the forest, they didn't linger in the dark, they didn't hunt only Thomas.

It didn't make sense. Andrew had destroyed the rest of Thomas's art—hadn't he?

Now this monster clawed from the walls with a sultry grin as if it knew what the Antler King had tried and now promised, *I can do better.*

Screams rippled down the hall, teens rising from their seats and conversations splintering. No one understood what they saw. Reality smudged and logic crumbled.

Color drained from Thomas's face, and he shoved Andrew behind him as he reached for the hatchet he didn't have. But a strange, numb calm flooded Andrew's chest. He should be freaking out, but he barely felt there at all.

"It's a dream ravager." He sounded far away.

"I didn't draw that," Thomas said, hoarse.

But it had to exist in some sketchbook they hadn't destroyed yet. This was why they couldn't win—because Thomas had drawn fierce and free for years, his drawings packed with his pain and anger and cathartic vengeance. It was impossible to collect and destroy them all.

There would also be no end to the monsters until they met the forest's demands. And Andrew hadn't told Thomas about that yet.

—cut out a heart

"You must have," Andrew said. "You draw all the time—"

"Not anymore," Thomas snapped.

The monster began to move. It didn't walk so much as flowed, its body a swirl of misting shadows that re-formed into triangular elbows and long, twiggy fingers and a sharp jaw that cracked to show an endless throat. Everything about it stretched as it moved, and its skin looked like bark under its shadows. Only its eyes glowed red.

Before the dining hall had a chance to dissolve into pandemonium, the monster howled and plunged its shadows across the room.

It was like throwing a blanket of black ink over the chaos. Where the darkness touched, everything went still. Frantic cries and attempts to run ended as everyone slumped into the tables. Bodies folded like their strings had been cut. Heads slammed into their plates, faces went slack.

A horrible, suffocating quiet seeped across the room.

Thomas sagged and Andrew barely had time to loop arms around his chest and hold him up before the darkness slid over them. The shadows felt alive, pressing against them, the slippery taste of earthy, rancid leaves and spilled ink suffocating them all.

The lights went out.

No sound touched the dining hall except for the click of the monster's fingernails as it slithered onto the table. It hovered over an unconscious student whose hair was soaked in gravy, their breathing shallow and slow. Then the monster's fingers began to grow. They stretched like sticks, knotted and nobbled, and grew over the student's face before sliding into their mouth and ears and nose.

The ravager was after their dreams.

All around Andrew, ribbons of darkness slipped into the students' slack jaws and curled down their noses.

Pain spiked through Andrew's ear, and he clapped a hand over it. As if he needed reminding what happened when the monsters got inside of you.

None of this made sense. The monsters came for him because he was close to Thomas—but the rest of the school? No, this was wrong.

Either the monsters' strength had doubled thanks to Halloween, or Andrew had never understood how they worked this whole time.

Maybe he didn't understand anything.

It's not real—

He had to think.

He dropped to his knees and dragged Thomas under the table, limbs tangling as Andrew shook Thomas to wake him up. Thomas was struggling to keep his eyes open, but his mouth had gone soft with sleep.

"Fight this. This is *your monster*." Andrew cupped Thomas's face. "Pen? We need a p-pen."

Thomas fumbled in his pockets.

Andrew reached around him to pull Lana and Chloe under the table, too, trying not to bang their heads as they slumped lifelessly into the cramped space. It bought them all time, but not much.

He had to tell a story.

"I don't remember drawing this . . ." Thomas trailed off, his cheek resting against Andrew's shoulder. He had his arms wrapped around his stomach, over the hole the monsters had already left in him.

"Stay awake. It won't touch you again." Andrew snatched the pen from Thomas, but his fingers shook so hard he struggled to press it to the underside of the table. Without a birch to write on, this seemed like the best option.

Think of a story. *Now.*

Before the ravager drank everyone's dreams and their lives along with it.

"Thomas, I c-can't think. I—"

But Thomas's eyes had closed. He looked so vulnerable, mouth open and body limp, all the fury of their fight drained until he was no more than a wisp. Andrew's eyes felt thick and cottony, his eyelashes dipped in molasses, but he bit down on his bottom lip until blood slicked his teeth.

Stay awake.

Thomas had fought monsters alone for countless nights. Now it was Andrew's turn to save them all.

He laid Thomas's head in his lap and dug fingers into his soft curls. *Hold on. Ground yourself.*

He began to write.

Once upon a time a boy collected nightmares and put them in terra-cotta jars. He traveled across many kingdoms to add to his collection, and if anyone refused to give over their foul dreams, he'd wait till they slept before peeling out their darkness with his long, needle fingers.

Above Andrew, the table shook under the weight of the monster. Sweat beaded around his mouth and he licked it so it stung against his bitten lip.

Nightmares swirled like black galaxies within his terra-cotta jars, beautiful and wicked and mesmerizing, and it did not take long before he opened the lids and took a sip. Then another, then another. Soon he could eat nothing but this. All other food poisoned him and he forgot he had been a boy. He ravaged a thousand dreams a night and still he starved.

Until one night he could no longer stand the hunger. He put mortal food to his lips. He ate, and for that he died.

Ink bled across Andrew's fingers and he wrote until he felt dizzy. Tendrils of shadows coiled under the table, sliding over Lana's face and between Chloe's lips.

This was the part where Thomas would use Andrew's stories to win the battle. Andrew would write how it would go—swing an ax, spill some blood, wrap a noose of vines about a monster's neck, scream enchanted words—and Thomas would make the story come true.

But Thomas was a dead weight, sprawled in Andrew's lap. Panic rose in his throat, and it took all his strength to hold it in, to believe he could do this by himself. He could be the prince, just this once.

Then a crooked hand shot under the table and grabbed him by the hair.

A cry ripped from his throat as the monster dragged him out. He thrashed like a caught fish, but the creature drew him into the air and then slammed him onto the tabletop. Plates shattered. Cutlery skidded away as glasses tipped over and drinks sloshed across the wood.

"WAIT—" It tumbled out like a gasp, but monsters didn't wait.

And no one was coming to save him.

The monster hauled Andrew down the table by his hair. Broken crockery sliced at his back and food smeared across his pants. He held on to the monster's wrists, trying to take some of the tension off his hair, but the pain splintered his vision.

The monster stopped in the center of the long table, surrounded by an audience of unconscious bodies with ribbons of darkness streaming from their heads. They looked like dolls, stitched with black thread, sightless and horrible. Andrew choked on a whimper. He tried to worm free, but the monster's twig fingers went tight. Then it slammed Andrew's head down on the mahogany table.

Once—*stars, dazzling and bitter—*

Twice—*ears ringing, piercing whine—*

Three times—*blood in his mouth, the world turned doughy and unsteady, the back of his head wet, wet, wet—*

He closed his eyes while the world spun, and when he pried them open again, the monster leered over him. Its jaw opened and long, needle teeth extended.

Andrew fumbled a hand around the table, dizzy and gasping.

His fingers closed on silverware. *Please be a knife, please be a—*

He screamed and arched his body upward in a frenetic surge of energy, stabbing the monster in the face.

Butter and bread crumbs covered the knife as it punctured the monster's cheek. Its skin tore like papery autumn leaves, and clumps of moss tumbled out. The monster screamed and twisted its head in agony.

Andrew wrenched free of its grip with a terrified cry. He didn't let go of the knife. He stabbed the monster again, and then again, and the creature bent in half and its bony fingers clawed its face.

But its tongue had touched mortal food. Poison.

This was Andrew's fairy tale, his tragedy, his beautiful suffering coming true. He'd won. He'd bested it alone.

As the monster disintegrated to rotten leaves, Andrew pushed to his feet and stood, bruised and fierce, atop the table. His chest moved fast and ragged, and he didn't know if he wanted to laugh or cry or keep screaming. He stayed silent as the shadows sank back into the walls and faded into the carpet.

Lights flickered back on over the trashed dining hall. There were tangled bodies and broken plates and splattered food everywhere as if a war had taken place while they all slept.

Someone groaned and raised their head.

They'd all be awake in a second, but Andrew still stood there with the bloody butter knife. He licked his lips, tasted blood and decay and the forest. He should . . . he needed to . . . He didn't know. He felt alive, powerful, *effervescent.*

He started to shake.

He was still shaking when arms wrapped around his waist and half lifted him off the table while everyone woke and confused cries filled the hall. The knife slipped from Andrew's fingers, but he didn't care. He touched his mouth as he was dragged out of the dining hall.

He was smiling. He couldn't stop.

Outside the hall, Thomas dumped Andrew against the wall and knelt beside him, cradling his face and brushing a thumb over his busted lip.

"Your head's bleeding, shit, *shit.* Stop smiling. You're freaking me out." Thomas's voice cracked. "Damn it, Andrew, *stop smiling*. What did you do?"

"I killed it myself." Andrew dug fingers into Thomas's shirt. "I'm s-s-strong enough now. I'm so-so-so much—so much more than I used to be."

Thomas swallowed. He still looked too pale and his voice sounded more wrecked with each word. "I woke up and saw your story. You didn't fall asleep, too?"

"I'm *strong enough*." Andrew was laughing, or maybe crying. Their fight seemed so meaningless now. "I want you. Please, I-I-I want you more than anything. Don't let me go."

Thomas pressed his mouth to the top of Andrew's head, and for a long, long moment he said nothing. He should have been fierce with pride or relief that Andrew could take care of himself. But Thomas's eyes looked haunted.

Then he crushed Andrew to his chest. "I want you always."

They stayed there, tangled in each other, heartbeats racing.

Nothing mattered but this.

TWENTY-EIGHT

The world had thinned.

Andrew felt it as he sat in class, as if he could press fingertips against the air and the gossamer threads separating this world from the next would part. A small push, and anyone could fall through.

Or maybe they'd already fallen.

His mouth felt full of graveyard dirt, his head bent over his notebook as he wrote feverishly. He needed to change their story. He needed to think up an ending cruel enough to appease the monsters, but soft enough so when this was all over he could fit himself against Thomas's side and be safe.

cut out a heart—
and bury it in the woods.
but you already
knew that, prince.

There had to be another way.

Class had been going on for fifteen minutes and their history teacher still hadn't arrived, but no one complained. They clustered in groups with their phones and talked about the principal's lecture during assembly hall that morning. *Food poisoning after a senior prank gone too far.* Wickwood was bent on convincing themselves nothing was wrong with this school, that no goddamn monster had ripped out of the wallpaper.

It seemed impossible they would stick to this story, but then maybe everyone had only been blacked out for a few minutes. It had felt like hours. Andrew alone had been suspended in time, choked on shadows and vines and forest decay, and if he told the truth, he'd sound like he'd lost his mind.

"Happy Samhain," Thomas muttered. "Pretty sure that means all the ghosts and demons and monsters will be at their strongest tonight. And probably their most hungry. We're so screwed."

Andrew shook out a hand spasm and kept writing. "The Halloween dance is still on."

"Of course it is. Can't have kids whining to their loaded parents that the school is creepy and, worse, boring." Thomas's fingers subconsciously pressed against his stomach.

Andrew should have asked about the wound, checked if the hole had grown or changed. His headaches had grown almost unbearable, and part of him knew that was because the forest had gone deeper inside him, nested down and rooted into his darkest places. If he put fingers in his mouth, he could feel it—moss growing at the back of his throat.

The kids in the desks in front of them were whispering about an after-party and who had smuggled alcohol. Listening gave Andrew a disjointed, untethered feeling, as if it was impossible everyone else planned to have fun tonight while he and Thomas would be fighting for their lives.

He flipped back a few pages to the story he'd written last night. A melancholy thing; he wasn't going to let Thomas see it. A poet with his chest held together by rose vines climbed a tower to kiss his true love, but as their lips touched, a monster with a charming smile snaked into the room. It tore into them and stole a piece of their lungs, a liver, a cracked rib to gnaw on. The end only came when the poet sent his rose vines down the monster's throat to strangle him. But when the poet tried to kiss his true love once more, he couldn't. Thorns grew in both their mouths. All they could do was bleed.

He should have ripped it up. All his focus had to channel into figuring out the perfect story for tonight.

Cheek still on his desk, Thomas watched Andrew with a kind of hollow, aching want. "Are we . . ."

"We're fine." Andrew bent over his notebook.

They didn't need to talk about it, not when he should have apologized as much as Thomas had for all the foul things that had been said yesterday. There would be time enough to figure it out later. All that mattered was the way Thomas had held him last night, reverent and desperate and terrified all at once, and how he'd pressed his mouth to Andrew's head. It felt right. It felt perfect.

I want you always.

The history teacher finally hurried into the classroom, frazzled and stressed, and she gave them a waspish lecture about wasting time instead of doing independent study while they waited. She broke off as someone rapped on the doorframe.

"Open your books," she snapped, and went to answer.

"What are you writing?" Thomas whispered.

But Andrew didn't have time to answer, because the classroom door opened again, and this time Principal Adelaide Grant appeared, her white hair in a merciless, tight bun and her pantsuit impeccable. She cleared her throat, but she didn't need to bother. The entire class had already ground to a halt to stare at her.

"Andrew Perrault. I need you to come with me, please."

The wave of icy panic that swept through Andrew left him nauseous, too frozen to move, to understand why she would pull him of all people. All he could think was, *She knows.*

That he sacrificed Clemens.

That he killed the dream ravager.

That he hit a boy instead of confessed he loved him.

That if anyone peeled apart his ribs, they'd see the darkness knit into his flesh.

"Leave your things." The principal looked impatient at his failure to comply.

He stacked his books, numb and clumsy, but grabbed his notebook at the last second because he always felt better with it in hand. One glance at Thomas, whose face had gone white under his freckles, made Andrew's stomach flip over. Thomas started to rise, but the principal gave a dismissive wave of her hand as if he were but a moth drawn to the flame she was about to extinguish.

Dead silence followed Andrew out of the classroom and into the corridor. He should ask what was going on, protest this—or should he stay silent? His limp, traitorous tongue made the decision for him by turning to wood in his mouth, and he said nothing as he followed the principal up to the faculty floor. He had to pull it together because he looked guilty: his darting eyes, his trembling fingers, the way he could barely get a word past the mud in his throat. Walking down the newly refurbished hall where Clemens had been murdered made his head spin. The worst part was how he was right next to the most powerful woman in this school and he couldn't even tell her what was really going on.

There are monsters in the woods. You need to get everyone out—

The principal opened the door to her office and ushered Andrew inside. It looked more intimidating than usual, the ceiling-high mahogany shelves and austere dark wood of her desk seeming to smother any light that crept in past the thick, burgundy drapes. A commanding heaviness filled the room like a hand pressed against the back of his neck, and everything smelled of stale, old books and suffocation. Or maybe he'd just forgotten how to breathe.

Two leather armchairs sat before her desk, and Dr. Reul rose from one, buttoning his tweed jacket. The old professor was known for his grandfatherly smiles and kind words, and he always smelled like something between mothballs and Earl Grey tea. Having him here meant he was playing good cop to the principal's bad cop. What was going *on*? Shouldn't Dr. Reul be teaching Classic Literature right now? Andrew had only enough time to register the pensive expressions the adults wore before he noticed Bryce Kane sitting in the other armchair.

He looked calm and tidy, uniform blazer spotless and golden hair combed back, and his smile was bloated with self-satisfaction.

"Have a seat, Andrew," Dr. Reul said.

He felt too light, his skin so thin that if they pulled back the throat of his shirt, they'd see his heart pulsing, raw and bloody, through his glass chest. He slid onto the vacated armchair and looked anywhere except at Bryce, who reclined in his seat as if he'd been invited to a meeting where he'd be announced king of the world.

The principal sat behind her desk and laced her fingers on the wood, casting a meaningful look at Dr. Reul before she cleared her throat. "There are two matters I need to discuss with you, Andrew, but first I would like to impress upon everyone in this room the need to conduct yourselves with honesty, courtesy, and behavior befitting ambassadors of the Wickwood name. Now, Bryce has brought me some troublesome news, Andrew. Have you been climbing the fence and venturing into the forest?"

Somehow it hadn't occurred to Andrew to worry this could happen. He'd freaked out very efficiently about everything else, but being caught in the forest? There was no way any students were up before dawn to spy on their return.

And everyone should be grateful.

They were being saved from having their throats torn open by monsters.

They should be *grateful*.

Everyone stared at him and he didn't know what to say. His mouth had gone bone-dry and when he tried to speak, the kind of voice-cracking wheeze of a prepubescent teen squeaked out instead. He had to try again, his hands sweaty around his notebook.

"No."

His word against Bryce's. It already felt like he'd lost.

"Obviously, I don't want to be a snitch," Bryce said, voice earnest and warm. "But I'm kind of worried about Andy. He looks so unwell, and after everything that happened last year—"

"What, like you bullying me?" Andrew snapped, and then closed his mouth, surprised he'd even had the guts to say that. He felt too hot, his whole body starting to shake, and he wanted nothing more than for Thomas to explode through the door and take this battle for him.

Bryce faked the most convincing *who, me?* look ever to be seen outside of theatre.

"That is the second matter we need to discuss." The principal sounded clipped, her gaze slicing the tense weight in the room. "It has been brought to our attention that Bryce has made some concerning comments about Andrew, and this is something we need to address since, as you both know, we do not condone any sort of harassment at this school."

So Lana had reported him, just like she'd threatened. Relief and panic swept across Andrew's chest.

Anger flashed across Bryce's face, but his brow smoothed and he was all benevolent charm again. "I can explain that. It was just a joke out of context. I made a comment about Andy going out with Thomas and they both got super defensive. Like"—he raised his hands in confused innocence—"I didn't know it was a sensitive topic. Good for them, honestly. I'm not homophobic or anything."

"No one is throwing around accusations like that," Dr. Reul added in hastily.

Andrew could not believe this. "That's not what happened." But the words came out too small.

"We welcome and cherish a diverse body of students here," the principal said. "I'm sure some unfortunate phrasing is at fault here and the mistake won't be repeated. Will it, Mr. Kane?"

"Absolutely not," Bryce said. "I feel terrible that I came across wrong. I've been in class with Andy since we were *twelve*. I'm fond of him. I know he's having a tough year."

Andrew could almost see himself peeling out of his skin, walking over to Bryce, and hitting him in the mouth. It would be like the night of the dream ravager, Andrew standing atop the table with his heart racing with horrible, wordless elation, butter knife in hand, his head full of screams.

Instead, he sat soundless, his throttling grip on his notebook leaving dents in the cover. He never had words when he needed them. He blinked hard and quick.

The principal looked relieved this was an incident to be tidied briskly and not something that required reports and phone calls to parents. "Well, that's settled, then. How about you two shake hands and then, Bryce, you can get back to class."

Bryce bounced from his chair and stuck out a hand toward Andrew, his smile all teeth. "Maybe you just didn't know the forest was out-of-bounds now. Hope you don't get in too much trouble, Andy."

Andrew stared at the proffered hand long enough for the room to grow tense. Dr. Reul shifted with a light cough and the principal looked weary as she rubbed a thumb against her temple. She seemed about to command Andrew to accept the handshake, to throw this little *mess* under a bridge where they wouldn't speak of it again. It was a reminder of who this school really protected, so he quickly grabbed Bryce's hand. A firm shake. Release. Bryce did not stop grinning as he sauntered out the door.

After it clicked shut, Dr. Reul moved to take Bryce's vacated chair, looking even more somber than he had before. His gray eyebrows drew together in concern.

"Before you deny anything again," he said, "we have already had several reports from the groundskeeper about finding . . . disturbances in the woods."

Monsters, monsters, *monsters*.

"May I have this?" Dr. Reul slid the notebook from Andrew's hands before he could think to argue.

Loss hit him like a fist to the stomach and he stopped breathing as he stared at his empty hands. No one read his stories, no one touched them. He should have held on—why hadn't he *held on*?

Dr. Reul paged through and then shared a meaningful look with the principal.

"The groundskeeper found writing on the trees," the principal said. "Strange little stories. Then after Bryce Kane shared what he had seen with us, Dr. Reul seemed to recall you often wrote tales in a little notebook."

It was a leap. They couldn't pin this on him. But all Andrew could think of was the way they could confiscate his notebook, match the handwriting, pin him to the wall with their disapproving, disgusted looks. This belligerent, rule-breaking student. Dr. Reul was still paging through the notebook, and Andrew's brain felt like a fogged mirror, his stomach so seasick he thought he'd empty himself all over the floor. He knew how those stories looked.

Violent. Macabre. Wicked. Twisted.

"I'd like to know why." Oddly, the principal had lost her sharpness and she swept an almost pitying look over Andrew.

"I would think you'd have little interest in the forest now. You've always been such a nice, mindful student. I must admit, I'm disappointed, Andrew."

"I'm . . ." But he couldn't find any words.

The only thing he could cling to was the fact that they'd only brought in him. Not Thomas. Bryce must have seen both of them walk out of the woods, so the fact that he'd only ratted on Andrew meant he had some sort of warped plan at play.

"We're sympathetic to what you're going through." Dr. Reul took off his glasses to rub at a lens. "But we're concerned you're not thriving here, Andrew. You've not completed a single assignment from my class this year and, unfortunately, the other professors have concurred the same. Perhaps a break is needed. For your mental health."

He said it in such a comforting way that for a moment Andrew didn't register what it meant. A break.

They were kicking him out.

"We care about your well-being," the principal said. "I have been in contact with your father and we all think it's wise if he picks you up this weekend. We can discuss where to go from there."

Andrew cupped a hand over his ear. It *hurt*. Everything pounded too loud, too fast.

He needed

Thomas.

"Wait," he said. "I'm f-fine. I don't need to leave." *Thomas can't be left to the monsters alone, he won't survive.*

No one would ever believe that they were protecting the school from the horrors crawling the forests at night. They were screaming for help, and no one could hear.

The principal gave him a long, careful look. "I don't think it's productive to bring disciplinary action against you for exiting the school boundaries, Andrew, so understand that this is a lenient outcome for us all. I understand you're not . . . well."

They saw him as a fragile thing, made of fractured glass, full of hairline cracks, and this was the gentlest way they could say: expelled.

Dr. Reul handed him back his notebook and he took it too fast, his head low so they didn't see the moment when his eyes shone bright as the surface of a river. He had to get out of there before he vomited leaves into his lap.

Outside the office, it was all he could do to keep moving, to stay upright when what he most wanted was to curl into a ball. No point going back to class. One look and Thomas would know. He'd explode. He'd go after Bryce—

Andrew pressed his face into the crook of his elbow for the barest second, but as he turned the corner, someone ducked out and crashed a shoulder into his chest so hard he tripped. He hit the ground with a breathless gasp, his chin clipping the carpet, teeth sinking into his tongue until copper bloomed against his teeth. All air left his lungs. He was twelve years old again with scraped knees, looking up at Bryce Kane's leering grin as he stood like a lord over his fallen prey.

"Hey there, you little shit," Bryce said, his affable tone not matching the fury in his eyes. "Your friends slandered me, and now they're going to regret it."

Andrew pulled himself shakily to his feet, his notebook clutched to his chest. The hall was empty, lined with closed office doors and not a teacher in sight. Blood ran down his chin and hit the carpet in a vermilion kiss.

"Did they kick you out? Sounded like they were going to. But don't worry, I'm sure Rye will cry for you." Bryce folded his arms, smirking. "It hurts that little murderer more, you know. Losing you. Way more than if it had been him."

Andrew wiped at his chin, his breathing shallow, his eyes unfocused. *Walk away, just walk—*

"Why do you even hate him so much?" he whispered.

"Pfft, I don't. I couldn't care less about him."

Liar, Andrew wanted to say.

"But," Bryce conceded, sounding almost magnanimous, as if he was sharing a coveted secret, "I think it's sick that he's screwing you, but still led Dove on. She could've dated me. I was going to ask her."

Andrew just stared at him. "She would never—" He broke off.

"She would have," Bryce snapped. "He's over there with some gross twin fetish and I would've been perfect for her. Would've looked out for your sorry ass, too. You should choose your friends better, Perrault, then maybe you wouldn't be hanging out with a murderer who's the reason your sister—"

Andrew shoved him.

Bryce's shoulders thumped against the wall and genuine surprise crossed his face, as if he didn't expect Andrew's feather-fine bones had the strength—or the courage. Andrew stood there breathing too fast, blood and forest mud clotted under his tongue, and he let anger pool in all his hollow places. He could feel it against his teeth, his hate for this boy, this moment, this school. He was about to lose everything.

He was losing himself.

"Touch me again," he said, "and I'll kill you."

Bryce glanced down at his blazer, where Andrew's hand had landed for the shove, and he stared at the thin layer of moss clinging to the cloth. He tried to brush it off, his surprise deepening to dismay when it clung on.

"What the . . ." But when he looked up, Andrew was striding away, holding tight to his notebook.

He refused to check his own hand, but he could feel it.

Moss flourished along the underside of his skin.

TWENTY-NINE

The doorknob didn't work, or maybe it was Andrew who was broken. He dropped his dorm key for the third time. Electricity bit at his skin, and he felt hyperaware of everything; his book bag digging into his shoulder, the skin over his ribs stretched so tight it hurt, Thomas hovering at his back. They hadn't had a chance to talk yet after Andrew's trip to the principal's office since Thomas had been in detention for skipping assignments. But what was there to say?

I'm leaving you alone alone alone—

Andrew couldn't tell him.

It was already late, dusk crawling across the sky while the forest stretched shadows right up to the school. Wickwood should have canceled the Halloween dance. Everyone should be behind locked doors tonight. Instead, the dorm thrummed with the chaotic laughter and shouts of boys getting ready for the party, ducking in and out of their rooms in tuxedos or ridiculous costumes.

"Just tell me what she said. Are you in trouble?" Thomas snatched the key from Andrew and opened their door.

Andrew stumbled in, book bag slipping from his shoulder and thumping to the floor. He wanted to dig fingernails into his skin and *peel,* but instead he checked his phone and found three missed calls from his father. He threw it on his cluttered desk.

He couldn't leave Thomas alone with the monsters, with stories he couldn't write, with no way to end this because Andrew had never told him the truth of what monsters demanded. They couldn't be apart; their lungs would be torn out from inside each other and they would suffocate.

Andrew's voice sounded rusted. "Bryce told the principal he saw me in the forest."

"What? He couldn't have. We could get expelled for—"

"I KNOW." Andrew slammed their door and Thomas leaped out of the way before it caught his fingers.

He looked startled, but said nothing as Andrew stripped off his blazer and fell face-first onto his bed. He needed to think, but his head throbbed and black spots kept nipping the edge of his vision.

Slowly, Thomas crept over and perched on the edge of the mattress.

Andrew stuffed a pillow over his face. "We have to tell someone about the monsters."

"If we say monsters are attacking the school, we'll sound insane. No one would believe us, literally no one." He yanked the pillow off Andrew's face. "You look really shaken up."

Andrew rubbed at his eyes, so desperately, achingly tired it was all he could do not to tug Thomas to lie down next to him so they could survive Halloween like this—tangled in each other's arms like two licorice twists.

"I'm just tired," he said.

Thomas leaned in suddenly, an arm planted on either side of Andrew, their faces close enough they could eat each other's words right out of their mouths. He ran a thumb over Andrew's

bottom lip and then traced down to the fluttering pulse in his neck. "Someday do you . . . want to be kissed?"

Something wicked and wanting surged in Andrew's chest, but the guilt followed like a swift uppercut. For the way he'd treated Thomas yesterday. For how he'd won their fight and made sure everything would go his way. It wasn't fair and he didn't know how to fix it. What to give and what to take.

But as he stared up at Thomas's face, all he could think of was kissing every one of those freckles. He nodded, his throat tight.

Thomas's smile was crooked and full of tentative delight. He shoved off the bed and Andrew felt robbed of his touch.

"Let's get dressed. I've still got my dad's suspenders around here somewhere. My tux hasn't fit for like two years now."

Andrew felt too washed-out to get up. He needed to slow down and focus on what he had to do before his dad arrived. Destroy the last of Thomas's drawings, that had to be the main priority. If the monsters wouldn't stop, that meant there had to be some art still left.

After that, he needed to—

Kiss Thomas. Somehow, somewhere.

Find Dove and tell her everything. Absolutely everything. If she wanted to stay at Wickwood, she could. He wouldn't blame her for putting her senior year over him.

Then Andrew had to stop the monsters, whatever it took. He would not leave Thomas alone with them.

Thomas left for the showers and Andrew took his sweet time hauling himself upright and rummaging through his wardrobe for his tux. He'd rather skip the dance, but they needed to look normal—not guilty, not unhinged, not like boys about to lose everything. The pounding of feet up and down the hall and the collision of voices said that everyone else was overexcited for tonight. It took their minds off exams and all the creepy things that had been spilling from the school.

But nothing guaranteed the monsters would stay away from the auditorium. Andrew and Thomas would need to be in the forest early to fight them back and spill enough blood to satisfy the monsters' appetites. It didn't matter whose blood, theirs or the monsters'.

Someone just had to suffer.

Andrew unbuttoned his shirt. Then he stopped.

His ribs had hurt so long he'd grown used to the way they pressed sharp against his skin. How he could fit his finger between the grooves. How he was starving and yet felt too full to fit anything in his mouth.

But this was new.

His stomach looked distended, skin stretched like rice paper. He spread a hand over his belly, fingers trembling, and he pushed.

Tentative, careful.

"What the—" he whispered.

His skin didn't give. It was like pressing fingers to a tree trunk, smooth and unforgiving. Hard lines coiled under the skin and crisscrossed over his stomach, and his shaking fingers followed one line and then another, tracing all the way to his hip.

Vines. Leaves. Roots.

He could see their unmistakable outlines.

This couldn't be—

No.

Instead of feeling the soft, forgiving skin of his stomach, he felt vines growing through his intestines. They shifted under his touch, still growing as they twisted and tightened around another organ.

Horrible, hysterical panic rose up his throat, and he was going to be sick. He had to get it out. He had to slice his stomach open and get it out, get it out—GET IT OUT GET IT—

Andrew sank to the floor, knees to his chest, hyperventilating as the room spun. He couldn't show Thomas. Not yet. They had too much to finish tonight.

He couldn't do this. He gripped his wardrobe door and concentrated on breathing, but he could feel the briars in his lungs, taste the blood in the back of his throat where thorns had pricked his tongue.

The forest had been growing inside him for a long time, he'd just refused to think about it.

The door swung open and Thomas ambled in with wet hair and a towel slung over his shoulders. He looked roguish in suspenders and white shirt with collar popped, his dress trousers cuffed to hide the fact they were too short.

Thomas stopped, still drying his wet hair. "Are you okay?"

Andrew dragged on an undershirt fast. "Yep. You go ahead. I need to find Lana and ask her something." He knew Thomas wouldn't offer to come if it was to do with Lana.

Thomas frowned, but he only said, "Meet me in the auditorium?"

First, Andrew needed to search the art classroom.

Then he needed to find a sharp knife.

It only took a press of fingertips to wood and the library door swung open. Normally the lights stayed on until 8:00 p.m. for independent study, but tonight everyone was up at the main school for the dance. The library should be locked, but Andrew stepped inside and the darkness greeted him, inky and black and forever.

He felt his way upstairs, cursing his lack of a flashlight. He could barely see his feet, and it made him agonizingly aware of everything else. The utter silence. The fresh dampness of the air, like the forest after rainfall. How the carpet felt like moss.

Inside him, vines stretched.

Upstairs, he put his hand to the wall and felt his way to the end. The art classroom would definitely be locked, but he was desperate enough to try kicking the door in if he had to. Add property damage to his list of sins. It was too late for remorse.

But the door gave at his touch. Something broke and fell from the knob as he pushed, and he frowned. Rope? It wasn't until the door stuck and wouldn't open wider and he had to squeeze through the gap that he understood what had been tangled in the lock.

Vivid, green vines.

He hit the light switch.

One bulb lit up in the center of the room and flickered a melancholy dance that barely cut the gloom. He recoiled, his back hitting the wall as the urge to cry out rose up his throat.

The forest was here.

It was impossible, it broke *his whole mind,* but inside the room grew a wonderland of trees and vines and lush greenery.

Vines crawled over the windows and fungi flourished over the desks. Tree trunks shot from carpet to ceiling, their branches cramped around light fixtures and cornices. Delicate violets bloomed along the floor and vicious rosebushes sprouted through Ms. Poppy's desk.

It couldn't be real. He reached out and the soft, furred edges of leaves brushed his palm. They leaned toward him as if hungry for his touch.

He had to get the drawings and run like hell. How the school would explain this away, he had no idea, but they couldn't pin it on Thomas—even though, for once, this was actually his fault. He must have lied and hadn't stopped drawing at all. That was the only explanation for why the monsters wouldn't stop.

Except there was never ink on Thomas's fingers, never pencil lead smudged up his hand, never paint tracking over his mouth because he'd bitten his paintbrush while concentrating.

Andrew crept through the classroom forest. He tried not to touch anything, though every thicket and branch reached for him, brushing his arms, his neck. Maybe it sensed he belonged here since he, too, was growing a forest inside himself.

He ducked under a branch heavy with apples rotting to their cores and found Thomas's desk. Vines grew through everything: his easel, his seat, his boxes of charcoals and pens. Andrew ripped handfuls of leaves off the easel, green staining his hands. His tux would be wrecked, but he didn't care.

He only had eyes for this.

No monsters sprawled in wicked ink across the canvas, no things with teeth and claws and blacked-out eyes.

Thomas had drawn in pastels, something he rarely did, the

pencil so light on the page that it looked like it was fading away. It was almost finished.

The three of them.

Thomas, Andrew, Dove.

Their faces pressed close together, cheek to cheek, Thomas in the middle with his freckles and frown and sour mouth parted so that roses could grow between his lips. A crown of feathers slid over one of Dove's eyes and her face was turned toward the sky with such aching sorrow it bled off the page. Andrew was the one half unfinished. The hardest for last. His hair curled in soft honey waves, dandelions woven between the strands. But his mouth was missing.

As if Thomas had been waiting to learn the shape of it first.

It hurt to look at them like this, at their grief and rage and joy. But they were all together, weren't they? In this papered reality, nothing had driven them apart.

Andrew was not himself as he took hold of the paper and tore it down the middle.

He was something else entirely as he ripped Dove's face in half. Then Thomas's.

Then his.

He knew doing this meant he'd slid a knife between Thomas's ribs and twisted. Thomas could hate him, but at least they'd still be alive tomorrow morning. This had to be the last of his work.

No more drawings. No more monsters.

He rummaged around the desk until he found a box cutter, which didn't seem enough of a weapon against monsters, but it was all he came up with. He turned to go, stumbling on the ground rutted with tree roots and damp leaves of gold and russet and crimson. Find the door. Get out of here. His foot slid on a damp patch and he struck out his arm in a desperate attempt to catch himself. He thought he grabbed at a low branch, muzzy in the dark.

But his fingers tightened over smooth, slick skin.

He was still looking down on the damp patch on the leaves; a pool of rainfall in a room where rain couldn't reach. Except it looked metallic and thick. Except it looked like blood.

That's when he made himself stare at the ankle he gripped with shaking fingers. It dangled at his eye level, no shoe, just a bare foot with mud between the toes, porcelain white and so, so cold.

He would always be in this moment, his fingers on dead skin, his neck tilted back so he could look up and up and up while inside him a scream began that would never stop.

A boy hung from the trees, vines noosed around his neck and thrust down his throat. Leaves curled out of his ears, still growing, his clothes torn where rose thorns had caught against flesh, all the better to find blood on which to feed.

touch me again and I'll kill you—

aren't you pleased?

this is exactly what

you asked for

Bryce Kane stared down at Andrew while a forest grew from his hollowed-out eyes.

THIRTY

Nothing mattered but this—find Thomas.

Before the forest did.

Andrew shoved through a wall of shoulders, tuxes and dresses and costumes, glittering laughter and cruel cut eyes. Everyone wore masks and wings and gold-dusted horns, and their smiles were bloodred slashes against the strobing lights. Monsters danced hand in hand with Wickwood students, all of them fusing together into one shapeless, melting terror while Andrew was the only one who could see them for what they were. The forest dressed up in human skin. It had come for its prince.

Bass shook the floor as he stumbled through the Wickwood auditorium. The rows of velvet chairs had been removed and stored, and the stage was decorated with pumpkins and scarecrows, the ceiling ribboned with thousands of streamers and orange balloons. Every beat of the music pounded inside his skull until he had no room to think. Sweat ran in rivulets down his forehead and he couldn't stop shaking, couldn't steady the floor under his feet, couldn't see as the world undulated and warped before him. He, too, was in costume after all—he pretended to be a slender boy with a serious mouth and eyes always searching for Thomas, but strip that away, and here was the truth.

He was a wretched thing, a rotten thing, a skeleton with his insides already devoured by the forest.

It was too late to save him.

Dancers churned in the middle of the floor, colorful lights pulsing until their faces blurred like water smeared over a painting. Teachers moved through the crowd, scanning for dangers and yet seeing none of them. The clawing need to warn them that monsters filled the dance floor choked Andrew, but he knew how he looked. Fevered and sweaty, wild-eyed and insane. In both fists, he gripped torn-up drawings of friends who were never meant to last.

He had to tell someone about Bryce, but it would be as good as a confession. He'd all but told the forest to do that. It was his fault, his rotted, corrupted, monstrous *fault*.

He tripped on the train of a long, lacy dress and stammered an apology as the wearer turned to yell at him. Then he backed up straight into a broad chest.

"Here's the little shit."

Andrew tried to duck out of the way, but one of Bryce Kane's vultures grabbed his arm and yanked him sideways with such abrupt violence that he nearly lost his footing. His startled cry was lost under the music, the laughter, the pounding feet and swirling dresses.

"If you're looking for your girlfriend, he's busy." The boy stood taller than Andrew, muscled and swift, his usual smirk replaced with twisted disdain as he grabbed Andrew's chin and forced him to look toward the refreshment tables at the back of the auditorium.

Because the school was so rural and the kids rarely had a

chance to let off steam, Wickwood allowed extravagance for their annual dances. Catering had piled the tables high with hors d'oeuvres, everything from salmon canapés to cheese platters and pastries. Hollowed-out pumpkins sat next to chocolate fountains, and the punch bowl billowed with dry ice. Thomas stood near the end of the tables with a plastic cup dangling nonchalantly from his fingers. He looked beautiful and bored, hair perfectly disheveled and white shirt tight around his biceps. Andrew hadn't noticed that before. Swinging an ax to carve apart monsters had made him stronger.

Beside him stood Lana.

Which peeled apart Andrew's lie about who he was with, but did it matter anymore? He had to tell Thomas about the art room. He had to—he—should . . .

He couldn't think. His vision blurred and his throat felt wrapped with thorns.

From this distance, he could barely hear them, but Lana gesticulated wildly with her hands, her floppy witch's hat half obscuring her dramatic stage makeup. She wore a stiff black tulle skirt with bright black-and-purple leggings, and her arms were sheathed in fishnet gloves. Bracelets of tiny plastic skulls hung around her wrists to complete the look. Thomas frowned at whatever she was saying and then shook his head dismissively.

Andrew thought he heard Lana say, ". . . calling for Dove. You need to make sure he knows."

Thomas stared at her. "*Knows?* The hell? He freaking knows, Lana."

Bryce's vulture moved his grip to the back of Andrew's

neck and started pedaling him toward the exit. Andrew slipped trying to stay upright, the need to shout for Thomas tangled in the thorns growing up his throat.

"Let's have a little chat. Specifically about where Bryce is." He shoved Andrew harder. "He told us about your little *threat.* Was taking it straight to a teacher and then suddenly he's vanished? What did you do, dipshit?"

More of Bryce's friends cruised over, all bright eyes and shark teeth in their immaculate suits and perfectly styled hair. The boy holding Andrew let go suddenly and shoved him at one of the others, and they mussed knuckles through his hair before shoving him sideways to the next one. Panic seized Andrew with such violent velocity he couldn't breathe. They were everywhere at once—shoving him, digging fingers into his skin, spinning him around, cracking knuckles against the back of his skull. He couldn't keep his balance, but every time he nearly fell someone hauled him upright and shoved him again.

He was not-not-not—

okay

"Did you tell your psycho boyfriend to do something to Bryce?" one of them snarled.

"Get him outside. Behind the school."

A hand gripped the back of Andrew's shirt and half lifted him toward the door, and all he could think was how pathetic it was that he could stand against monsters in the forest but here, under swirling bright lights and pulsing music and laughter, he had been reduced to a tremulous, terrified slip of a thing in desperate need of rescue. He was suffocating, he was drowning. Apparently, they all just looked like boys messing around, because not a single teacher walked over, not a single head turned. No one cared. No one noticed.

Except one.

Thomas slammed his shoulder into one of Bryce's vultures so hard he stumbled. He broke into their knotted circle with eyes blazing and teeth already bared in a snarl. But when he reached out for Andrew, someone blocked him with their arm.

"Stand back, creep. Unless you're here to confess to murder."

"Yours? Keep touching Perrault and we'll find out." Thomas rammed the next boy with his elbow.

He'd start a fight like this, an all-out brawl. Andrew couldn't let . . . he had to stop . . . His skin was a fevered oil slick and they all held matches.

"Where's Bryce?" One of his friends took a menacing step forward. "What the hell did you two sickos do?"

Someone grabbed the torn-up drawings from Andrew's sweaty hands. "Look, Rye is still obsessing over Dove. After everything he did to her." He flung the pieces at Thomas.

"*Stop.*" Andrew thought of the box cutter blade in his pocket.

Thomas slowly bent to pick up the shredded paper as it fluttered to the floor, and his face went blank. His eyes caught Andrew's and for a second they stared at each other as grief hollowed out Thomas's face. He had become nothing, just an empty box of desolation as his mouth formed the words, "That was all that was left of us."

His last drawing.

His last piece of Dove.

A vulture shoved Thomas back, hard. "People heard you fight with Dove. You should've been expelled and got your ass sued to hell and back. She told you not to touch her brother and you went and did just that."

Time slurred, tilting to the left as Andrew began to slip. He would fall off the edge of the world, and he would never stop falling. His mouth throbbed as if he'd just been hit, blood wetting his lips as if he'd torn open his own tongue. Or maybe that was the fungi digging into the cracks between each tooth.

So Dove had sabotaged him.

A small part of him had known it, really, had known she was angry at the way Thomas and he had grown close. But if she'd told Thomas he couldn't have Andrew and Thomas had obeyed for so long . . .

"Wouldn't be surprised if you hurt her," the vulture spat right at Thomas's face.

"For the *last time*," Thomas yelled. "I wasn't in the forest with her! I wasn't there! I *wasn't there*."

People were looking now, teachers taking note. The music seemed to tilt up a notch to cover the disturbance, but it would only take a moment more before everything broke. A teacher intervening. Or Thomas hitting someone.

Andrew had spent all this time wholly believing Thomas, but what if—what if he was just ignoring the evidence? This boy had something monstrous living right under his skin, something that leaked out of his drawings in ink that turned into flesh and bone. Dove had cut him out, had refused to forgive him when usually she would. Why was he siding with Thomas when he should be loyal to his sister? Maybe she didn't want Andrew with Thomas because Thomas was—

Sometimes there was no stopping pain. There was just

seeing how much you could swallow before it spilled out your throat.

Andrew tore free of the vulture who still had claws in his collar. "If you want Bryce, he's in the art room. The forest ate his eyes. I-I-I need to talk to Dove. I'll go get her."

The boys all froze, expressions ranging from confusion to horror, but no one looked as stricken as Thomas in that moment.

"Andrew . . ." He stopped, his face naked and wretched and aching.

But Andrew had already turned away and run for the doors, for the night, for the forest's fetid, terrible beckoning.

THIRTY-ONE

There wasn't enough of Andrew to hold on to, so it was easy for him to slip away into the dark. The night air soothed his feverish skin, and when he wiped at his mouth, his palm came away smeared with thick, bloodied dirt. He wasn't crying, but it probably looked like he was.

He stumbled along the outside of the school, his hand trailing across the ivy-covered bricks, while golden light poured from the arched windows as if promising only warmth and safety resided in there. He knew the truth. The monsters were everywhere now and all chance at escape had been lost.

"Dove." His voice rose against the velvet dark. "I need you. DOVE."

He wrapped his arms around his aching stomach and tried to ignore the way the forest writhed inside him. Get it out. That he could do. If he just took the box cutter from his pocket—

His next breath caught in a sob. Maybe he *was* crying. He reached up to wipe his cheeks—but two cold hands pushed his away and brushed at his hot tears.

"Oh, Andrew."

He looked up into Dove's concerned face.

"Dove." His voice cracked. "Everything is really, really screwed up right now and I-I-I need . . . I need you."

Dove went still, and for a harrowed second, he thought

she'd walk away, tired of him and his riotous emotions that always spilled out in disarray when he should be put together, cool and clever and confident like her. He was sick of being the broken sibling, the incapable one, the slip of north wind more likely to fade away than deserve anyone's affections.

Dove settled down on the path beside him and wrapped her arms around her legs. Of course she'd skipped the needless frivolity of the dance, remaining in her neat, pressed Wickwood uniform with her hair in a tight ponytail and a pencil still tucked behind her ear. Only Dove would choose studying over literally anything else. She had the future planned out, Ivy League colleges, internships, and the stars all within her grasp.

"Did Dad call you?" Andrew scrubbed at his face again, embarrassed at his running nose and reddened eyes. "They're expelling me. But you can . . . stay here. You don't have to leave because I'm a pathetic waste of space." He couldn't help but add in a wounded mutter, "You prefer studying to being around me, anyway."

"I need to study," Dove said. "I need . . . something to hold on to."

"But *why*—"

"Andrew, leave it." She sounded firm then, and if he pushed, he knew she'd stand up and leave him. "Maybe they're right, you know? That you need a mental health break. You know you're dangerously thin, right? Not to mention . . . Well, you seem like you're in your own world."

He let out a shuddering breath. "I need to show you something. In the forest."

Dove shot him an incredulous look. "Absolutely not. Did

you forget the whole reason you're in trouble is because of sneaking into that forest? Plus, it's pitch black out there. It's totally not safe. Let's go to the nurse and tell her you're not feeling well." She pushed to her feet and offered a hand. "Come on. I'll take you."

"Is that why you're sick of me?" His jaw set, and he didn't take her hand. "Because you're done with having to babysit me and patch me up and fight my battles?"

Dove sighed, equal parts exasperated and fond. "Would you please get up?"

Slowly, his body throbbing with the effort, he climbed to his feet without help. "I'm going down there, with or without you."

"You are not."

He forced himself down the garden path that wound toward the sports field while Dove spluttered in disbelief behind him. If she stormed off, then whatever. Thomas had been right about the strength of Halloween, and it seemed unlikely the forest would stop after devouring one student. It still hungered.

He slipped a little on the mossy, dew-slick pavement and then startled as Dove appeared beside him. She folded her arms and glared, but she followed.

"I know you won't believe me," Andrew said. "But try, okay? Please? There are monsters in the woods. They crawl out of Thomas's drawings, and every night we fight them, and every night we nearly die for it. They want a . . . a sacrifice from the prince."

"Andrew." She sounded careful. "Let me take you to the nurse. I promise I'll stay with you."

His fingers clenched into fists. "I'm not crazy. I'll prove the monsters exist. Just come."

Dove said nothing, but he knew she thought he was having a mental breakdown. Logical, factual Dove who thrived on color-coded spreadsheets and itemized to-do lists would only ever see her delicate, dreamy brother as the unstable one. Well, she'd find out the truth soon enough.

He needed her to see.

He was so tired of suffering because he moved through the world differently from everyone else. This wasn't only about goddamn monsters. It was about how he never seemed able to cope, how the world didn't fit against his skin, how he felt too much and hurt too often and couldn't pack his emotions into neat, palatable boxes. He needed help. He needed someone to hold on to. He *needed* to be believed. It didn't matter if what hurt him was an invisible weight inside his head or something that left real bruises against his skin: His pain was real.

Moonlight lit a silver path across the sports field as they walked toward the fence, looming tall and ominous against the dark. Dove kept a step behind him, her fingers fluttering at his sleeve in a half-hearted attempt to slow him down, but he moved with dogged determination. He saw the problem first.

The fence had been ripped open, the hole wide and jagged with bloodied, matted bits of feathers and fur caught against the serrated chain links.

"See? The monsters busted through here. They got into the school." He whirled on Dove, but her mouth stayed a thin line. "They murdered Bryce Kane."

"You know seniors party in the woods, right? Obviously cutting the fence is an entirely new brand of stupid, and people are totally going to get expelled for this." Dove picked up a gore-slick feather. "The sad part is some animal's been hurt because of it."

He snatched the feather off her. "This is from a *monster*. You're literally holding the evidence and you still don't believe me."

"Can you even hear yourself, Andrew?" Dove waved helplessly at the forest. "It's a bird feather because birds *exist*. Maybe there are wolves out there . . . I don't know. Do they have wolves in Virginia?"

Frustration turned hot in his chest and he plunged through the hole in the fence. She followed, taking her time so as not to tear her uniform.

He stormed deeper into the trees, not caring how dark it was or how far Dove lagged behind, her footing unsure against the roots and tangled undergrowth. She broke into a jog, calling for him to wait, and he felt vindicated that she seemed spooked.

"Five minutes," she said, as if her compromise was a gift. "Then we go back, okay? Together." She said it like a treat, and it felt so patronizing he wanted to scream.

The forest licked its wicked lips, watching them. Still and silent. Nothing moved in the underbrush, nothing breathed out with lungs of vines and brambles. The thick smell of loam and leaves stuffed up his throat, but no monsters lurked in the shadows with viscid intestines unspooling from their perforated skin or poison drooling from their sharpened teeth.

No wind touched the trees. It had never been so perfectly

s t i l l

Dove touched his shoulder and he flinched.

"Thomas is probably down here," he said. "He would've gotten the hatchet and then come to find me."

"Andrew . . ."

But he cupped hands around his mouth and called, low at first because he knew this would invite an attack and he'd forgotten until now that he was unarmed. But when no response came, his voice rose. Nothing moved in the forest, no monsters, but no Thomas, either. Maybe he was still in the dorms, snatching the hatchet from under the bed and swapping his too-short dress pants for jeans that could take the gore and mud of battle.

But something felt . . . wrong.

Andrew kicked through the leaves until he found a rutted path. He turned in a slow circle, but only trees stretched out as far as the eye could see. The air shivered, both tremulous and expectant, as if it hid a boy, or a monster, and it didn't want to show either.

"Thomas isn't coming."

Andrew stiffened, a sick dread fisted in his gut. He struggled to keep his voice neutral. "How would you even know that?"

In the dark, Dove's face had been lost, only the shadowy outline of a nose, a jaw, the curve of an eye socket pooled with black. "Maybe I was wrong staying away from you this semester. But I thought you needed space to adjust."

Dread thickened in his mouth. "What are you talking about?"

Dove took a tentative step forward. "Sometimes you choose your own reality, Andrew. You've always been like this, and I'm not angry at you. I understand. It's like when we were little, you'd tell these sprawling, fantastical stories, but they never *ended.* Even when I got tired of playing, you wouldn't. You'd lie on the carpet for hours just playing alone . . . in your head." Her voice had gone thin and rusted, and she fought to steady herself. "Thomas made you interested in *this* world. And I get it. I'm grateful to him. But . . ."

His ribs began to buckle inward, roots twisting and snapping as her words took him apart like scissor blades.

"What are you . . . So I had a big imagination as a kid? What's that got to do with any of this?" He started to shake. "I'm not *hallucinating* monsters."

Dove's fingers brushed his hand, and his scars seemed to light up like they'd been brushed with acid. "No." She'd never sounded so gentle. "I think you're hallucinating Thomas."

He snatched his hand away like she'd cut him.

"When school went back this year," Dove said slowly, "Thomas was arrested for murdering his parents."

Andrew stared at her.

"He didn't come back to Wickwood after that. It's horrible. It's . . . hard to accept. So I guess you didn't accept it. In your head, he's still here." She wiped her eyes quickly. "I didn't think you were struggling this much, or I would have told Dad about it."

"You're lying." The words hardly left his lips.

"I know things are tough for you—"

"YOU'RE LYING." He whirled on her, and there was so much pain and fury and hysteria spilling from him that it felt like it would burst from his chest and tear open a hole in the world. "He's been in class with me, and he fights monsters with me, and—and Lana! Ask Lana. He argues with Lana all the time."

The pity in Dove's eyes landed like a lash against his cheek. "Lana doesn't talk to you. She's never been your friend."

"She started talking to me this year. She . . ." He trailed off.

"What about Chloe? She rooms with you and Lana. She's . . . my friend."

"I don't know who that is and, um, Andrew, you don't have friends."

Andrew wanted to rip out a thousand trees and hurl them into the stars. "You're messing with me and—and stop it! Just *stop*." He jerked back when she reached for him. "Don't you *dare touch me*."

"I'm sorry. I shouldn't have told you here. Please let me take you back up to the school and we'll calm you down and call Dad and—"

"This is not all in my head."

"Andrew."

"It's real. It's all real and you're *lying*—"

"Stop yelling at me!" Dove grabbed him by the shoulders, getting in his face before he could twist away. "God, Andrew. I am trying to help you. You. Need. Help."

Across the forest, a low wail rose and then suddenly splintered into a bloodcurdling scream.

Then there was the thudding *whack* of a hatchet.

The scream cut off.

Andrew's pulse leaped. Relief exploded in his veins, and he grinned at her, wild and unsteady and completely terrifying, but he couldn't stop. "Did you hear that? Did you? Monsters. Thomas is killing them."

Dove cupped his face with cold fingers, and she looked close to tears as she searched his eyes. "I want you to know, whatever happens, I love you and I'm going to get you help."

It sounded like goodbye. It sounded like giving up on him.

"You don't . . . hear it?" he whispered.

Tears slipped down her cheeks as she shook her head. "It's going to be okay."

But it wasn't.

He was falling.

He was tipping toward nowhere with nothing to hold on to. Inside his chest, the forest grew, vicious and alive and hungry, and it filled him right up to the top of his throat.

He could feel the way this was the end, how he soon would not be able to hold it in.

He turned away and started to walk, slow at first, ignoring Dove as she called helplessly after him. Then, without even thinking, he started to move fast, faster, nothing in his head but rose petals unfurling and the soft lisp of rustling leaves. Then he was flat-out running.

The forest swept past him, black and endless, as he tore along the path so fast he felt like he was flying. Dove tried to come after him, but she couldn't keep up on the uneven ground. He knew this forest intimately, wholly. He would not fall.

His lips parted, and he was screaming.

One word, the only one that mattered.

"THOMAS."

"THOMAS."

"THOMAS THOMAS THOMAS—"

Around Andrew, monsters peeled their teeth from the trees, and trained their yellow eyes on him. Bones rattled and the underbrush turned over in a snarl. Their rot, their malevolence, washed over his face and he sucked it in with a sob.

Ahead of him, a shape formed among the trees and began to

move toward him. It came up quick and lithe, and he was moving too fast to stop even if he'd wanted to. But he didn't want to stop. He was a boy close to the end of infinity and he would run off the edge of the world if that was what it took.

He was anguish and speed, his fingers outstretched for the only thing left in the world that made sense.

They collided like trees felled in a storm, arms flung around each other and heads cracking together from the force of their entwining.

He flung his arms around Thomas's neck and crushed him breathlessly close, breathing him in, all forests and charcoal pencils, his body hard and lean and impossible to break. Thomas tossed his hatchet to the side so it thumped dully on the leaves. Then his mouth pressed hard to the side of Andrew's sweaty hair, then against his jaw, so close to his mouth it felt like dying. He palmed tears from Andrew's cheeks and then simply held him like nothing else mattered.

"I n-n-n-need you to be real." Andrew could barely pull the words bound in thorns and wicker switches. He wanted to bite Thomas's jaw just to feel that hot, sweaty skin, already flecked with blood and damp dirt.

"What?" Thomas said. "Of course I'm real. I figured you ran down here, and I came as fast as I could but—"

"Bryce is—"

"It's not your fault." Thomas slipped from Andrew's arms and scooped up his hatchet.

He spun with a graceful agility that made Andrew's heart skip a beat and then slammed the blade into a monster scuttling across the leaves. It shrieked, and blood splattered the front of

Thomas's white dress shirt in a hot streak of red. One of his suspenders had slipped, but he didn't seem to notice as he flipped the hatchet with deft ease and cut down another monster.

Then he turned back to Andrew, blood flecking his cheekbones, his eyes smoldering coals. He reached out a hand to see if Andrew was okay, just as he always did.

But Andrew stepped back. He grabbed at his hair, his head shaking, a low moan escaping from his raw throat. "I don't know . . . I don't know if-if-if you're real."

Thomas took Andrew's wrist and turned it over, placing his thumb on the frenetic pulse. "Hey," he said, so softly. "What do you need me to do?"

"Is this all in my head?" Andrew went on, barely coherent. "Did I make this all up? The m-monsters, the-the stories, the—"

"I'm real, Andrew. Do you see the blood on my shirt? How can—"

"Kiss me, then." It burst out of him, frantic and feral. "Kiss me."

Thomas took Andrew's face in his hands, thumbs tracing his lips as he tilted his head down. Their lips almost touched, Andrew's swollen and crusted with blood, Thomas's warm and soft as a story.

Then he whispered, "I am real. You are real."

"*Make me* believe you," Andrew said.

And Thomas kissed him, hard and fierce and merciless. All teeth and tongue as he took everything from Andrew and devoured him whole. Andrew's teeth sank into Thomas's lip until the old scab burst open again, and then it was impossible to do anything but breathe as one.

They were a catastrophe, exploding.

Thomas pulled back and grabbed Andrew's face, rough and hard. He pressed their foreheads together. "Do you feel this? I am here and I am here and I am here."

He couldn't make this up, could he? The extraordinary wonder of pain and blood and Thomas.

"Dove said it was all in my head." Andrew could barely get the words out, he shook so hard. "She s-said I make stuff up and you were gone, but you can't leave me, I-I can't be without you—" He choked on a sob; he felt like an autumn leaf, disintegrating to the touch. "When she catches up, you have to—have to make her see the monsters so that—"

"Wait." Thomas pulled away slightly, his hands still cupped around Andrew's cheeks. "When she . . . catches up?"

"She was right behind me." Andrew twisted, looking at the empty track. "I just don't understand why she lied. I'm so confused, I'm always—I'm so confused."

"Andrew." Thomas's voice came sharper this time. "Look at me."

He drew in a shuddering breath, trying to center himself as he leaned into the one person who would always hold him up. But almost too late he registered a growing panic in Thomas's face, a worry not stoked by monsters or the night or all the rules they were breaking.

He kissed the corner of Andrew's mouth so tenderly it could make him cry.

"You need to listen to me," he said, low and urgent. "You were not talking to Dove."

"I was—"

“That . . . that *thing* you were talking to. It wasn’t her.”

“She’s my sister. I know her—”

“Andrew.” Thomas’s voice cracked. “It can’t be her. You know that.” His eyes looked like a thousand shattered mirrors as he pressed his thumb to Andrew’s mouth. All he could taste was blackberry briars and dirt and forest rot. “That thing was not Dove because Dove is dead.”

5 MONTHS EARLIER

Andrew had bitten his pen until ink had bled across the corner of his mouth. Thomas kept looking at Andrew's lips, and this had to be why. What other reason was there?

They lay on the grass in the Wickwood rose gardens, books strewn around them in a fruitless display of studying. Sun warmed their heads in a dangerously comfortable way. It would be so easy to fall asleep, cheeks cushioned on arms, the echoes of a busy afternoon at Wickwood humming around them. From the sports field, whistles blew as the soccer team did drills, and students chattered along the garden paths as they wound in and out of the library. Exams would be over soon. Then summer would be here, glorious and long and free.

"Come home with us for the holidays." Andrew lay on his stomach on the grass, notebook open and half a story fallen from his pen.

Thomas sat cross-legged, his brow furrowed in furious concentration as he drew a crown of hollyhock and blueberry vines onto a wicked fairy king. "Sure, let me whip out a couple of thousand dollars for a plane ticket."

"My dad would pay." Andrew bit his pen again. "It's not like your parents would miss you, right?"

"They won't even remember to pick me up." Thomas sounded unconcerned, but his shoulders had tightened. "Maybe

I'll just nest in the forest like a goblin child and eat summer berries and go entirely feral."

He was halfway there already, his frowns always a little too sharp and chaos spilling out of his pockets all through classes. He'd stood atop the garden shed when they stargazed last night and howled to the moon while stardust brushed his cheeks.

"What are you writing?" Thomas tossed aside his drawing and leaned in, but Andrew covered his page with an elbow.

"It's not done yet," he said.

"I want an exclusive preview."

"When it's done." Andrew slapped the notebook shut and stuffed it beneath him. He had yet to decide if he was embarrassed about this one. In it, two dryads kissed and tangled their wooden arms together as a woodcutter split them apart for firewood. It was beautiful and anguished. And he'd written them both as boys.

It felt thrilling but strange to write. He'd never looked at a boy and wanted him.

Except one.

A wicked gleam caught in Thomas's eyes. "I challenge the bastard prince to a duel with birchwood swords for the right of constant access to his stories."

Andrew gave him a skeptical look. "You're the prince, not me. I'd be the poet or something."

"Fine, the prince demands it from his loyal poet. Disobey and feel a bone blade at your throat."

Andrew started to argue against this poor storytelling, but Thomas pounced. He flung himself onto Andrew's back and hooked arms under his shoulders to send them both rolling across the grass. They knocked into their textbooks and pages fluttered everywhere. Andrew drove his elbow into Thomas's stomach and got a solid *oof* in reward. But then he was laughing too hard to do anything but lose.

He ended up on his back, Thomas straddling him. When he dug fingers into Thomas's ribs to tickle, Thomas pinned his wrists to the grass.

They were both breathing hard.

Thomas stared down at him with eyes bright as the forest after rain. He was so real right then, so alive.

The world smelled violently of roses.

"Now what." Andrew tried to look unimpressed. "You'll have to let go of me to reach my notebook and I know exactly how ticklish you are. I'll murder you."

Thomas leaned forward, his whole weight pressing Andrew thin as paper. But he'd forgotten he'd wanted to struggle.

"Can I ask you something?" The mischief had gone from Thomas's eyes and he sounded unsure.

"Denied," Andrew said easily. "Get off before I headbutt you and there ends your perfect nose."

"You think my nose is perfect?"

"Well, it's straight," Andrew said.

Thomas's mouth quirked a little. "At least one part of me is."

Andrew frowned and started to contest this, because Thomas also had straight teeth, but someone cleared their throat with dramatic annoyance, and he peered over Thomas's shoulder to see Dove.

Thomas flung himself off Andrew and somehow put a thousand miles between them in the space of a heartbeat. He had his sketchbook in his lap. Grass in his hair. His eyes looked electrified as if he'd been caught breaking all the rules.

Despite a long day of classes and a rigorous English exam, Dove looked pressed and composed, as if she meant to give a presentation or head to a formal dinner. Not a wisp of hair out of place. Not a smudge on her uniform. She folded her arms as she surveyed them with narrowed eyes.

"We were studying," Andrew said. "I've got your flash cards . . . um, somewhere."

"There are twenty-seven," Dove said. "You have to memorize *twenty-seven* before tomorrow, Andrew. Why do you two need supervision to get anything done?"

"You could study with us?" Thomas said.

Dove gave him a cool look. "Pretty sure I'm not studying the same things you are, Thomas Rye."

He shot her a frown, but Dove ignored him and smoothed out the pages of one of the textbooks they'd messed up while wrestling. She collected the scattered flash cards and smacked them over Andrew's head, which he grumbled about without any heat. Without her organizing his exam prep, he'd have flunked out of Wickwood long ago.

What he wanted, though, was to lie among the roses and sleep away the warm afternoon. Maybe with Thomas's head on his chest.

"I want to talk," Dove said.

It sounded like *Talk* with a capital *T*, and Andrew immediately folded into avoidance mode. At home, if their father tried to have a discussion, Andrew would bury his face under pillows in the sofa or block his ears and sit in the linen closet until everyone gave up and left him alone. It was childish, sure, but he had panic attacks that felt like willow switches against his bare back. They all knew this. They knew he couldn't cope.

He could only handle life if he looked at it carefully from the corner of his eye. It was easier this way.

Thomas scrambled to his feet. "Let's go to the forest. To the Wildwood tree. Then you can talk."

"Aren't we getting too old to climb trees?" Dove said.

"Never." Thomas snatched up his sketchbook.

"It's out of bounds . . ." But Dove sighed and flung her hands in the air as if she didn't have time to fight Thomas today about rules. "Fine. I guess we can sneak past the soccer field while everyone's distracted by practice. But we have to be quick, all right? I have a study session with Lana."

Andrew hadn't moved and they didn't notice yet. When Thomas and Dove were together, this happened every time. Private conversations with their eyes. Their bodies both magnetizing and yet repelled. Their words thorny and sweet as their bickering turned to jokes and back again with such swift speed Andrew always felt left behind.

He watched how close they stood, how Dove's finger brushed the back of Thomas's hand as he argued about if one could grow out of loving a tree.

"I don't want to." Andrew collected his homework as he stood. He skin felt itchy from the grass, his chest tight.

"Please?" Dove had on her softest, wheedling voice. "We need to talk, all three of us. *About* us."

"I'm too tired." Not a lie. His cottony weariness of earlier had turned to a sludgy sort of ache against his bones. Too many late nights studying. Too much holding his breath during exams.

Annoyance edged onto Dove's face. "I'm literally begging here."

But Andrew's jaw had gone tight and he turned away. "You two can go."

"I need all three of us—" Dove started.

"And I don't want to go with you." He said it too sharp, and Dove wilted.

She liked to corral them, her boys, her two best friends, and usually he was relieved to follow dutifully in her wake, to feel safe knowing she made all the decisions and he wouldn't have to. But right now he was too scared of what she might ask.

Maybe she would ask for Thomas, and maybe Thomas would say yes.

He was a hurricane and she the whole sky, and even now they were having a vehement conversation with their eyes as Andrew walked away. Neither went after him.

As he vanished behind the hedges, he heard Thomas say:

"You have to give him warning. You know he hates confrontation."

"He could do something for me for once." Dove sounded tired.

". . . come on, let's just go."

Andrew felt sick, his stomach full of stones, as he trailed to the dorms alone, wincing at the two boys who bumped shoulders with him on purpose so he'd slam against the wall. This had been his whole year, everything from snide remarks and casual shoves to his books being wrecked and disembodied hands shaking the shower stall while he was in there, shivering and terrified. Always, it was Bryce Kane behind it. Andrew wanted to tell someone, but Dove would report them and the bullying would for sure get worse because rich kids didn't get more than a slap on the wrist at Wickwood. And Thomas would—well, he would start a war and beat someone into the ground for Andrew's honor. And then he'd get expelled.

So Andrew kept his mouth shut.

At least his dorm room remained a luxurious, quiet sanctuary. The sun flung golden afternoon rays over Thomas's bed and Andrew couldn't resist. He could steal an hour, Thomas and Dove would be at least that long, and he could study the flash cards after dining hall to win back Dove's favor. No one would catch him caving to this indulgence—dumping his books on his messy desk, toeing off his shoes, unbuttoning his shirt so that when he slipped into Thomas's bed, his skin lay against where Thomas had been. It was an easy way to sate the craving of something he could never ask for.

Laundry and extra blankets had been tumbled on Thomas's bed, and the cottony warmth dragged Andrew down into sleep. His muscles uncoiled, his stomachache eased. He pulled pillows over his head so his world muffled and all that was left was the smell of soft laundry and traces of paint and the warm, earthy taste of Thomas.

Somewhere, through the dregs of unconsciousness, he heard the dorm door open and then close. He wasn't awake enough to care.

A cool hand touched his cheek.

He pulled from sleep hard, sucking in air like he'd been underwater. It felt like his heart had stopped. Like he'd been lost. Like he'd had a fist on a branch and then—

snap

But he was still buried under Thomas's mussy blankets, sweaty and muddled from waking so abruptly. Someone had flicked on the lights and the glare burned his eyes. He sat up, blinking hard.

Ms. Poppy hovered over him, bangles clinking lightly as she placed a cool palm on his forehead.

"S-sorry." He sounded slurred. He felt undead, not awake, like he'd slept under a thousand-year enchantment instead of just the afternoon.

The clock on Thomas's desk read 8:39 p.m. Damn it, he'd missed dining hall and tutor sessions. Sending a teacher to find him meant incoming detentions.

"Darling, you're a little feverish." Ms. Poppy made a soft, distressed sound. "We had someone come look in here, but they must not have seen you under all these blankets. I need you to come with me."

Sleep had left Andrew so foggy he couldn't find words. He fumbled for a tee shirt, one of Thomas's maybe. Paint flecked the hem.

"I'm sorry," he mumbled again.

"You're not in trouble." But the way she looked at him was infinitely sad.

He followed her downstairs feeling too wrecked to stay upright. Something felt off. The dorm seemed subdued, the usual boisterous games in the rec room dulled, and everyone stared at them as they hurried past.

Outside, the summer night felt sticky and loud, cicadas singing from the forest and tires gravel crunching in the parking lot. Wasn't it late for visitors? The hedges ended and he saw it then. Cop cars and an ambulance, their blue lights still flashing.

Panic flooded his lungs, vicious and wild.

Ms. Poppy hurried him into the school, murmuring something that was meant to be reassuring, though he couldn't hear her past the roar in his head.

He was something.

missing

On the stairs up to the faculty floor, they had to step aside as one of the junior counselors walked down with arms around Lana Lang's shoulders. She had tissues pressed to puffy eyes, her breathing barely controlled. When she saw Andrew, she turned her whole body away and started crying harder.

He hadn't spoken to her often—she was slightly terrifying—but he knew Dove adored her. Her presence always turned Thomas snappy and jealous, a juvenile reaction that Dove shut down because she had no patience for his inability to share. Andrew understood him, though. Thomas was so used to no one liking him, no one caring, that when they did, he was always terrified of the day they'd stop.

Ms. Poppy took Andrew's hand and squeezed it.

In the principal's office, they sat him down. Two cops spoke to the principal, and senior teachers came in and out. The room felt too small and stuffy for this many people. Andrew thought he'd be sick; he had no idea what he'd done wrong.

He couldn't stop thinking about the ambulance outside.

The way he hadn't seen Thomas.

Agony wrapped fingers around his throat and pressed down hard enough to snap cartilage.

The principal perched in the other leather armchair beside him instead of behind her desk, an intimacy that made the situation even more disconcerting.

"Andrew, I have some difficult news, but first I want to assure you that your father is on his way. We would have him on the phone for you, except he decided to get on a plane immediately."

Andrew picked at the paint crusted on the hem of his shirt. Thomas's shirt.

"There has been an accident."

He wondered what Thomas had been painting since he usually gravitated toward ink and charcoal for his monsters.

"Your sister went into the forest. From what we can determine, she was climbing an old oak and a branch broke. She . . . well, she struck her head on a rock when she fell."

He said nothing. He thought if he were in one of Thomas's drawings, they could scrub charcoal over the top of his worried eyes and sad mouth and blot him right out of the world.

"She . . . passed away. I am so sorry, Andrew."

Andrew looked steadily at his fingers twisting his shirt. "No, Thomas wouldn't let that . . . Thomas Rye would have s-saved her."

The principal's voice sounded higher than usual, and she had to pause and clear her throat. "Lana Lang confirmed that she saw the two of them down by the tree line. They had some sort of argument, and then Dove went into the forest alone."

The principal went on speaking. Andrew wished she'd stop. There had to be a finite number of words in the world, and she wasted them going on and on about how students were forbidden from the forest without teacher supervision. How misplaced loyalty meant Lana hadn't reported Dove missing until after dinner. Then police had been called. A search party sent into the forest.

Thomas had been found, oblivious, in the art room.

Andrew had been searched for, but they missed him the first time under all the blankets, and then Ms. Poppy thought to check again and found him asleep.

His twin had been severed from him, and he hadn't even been awake to feel it.

They asked if he had questions.

He didn't.

People kept giving condolences.

He peeled paint from his shirt.

He said, "No," one more time, just softly, but nobody listened. They had already accepted the truth of this story they'd made up, this dark and treacherous fairy tale worse than anything he'd ever written.

Eventually someone said, "He's in shock," and they dithered around about what to do with him before deciding to send him back to the dorms.

Dr. Reul escorted him, making comforting comments about how bright and loved Dove was and how he understood Andrew didn't feel like talking right now, but when he did, there were people who would be there for him. All Andrew noticed, as they passed the empty parking lot, was how the ambulance had left.

They took her away. They didn't even ask him if they could.

Only the lights in the kitchenette had been left on, all students in bed and the counselor on duty waiting up with herbal tea and a pitying expression. Thomas sat at the table staring at a cooling mug before him. When he looked up, his expression was so raw and terrible that Andrew glanced away. They'd flayed Thomas alive, it was easy to see. If they took his shirt off right now, would he have skin left, or just muscle and sinew, throbbing livid and red and bloody as he struggled for each breath?

Andrew felt nothing as he stared at this boy with devastation bleeding from his eyes.

They climbed the stairs to their room in silence and readied themselves for sleep by the light of a single bedside lamp. Andrew shrugged off the shirt he'd stolen from Thomas and opened his wardrobe door to find his pajamas. Seeing himself in the slim mirror screwed to the inside of his wardrobe door gave him a jarring sense of vertigo—this angular, pale boy with collarbones made of twigs and hip bones sharp against his pants. It felt like someone else.

Thomas hovered behind him like a ghost. He took a step forward, his mouth trembling. "Andrew, I'm . . . I'm sorry. I should have been with her. I should never, never have let her go alone—"

"Yes." Andrew's voice was barely above a whisper. "You should have been with her."

Thomas shrank into himself. What had he expected? Forgiveness, absolution?

"It's all your fault." Andrew said it in a way that drove a knife into Thomas's gut and twisted.

He stared at the mirror, at the boy before him who looked like Dove: her honey hair, her warm brown eyes, that stubborn tilt to their mouths when they were upset.

Thomas wiped his eyes and dug fingers through his hair, trying to steady his shuddering breathing. "I'm sorry. I'd do anything to go back in time and—"

"Stop talking." Andrew didn't recognize his voice, cool and hard as river stones.

"—stay with her. She wouldn't have died alone. Shit, she wouldn't have *died*. I'd have caught her or carried her to get help and—"

"I said *stop talking*."

Thomas choked on a sob. "I'm sorry—"

Andrew hit the mirror.

He hit it again, *again*, until glass shattered and blood smeared across his reflection. He no longer looked like Dove, now he was a red-smeared thing in fractured pieces. He hit it again.

Thomas was crying out for him to stop, pleading with a voice gone high and cracked and terrified.

He would stop when he'd obliterated every last piece of glass into stardust that he could coat his tongue with and whisper a magic wish to the forest.

Give her back.

Arms wrapped around his waist, trying to pull him away. He wrenched free and smashed his hand into the mirror again. He felt nothing. His fingers looked like broken twigs dyed crimson and dusted with slivers of glass as he kept punching the mirror again and again and—

The dorm door burst open. People were yelling. Light blazed the room and seared his eyes with such brutality that he screamed.

Stronger hands took him by the shoulders and dragged him away.

Voices piled over each other, arguing, questioning. Doors squeaked open across the hall as sleepy faces peered out to see what was happening.

Andrew thrashed against their grip, a strange, unkempt violence spilling out of him as he snarled between clenched teeth. This wasn't him. He was never like this.

He didn't know how he ended up on the floor in Thomas's arms, rocking slowly, slowly. They sat in a sea of mirror shards while Andrew cradled his mangled hand to his chest. Thomas's cheek pressed to his bare spine, his tears tracking down Andrew's skin.

"I'm sorry . . . ," Thomas whispered.

"I said." Andrew placed each word like a rusted blade against Thomas's tremulous throat. "Stop. Talking."

Thomas didn't speak again. He held Andrew and cried to make up for the fact Andrew hadn't cried at all.

Everything inside Andrew had been scooped out, and he'd been left a hollow thing, impossible to fill.

Dove would absolutely freak out when she saw what he'd done to his hand. He'd explain it to her over breakfast, how it had been a tough, stressful year, and he'd spaced out for a minute.

He'd thought there was a monster in the mirror and he only meant to kill it.

THIRTY-TWO

Andrew's mind was a lit fuse, catastrophic detonation imminent, and everything inside his skull pounded and strained, as if it wanted out, *out, OUT*. His legs couldn't hold him, and he sank to the leaves with hands curling over his ears. A keening wail slipped between his bloody lips and he felt thorns curl deeper, harder into the soft meat behind his eyes. He needed to think, but he couldn't.

Someone was lying to him.

Yellow eyes flickered around them, the gnarled shadows of monsters tucking themselves between trees and roots as they wet their lips and waited for the right moment to attack.

Thomas swallowed hard, his gaze darting from the lurking monsters in the thickening dark to Andrew folded in on himself.

"I don't understand how you don't—" Thomas stopped, choking on a dry sob. "Lana told me that she didn't think you knew, like somehow you'd . . . blocked it or something. But I don't understand. You have to know. You . . . have to. I tried not to bring Dove up since you didn't, and I didn't want to hurt you." He put his fist to his lips, pressing so hard his teeth cut into his knuckles. "I feel so fucking *guilty*. I should have been with her, and I'm scared you still . . . blame me."

Andrew dug his hands into the leaves until his fingernails hit something hard and sharp. Not rocks. Teeth.

"I already told you." Every word shook as Thomas fought against tears. "I think someday you'll hate me."

He was gorged on guilt; he festered with it. Andrew could see it unspooling around his eyes and running like brackish tears down his cheeks. He could hear the way the monsters salivated for it, their claws tearing through tree bark, teeth clacking against bone in anticipation for their next taste of suffering. They wanted him to take a fistful of agony and stuff it in his mouth again and again until he was so full of decaying leaves and moss and the wet, rotting skin of trees. He would belong to the ground.

But none of this was Thomas's fault,

was it?

Thomas swiped a dirty hand across his eyes. "She would never have gone into the forest if not for me. She hated breaking rules. A-a-and I drove her to it. We fought . . . You know we fought, but it was about you."

Andrew looked up, his mouth stained with blood. "What."

"I was going to ask you out." Thomas sounded wretched. "I was just working up the nerve and she somehow *knew*. I guess she saw how I looked at you, even though you—you didn't notice. She didn't want us to change, us three. It had to be *us three*, she said, but I never would have cut her out. I just wanted to kiss you. I still"—his voice had gone so high and hoarse it kept cracking—"I still just want to kiss you all the time. We started arguing before we even got to the forest because she said 'I forbid it' and I-I flipped out and said you didn't belong to her."

They'd fought *over him.* Andrew almost didn't believe it. He thought Dove was sick of him, of watching out for him and mopping him up and keeping his tremulous ribs together when he was always seconds from bursting apart.

"I stormed off and she went into the forest alone. I don't know why. She was so mad. I guess she just wanted to stomp around and get her feelings out. And then . . ." Thomas trailed off miserably. "Then she fell. And I wasn't there to catch her. I didn't even feel it. I should have felt it or been there or *run to her.* I loved her like she was my family. But I love you . . . like you're my whole world."

"Stop." Andrew stared at the soil filtering between his fingers, at the scars like spiderwebs and lace across his skeletal hand. "You're . . . lying. She's not—"

He couldn't say it, because it couldn't be true. He had seen her, he had—

"But how shitty would I be," Thomas said, raw, "to kiss you after she was gone? This is why Lana hates me so much. She thinks I saw Dove's . . . she thinks I saw it as an opportunity to get with you, but I *didn't.* I'd rather die than be like that. I just don't want to be alone anymore. I just—I'm so scared of being alone."

He dropped to his knees. Energy sloughed from Andrew's skin, and his forehead slumped against Thomas's shoulder, but he cupped Andrew's face and forced him to look up.

"Listen to me." A fevered terror lit Thomas's eyes. "I don't think the monsters are going to let us go easily this time. Or at all. You have to get out of here."

"But I can't," said Andrew, his voice so dull and far away

it sounded smothered six feet underground. "They want the prince, and I'm . . . that's me. Not you. It was never you."

And it was the way Thomas didn't correct him that said he knew.

That he had known, perhaps, for a long time.

Andrew, who hadn't fallen asleep when the dream ravager came.

Andrew, who told a wicked fairy tale about a wolf that ate Thomas's parents.

Andrew, who had never stopped writing, even though Thomas had stopped drawing.

Here was a boy who made monsters, or perhaps was a monster himself. All because he couldn't face the fact, the guilt, the sorrow, the rage, of his sister being

dead.

The world slid sickeningly left, and pain shot behind his eyes in a white-hot spear of excruciating agony. He couldn't bear it. He was going to tear outside his own skin.

Monsters stepped out from behind the trees with masks of blackberry briars and vicious teeth curved over their jaws, limbs fused with riotous trees and claws extended. Perforated intestines and foul, viscid liquids, and endless decay slithered out of their concave bodies. Then Andrew noticed the writhing tangle of vines pulling themselves from the soil, thorns hooked and tipped with blood, bodies throbbing like snakes. He tried to scramble back, but a green vine looped around his ankle. In a flash, it tightened like a tourniquet.

"*Thomas.*" It burst from him like a plea, a prayer.

Thomas snatched up the hatchet and swung hard, chopping

the vine in half while maggots and festering black beetles burst from the severed flesh. But already another had grabbed his ankle, sneaked a tendril around his wrist, crawled toward his waist with leaves blossoming with a green so lurid it stood out like a scream in the dark.

Their eyes met and the grief was so visceral, so brutal, that a wail tore from Andrew's throat.

He clambered to his feet, unsteady and drunk on his devastation, kicking back the vines as more surged from the soil and with thorns looking to hook into flesh. They smelled blood. They wanted more.

"S-stop." He practically screamed it. "It's not him. It's *me*. You want *me*!"

"Andrew, shut the *fuck up*." Thomas sounded frantic as he tried to slice the vines tightening around his body. The hatchet slipped and sliced across his thigh, but he didn't seem to care. "I won't let them have you—"

"I'm the tithe," Andrew said, and his mouth was full of ink.

Thomas screamed at the same moment the forest dug fingers into Andrew's face and *pulled*.

Something slick and livid exploded from Andrew's eye, growing thick and fast down his cheek in a rain of warm earth. He clawed at his face, as roots tore through soft tissue and skin. He was screaming; he couldn't stop. Pain bloomed, vicious and bloody and red. With trembling fingertips, he touched his eyelid just as thorny roses unfurled petals dripping with the viscid jelly of his perforated eye. They grew. *Blossomed*.

He couldn't see.

Someone was screaming his name.

He couldn't see.

It shouldn't be a surprise that the forest had outgrown the confines of his thin, frail body and longed to stretch. He used to be an empty boy, impossible to fill.

Now he was so full of monsters.

THIRTY-THREE

Every good story ends with a wishbone snapped, a bloodied kiss, the prince's sacrifice.

—cut out a heart—

and bury it in the woods.

But he already knew that.

The hardest part was not what he had to do, it was walking away from Thomas as vines twisted around his wrists and tore open the buttons of his once-white shirt to find the hole the monsters had made—Andrew had made—that was impossible to fill. The hardest part was listening to the way Thomas screamed, terror unraveling him right to the core, as he watched the forest eat through Andrew.

But he had no choice but to go.

Someone had to finish telling the story.

Night slid an inky tongue across the forest as he walked, like it meant to swallow him whole. The weight of it pressed against his chest, drowned his lungs, smothered any pathetic whimpers escaping from his bloodied throat. He stumbled on gnarls of roots and thorny underbrush, but even as it bit at him, he felt nothing. Behind him, Thomas stopped screaming.

Don't think, don't *think*.

He didn't let himself cry; he wasn't even sure he could with the rose thorns sinking into the tender skin below his eye. He climbed over a fallen tree throbbing with fungi turned bioluminescent under the streaks of silver moonlight. It crumbled under his palm and clung to his skin with moist, decaying flesh.

The whole night made sense, in a brittle, circular way. He took in a lungful of air and felt it slide wet and tar-slick down his throat, a strange sort of calm folding over him. He wondered if anyone would notice they'd gone into the woods and never came out, if anyone would care. After this, everything strange and uncanny about the school would stop.

A shadow shivered behind a tree and the world seemed to crystalize around him, breath held, air turned cold enough that his breath was a white globe before him. He stopped and tucked his hands in his pockets.

"Come out," he said.

Silence stretched for one beat, then two.

Then Dove stepped from behind the roses. She still wore her summer Wickwood uniform, the last thing he'd seen her in, though her face had begun to change now as if the need to look like neat, fastidious Dove had passed. Moss grew across her cheek, soft green tendrils pulsed from the corner of her mouth, and her brown eyes had been replaced with the vivid, unforgiving green of the forest.

"Take off my sister's face." His voice did not waver.

"She wanted to protect you," the forest said softly.

"She wanted everything to stay the same," Andrew said. "And it couldn't. It didn't. We let our love for each other cut us to the bloody core."

"You didn't bring a pen."

It took everything in him not to stand there, not to cry. "I'm not telling that kind of story this time. Now take off her face."

The monster slipped backward into the trees, the dark taking hold of his sister's edges and unraveling them. Andrew watched as the monster grew, as its flesh turned to bark and its fingers to scraggly sticks, as it grew tall and then taller until its huge form blotted out the moon. Its jaws stretched open to show teeth, wicked and long, and when it pulled its feet from the ground, the earth tore as roots exploded free. Gripped in its mangled stick fingers was a notebook with spores of mold flourishing over the battered cover.

Andrew wiped the blood off his mouth and took his notebook of wicked fairy tales from the monster. He nodded once in thanks.

They walked into the forest, the monster huge and terrible behind him, shadows and malignant rot slick on its branches. He climbed fallen logs and let moss smear between his fingers and stain the knees of his pants. He took off his suit jacket and let it fall behind him. Then his shirt, streaked with dirt and leafy prints from the forest. He left it tangled in a thorny thicket.

From his pocket, he pulled out the box cutter.

As expected, the place where the Wildwood tree used to be was empty. It had yanked its roots free and gone walking, had packed its body down to look like a girl with honey-blond hair and a name of softened feathers. A distant part of him wondered how much of Dove's blood it had drunk as she died, quiet and alone under its canopy.

He nestled the notebook in the leaves at his feet. Then he traced fingers along the grooves between his naked ribs, across scars from monster bites and claws, until his palm pressed flat to his stomach where vines grew beneath his skin.

He cut, deep enough to hit wood. He wet his fingers with his own blood, feeling nothing but how warm and coppery it was.

He began to write, fingertips against skin, bloody letters smeared and slurred because he couldn't stop shaking.

The Wildwood monster fitted its root feet back into the hollow, and then it stretched for the midnight sky speckled with the chipped-off edges of diamonds. The way it looked at him wasn't cruel or vindictive, rather gentle, as if it realized he had run as far as he could and his tiredness was to be expected.

Its voice had turned deep and melodic and ancient. "You woke us, now sate us. A tithe was never going to be enough."

Andrew began to write.

Once a prince took a knife to his chest and carved himself open, showing ribs like mossy tree roots, his heart a bruised and wretched thing beneath. No one would want a heart like his. But he'd still cut it out and given it away.

He thought, far away, he heard someone cry out his name. The cold took hold of his naked shoulder blades and sent goose bumps rippling down his spine.

He gave his heart to the October boy with one thousand and one freckles and hair of autumn leaves. But almost at once, the heart began to corrode, and the prince turned into a monster. They should bury it, the prince decided, and see what it would grow into.

Andrew painted words on his arms, his chest, his throat. A slow, dizzy molasses began to pour across his mind, and it was so very hard to keep his eyes open.

In the distance, someone was running.

Air tearing through lungs.

A scream almost reaching him.

They decided to bury the heart deep in the woods, for monsters were ravenous things, not to be trusted. This way the October boy would be safe.

Blood dripped from Andrew's arm and splattered on the notebook. Or maybe those were tears finding their way around the roses filling up his eye.

Within the ground, the heart grew into a tree and the monster lived among the branches and forgot he had ever been a prince. But the October boy didn't flee. He climbed the tree and kissed the lonesome monster until it devoured him whole.

Andrew scooped damp soil and decaying leaves until he made a shallow hole, deep enough for the journal to fit. There was just enough room left to fit a throbbing heart. He let out his breath, slow and careful, and stayed on his knees as he put the tip of the box cutter to his chest.

His mouth trembled.

The forest watched him, silent, and the monsters stayed back in respect, though the hunger in their eyes was still terrible.

To cut out his heart was actually

such a small

thing.

"Everything stops," he whispered, "after this."

Something slammed into him.

Andrew hit the leaves with a thud, all the air punched from his lungs. His fingers curled tight and protective around the box cutter so it wouldn't fly from his hands, but someone grabbed

his wrist and pinned it to the ground. He tried to wrench away, to fight fierce and victorious, but he had so little strength left.

"Andrew, *wait*."

He smashed his head into Thomas's face and sent him careening backward, hands over his nose as he choked back a cry. Andrew dragged himself to his feet, the box cutter burning in his hand as if it was a dragon-tooth blade forged for princes who wore briar crowns. He stood over Thomas, his ribs moving raggedly, watching the October boy writhe on the ground with a hand cupping his bloody nose.

The world had begun to lighten with a graying dawn he wasn't ready for. He was running out of time. The Wildwood tree stretched its branches toward the sky, patience thinning.

"Cut out a heart and bury it in the woods."

Andrew didn't realize he'd said it out loud until Thomas looked up at him with swollen, glossy eyes and said, "Does it have to be *your* heart?"

He looked ruined, his clothes torn and blood seeping from dozens of cuts on his arms from where the thorny vines had pinned him down. He must have freed himself with the hatchet. Then he would have run so fast to get here in time because he, too, remembered the story Andrew wrote last summer and slipped into his back pocket.

Andrew pressed the palm of his hand against his good eye, squeezing until the world refocused. Dusty light shimmered like fairy dust around him and turned the edges of the forest sepia and soft. It seemed impossible they'd been scared of this forest for so long.

Thomas pushed himself to his knees and then stayed there,

a supplicant before his prince. He could unmake Andrew if he wanted; he could destroy him with the tender shape of his mouth. But he waited.

"I know it wants a heart," Thomas said, raw, "but it doesn't have to be yours."

Andrew's fingers brushed across Thomas's beautiful cheekbones, the curve of his perfect jaw, then through the thick, sticky blood spilling from his nose down his lips. Then he wrapped his fingers around Thomas's throat.

This was how they were, bones broken and mended crookedly, each entwined with the other. He thought maybe you could love someone so much you ruined them, and then you ruined yourself.

"If you cut open my chest"—Andrew's voice was wrecked—"you'll find a garden of rot where my heart should be."

Thomas tilted his head up, and the way he looked at Andrew was so tender and fierce, so full of fearless worship. "I don't care how dark the world is for you. I'll hold out my hand until you find it, and I won't let go."

Ribbons of blood traced Andrew's wrists and threaded around the box cutter. If he ignored what the forest demanded, this would never end. The monsters would keep attacking, more people would die. They hungered for guilt and grief and for the two boys who fed them relentlessly. So, in truth, this moment made sense.

"But just know this," Thomas said as he fought back tears. "Dove's death was an accident and she never would have haunted you in revenge. This is all your doing, and you could tell a different story if you wanted to. You're strong enough. You're brave enough."

Andrew slowly peeled Thomas's filthy shirt back just enough to show the trembling skin over his heart. He pressed fingertips against warm flesh, felt the throbbing, bloody beat. Hot and fierce and alive alive *alive.*

They didn't need two hearts. They could share Andrew's, even if it was a bruised and sorrowful thing. Their rib bones would twine together in a lattice to protect them from the worst of the world and they would always be together; they should never be apart.

He began to cut.

THIRTY-FOUR

Dawn dyed the forest in colors of the softest russet and gold. The air felt crisp on the tip of his tongue, wood smoke and pines and the musk of freshly turned earth. Blood stained the leaves and glistened in small pools, a red so deep and dark that if one dipped fingers into it, they'd touch another world.

He'd covered the hole with soil, packed it down hard with his palms before brushing leaves on top. The box cutter had been buried as well, resting gently on the notebook that held all his most decadent and lovely, and cruel and macabre stories. That notebook was his everything, his most precious possession, his heart made paper.

Before him, the Wildwood tree looked like an old white oak again with branches stretched in a wide, leafy arch, thick whorls and knots in the bark at the perfect height for handholds if one dared to climb. One branch was broken.

The forest had never been so still, so peaceful.

It had fallen asleep, worn to the weary bone.

He sat very still among the roots of the oak, his skin still covered in cuts and bloody letters from a story now too smudged to read. Rose petals flaked from his left eye, and the thorny vines had gone brittle now that there was so much less blood to drink. His bare skin had turned to cold alabaster, his long, delicate fingers absently tracing the branches grown from his split-open stomach.

"It will stop hurting soon," he said to the quiet between the trees.

They didn't answer; they were just trees again. All that was left of the monsters were broken wishbones and carved-out teeth scattered among the roots.

They'd devoured each other in this forest, these boys so ravenous and defiant and tearful, they'd not known how to stop. The way Andrew loved Thomas was terrible and eternal, but he couldn't remember if he'd ever said that out loud.

"Remember you love me." His words felt so small and sleepy against the forest's dawn. "All my stories are about you. They will always be about you."

He ran his fingers through Thomas's curls, his movements slow and careful so he didn't disturb the careful way he'd arranged Thomas's head in his lap. They were both so tired, they needed this moment just to rest.

He carefully slipped his hand into Thomas's and laced their fingers so they fit, scarred knuckles against freckled ones, both stained with forest dirt and blood. He kissed the back of Thomas's hand, tender and aching. They were beautiful together; they were magic and monstrous, and they had created a whole vengeful world between them.

Andrew lowered his head so his mouth was close to Thomas's ear. "Wake up. I need you to tell me if we're real."

Thomas didn't open his eyes, but his face had gone soft; all that fierce anger and lonesome fear slipped away.

"Kiss me," he said, low and sleepy. "Then you'll find out."

ACKNOWLEDGMENTS

I left a piece of my heart in this dark little book. If you've turned the last page and are now frowning at the wall, then everything is as it should be. I suggest not going near any trees for a while and keeping a tight hold of your eyes.

This book exists with deep and humble thanks to so many people. Thank you to Emily Settle for loving these horrible, beautiful boys; I am beyond grateful to work with you. To Claire Friedman, Jana Heidersdorf, Meg Sayre, Aurora Parlagreco, Helen Seachrist, Raymond Colón, Jackie Dever, Zhui Ning Chang, and Tara Gilbert, for all your work to make this book the best it can be.

Much thanks also goes to Maraia, Melissa, Kelsea, and Samantha. Thank you for telling me to be brave, for listening, for reading; I don't know what I'd do without you. And to my parents, for supporting me so much.

And to you, reader, thank you. May this one haunt you.

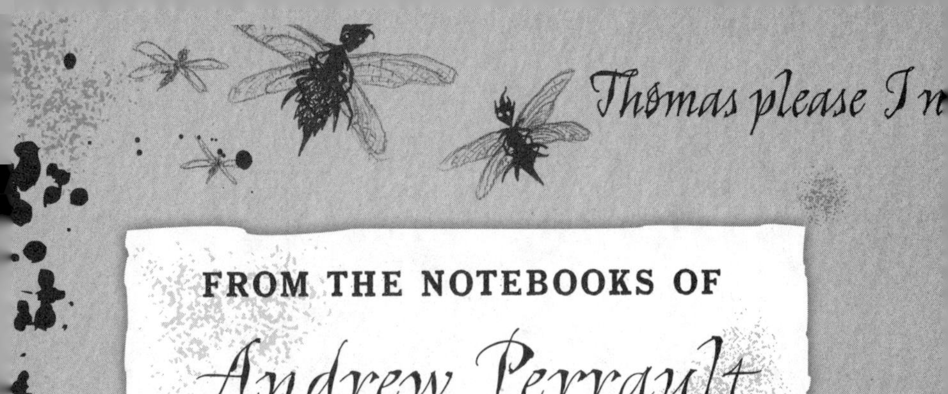

FROM THE NOTEBOOKS OF

Andrew Perrault

~~e cut out~~
~~is heart~~ he
ripped out
heir hearts

~~Andrew I~~
you don't understand

TR

~~like a Dove~~

Once upon
a time …

I.

The Antler King was a terrible creature, pulled straight from the wicked deep of the forest, and it hunted with vicious intensity.

Where it stood, grass wilted. Where it prowled, shadows festered. It sharpened its teeth on whetstones and polished its hooves in spilt blood. The weight of its inverted antler crown was monstrous, and the sharp tips often pierced its own skull and sent blood running from its eyes. But it had grown used to the pain.

Nothing pleased the Antler King more than when its prey ran and it could give chase. It liked to feel their fast-beating hearts under delicate rib bones before it snapped their bodies in two. When the prey cried prettily, the Antler King carved off their faces with a knife made of its own horns.

Few ventured into the forest for fear of this monstrous creature. But when it hungered, it crawled out of the rotten places between roots and mossy hollows and came for them anyway.

In the end, the villagers struck a bargain with the Antler King. They offered it a tithe of one mortal every month if it remained in the wicked deep and left them alone. The Antler King agreed. Finally, there was peace between village and forest—aside from the twelve who were tithed and died weeping each year. But all agreed it was for the best.

No one dared ask why the Antler King stole faces, and it never told.

The monster often sat by a frog-lily pond and placed the skinned faces over its own to see what it would look like if it could be human.

II.

Once an ancient crown had been lost to the woods and now lay grown through with roots and vines and feathered with soft moss. After a thousand years, the gold had tarnished and the opals had cracked. In the summer, fairy foxglove entwined with the crown's elegant curves, and in winter, snowflakes danced on its pointed tips. Many searched through the glens to find it, but unfortunately for them, the thistle fairies got to it first.

They crawled over the crown with glee, scraping their long, needle-sharp teeth on the gold and polishing the opals to a shine with their shimmering, incandescent wings. For they *wanted* the crown to be found.

A traveler stumbled upon the crown first and picked it up with awe, brushing off the moss and holly berries and setting it upon his head with delight. He didn't notice the tiny thistle fairies perched all over the crown.

The attack came swiftly. The thistle fairies detached in a wave from the crown and flew at the traveler's face and neck, sinking their teeth into his veins and drinking hungrily. Many underestimated these monstrous little green creatures with their faces as sharp as the tines of forks. In a few swift minutes, the traveler's blood was drained and his body rotted into the ground among the mushrooms and moss.

Next, a farmer picked up the crown and met the same fate.

Then a knight tried his hand and found that thistle fairies' teeth could sink straight through silver-plated armor.

Finally, a lonesome exiled king found the crown and wearily tried it on to remember his glory days. When the thistle fairies attacked and pierced their teeth into the jelly of his eyes, he did not fight. He simply opened his mouth and invited them to dive into the dark depths of his throat. The monstrous creatures could not resist, flying into his mouth and down into his lungs and ribs to feast.

But when the king clamped his mouth shut, they could not escape.

He died with his blood sucked clean from the inside out.

The thistle fairies died from suffocation as the corpse deflated around them.

III.

After the village boy fell in love with a queen, he was determined to prove his worth so she might agree to marry him. He brought her all sorts of gifts: thimbles full of fairy tears, moonbeams trapped in glass jars, clusters of azure roses, and crowns of fresh-cut hollyhock.

It delighted the queen, this love, and her eyes lit up whenever he laid the gifts at the foot of her wicker throne. She took him into her royal gardens and kissed him behind the hedgerows.

"But," she warned, "I cannot marry you until you prove utmost devotion to me."

Desperation stoked the lovesick village boy's heart, and he hurried away only to return the next morning with a curl of his hair in a silver locket so she might wear it against her heartbeat. The queen accepted it with a wan smile. But it was not enough.

Again, the village boy returned, this time with a filigreed dagger, sharpened on the edge of his own frozen tears. It was still not enough.

Again, the village boy returned, with a tooth pulled from his own gums, the bloody roots curved in the shape of a heart. It was still not enough.

Again, the village boy returned, this time with his hand cut off and laid in a golden box. It was still not enough.

Frustrated tears spilled down the village boy's cheeks as he wept at the foot of her wicker throne in despair. He was fevered from blood loss, yet all he received was the queen's sorrowful dismissal.

"What more can I do to prove my love?" he said.

The queen led him gently to the royal gardens once more and kissed away his tears behind the hedgerows, murmuring soft and lovely things. Then she pulled out the filigreed dagger and placed it in his remaining hand.

"If you gifted me your liver," she said prettily, "it might convince me that you are wholly devoted to me."

He cut his liver out then and there before her, careful to keep his blood from staining the gossamer lace of her gown. While he lay at her feet, his body split open in ruination, she ate his liver with delicate delight, marveling at the softness and the way it split open in her mouth like a sun-warmed peach.

The last thing he heard her say was "It is still not enough."

There is something

wrong

with the garden.

Keep reading for an excerpt.

Faint voices drift up the staircase, muted and indistinguishable.

There are people in Hazelthorn.

Evander can't breathe. His stomach is full of curdled cream and rotted violet stems and he can't wrap his mind around the *wrongness* of this. Aside from Carrington and himself, no one else is allowed onto the estate—the sole exception being Mr. Lennox-Hall's grandson, but even he's only permitted when school is out and his grandfather is home. Which he isn't. Mr. Lennox-Hall is still on his latest business trip.

That is the ironclad rule: Evander and Laurie can never again be left alone together.

Evander must have lost his goddamn mind, but he slips downstairs, his bare feet silent on the carpet. *Go back to your room,* something inside him hisses, but he can't stop himself.

He blinks to adjust to the moody light flickering from chandeliers that line the hallways as he passes an ornate dining room and stuffy library, everything drenched in shadowy shades of deep green. The voices, the music, have sunk hooks in his throat and he is helpless as he is drawn in.

". . . happens when you get yourself expelled."

"I was not expelled, Carrington."

"—your grandfather won't take this kindly."

"Since when does he ever take anything about me kindly? I hate the old bastard. Long may he rot."

"That's enough—"

Curiosity is a poison and Evander is furious at himself for being unable to resist. But he doesn't stop until he's in the wide archway. This parlor is an extravagant room, crammed with chaise lounges and bookshelves and potted plants, the heavy drapes and tasseled lampshades giving it a dim, boxed-in feeling.

And there is the person he should hate most in the world.

Evander stares.

The boy sprawls across an antique chaise with the languid disregard of a spoiled heir, unbothered and casual as if he's never been denied a thing in his life. His hair is a rumpled riot of insufferable gold, his white shirt open at the collar to reveal the arch of an aristocratic throat. Only a brace on his left wrist interrupts his indolent perfection.

Seeing him this close after so many years gives Evander a discordant rush of vertigo. He only just manages to pull himself back into the shadowed hallway as the old butler bustles out of the room with a tray of dirty dishes. Carrington still wears black suits and white piqué vests as if he's a butler cut out of a twentieth-century novel. His dislike of Evander is never hidden, but he still tends to him with rigorous dedication. It's his *job*.

He doesn't notice Evander flattened against the wall as he hurries off to the kitchen.

Evander waits until his rabbiting pulse smooths before

he pushes back into the mouth of the parlor. Leave. *Now.* But he can't.

He has to see Laurie again.

His fingers grip the archway, his knuckles gone white.

It takes only a second for Laurie to notice him, and he freezes.

Somehow Evander hadn't been prepared for this, for the way Laurie has grown up while Evander still feels caught in the past. He must look a mess: his hair dark and lank, curling past his jawline and long overdue for a cut, sweater grubby and plaid pajama pants clinging to bony hips, his limbs too fluid and elastic, as if at any moment they could bend the wrong way. He is shaking, ever so slightly, though from fear or rage he doesn't know.

He isn't supposed to get angry. It isn't good for his health.

Laurie sits up with a mocking smile tucked into one corner of his mouth. "Almost forgot you were real."

Heat eats at Evander's cheeks. "You can't be here." It's somehow shocking to hear his own voice, but his teeth clench and he keeps going. "You aren't allowed."

Laurie flops backward onto the chaise, one eyebrow raised. "I think you'll find this is actually *my* house. *You're* the transplant." He pulls out his phone as if this whole situation is uninteresting, though he seems to be breathing a little quickly.

As if maybe this is a shock to him too.

Laurie doesn't think about him, Evander realizes. He travels the country and attends elite boarding schools and does whatever he pleases beyond the walls of Hazelthorn, and he doesn't think of Evander or what he did to him at all.

While Evander has to think of Laurie every day.

He shouldn't. He tries not to. But he still thinks of this boy until his lungs seize and his mouth fills with rust from a bitten tongue.

"If he finds you've come back while he isn't here—" Each word trembles with a rage he didn't think possible.

"He knows." Laurie's eyes are half-lidded with boredom. "He's in the conservatory right now, messing with his stupid plants. I've been on summer break for a week already and he's been here the whole time."

Evander's fingers curl into fists and there is a high-pitched buzzing in his ears. He's trying to remember if it was like this before between them: Laurie dismissive and apathetic, Evander eaten through with jittery nerves.

"You can come sit down if you want." Laurie tosses the words like a bone to a dog. "You look pale."

Evander can feel himself winding up, his jaw clenched tight enough to crack. "This is just how I look."

Because I'm always ill, he wants to scream. *And it's all your goddamn fault.*

Though maybe he does need to sit down, because his vision has turned spacey and his stomach won't stop doing loops. But he doesn't understand. Mr. Lennox-Hall being back in Hazelthorn for days without bothering to visit Evander is unthinkable.

But then, who is he anyway except a charity case roped to them by guilt?

"I'll find your grandfather and talk to him. There must be

some mistake." Evander sounds raw, but Laurie's eyes track him with a sudden interest.

"Don't," he says. "He doesn't like to be interrupted. Stay here with me."

His gaze could pin Evander to the wall.

No.

That can never happen.

Suddenly Evander is in the garden again, caught against holly leaves and rose thorns, and he steps backward once, twice, before he turns and flees into the depths of the mansion.

His hate for Laurie is unmanageable, wild and bitter as wormwood on his tongue, and he should have lost all interest in him by now. He shouldn't watch for him through his window. Or crave snippets of his voice. Or think about his cornflower-blue eyes and the beautiful shape of his wretched mouth.

Evander can still taste blood and earth and rotten petals and a death that almost spilled like indigo ink.

Seven years ago, Laurence Lennox-Hall tried to kill him in the garden, down amongst the roses. But somehow, Evander is still obsessed with him.

RACHEL DEUTSCHER

CG DREWS is the *New York Times*–bestselling author of *Don't Let the Forest In, Hazelthorn, A Thousand Perfect Notes,* and *The Boy Who Steals Houses.* CG's work has been translated into over a dozen languages and won the 2020 CBCA Honour Award. Currently living in Australia, CG never sleeps and is forever buried under a pile of unread books.

CGDREWS.COM